'Penelope Todd's latest novel celebrates the beauty of a life of quiet stoicism, following a simple path. The clamour of twentieth century history fades beyond the richly observed detail of one woman's life: from childhood to youth and love, marriage, childbirth, loss and the consolations of friendship, a garden, and the wide vistas of Otago's high country. To read it becomes a kind of meditation.'

Fiona Farrell

A NOVEL

Penelope Todd

CLOUD
INK

Published by Cloud Ink Press
C/o Southside
1/110 Symonds Street
Auckland 1010
www.cloudink.co.nz

First published 2024

ISBN 978-1-7385943-3-7

A catalogue record for this book is available from
the National Library of New Zealand.

Typeset in Adobe Garamond Pro 11.5/15

Cover design by Caroline Pope

Internal design by Paul Stewart at Arotype

Author photo by Claire Beynon

Printed in New Zealand by Ligare

For my father, Andrew

Author note

I remember my grandmother as tall, kind and somewhat aloof; she was deaf in later years and died when I was thirteen. Nell grew up early last century in the Mackenzie high country, and raised her own family on a sheep station in the Maniototo. Then they moved to Dunedin. This novel of her life grew from impressions, anecdotes and memories. Nell's name has been retained; most others have been changed. Landscapes, buildings, events and people have been kept, created or re-created as imagination saw fit.

sound erupts

light rushes in: blobs   splashes   blazes & gulps of light
newborn, she knows milk-swoon

    lips   hair-drift   skin-feel   eye-hold
        mama

       green wobbles at a window
           shade looms, and shadow

in the warm kitchen: sizzle   splash   a-clattering
in the cool nursery: nanny brisk ... and calm
           brother   poop   wet   rough/kind

       she learns: aversion
                    desire
    dada

lavender   woodsmoke   coalsmoke   pipesmoke   mutton fat
    sunlight soap   wool grease   wet-dog

sofa she is propped up on
       verandah boards she is laid down on

   tea chest she is stood in
       frosty lawn where she takes her first steps

1898

Beyond the garden, trees crowd, then paddocks sprawl. Behind the house, a hill rises. Across the paddocks, larger hills.

Visitors bend her way and exclaim; she is trapped in a highchair with mess on her hands while at the table gruff men eat.

Wet, heavy pants (she is dry by sixteen months).

In winter, family and horses were moved from the station down-country, to the coast where the paternal grandparents lived on a smaller holding in a larger house.

Past the ears of horses, over the clop of hooves, Nell views an endless road from Mama's rocking lap.

Daddy calls her, 'Come and have a look.' He's crouched at the hot water cupboard. Yellow fluffs jostle in a box, cheep and fall over. Nell dares put her hand among them and hold it there. The sweet, sharp smell.

A horse *huge* crosses the lawn and towers over Nell, touches its nose to her hair then throws its head up at the sky.

Mama goes away and kitchen verandah wash-house bedroom are haunted spaces.

She brings home a baby sister. A sis-tella. Stella.

1900

Nell pedals her blue tricycle into the new century.

Nanny goes away. Brother Hamish, six, is Nell's fierce commander. He shows her the run of the pantry. Their attempt to make a cake in a cake tin with crab-apple jelly and eggs upsets Mummy.

A rough boy comes to stay. He bends the old cat over a sawhorse, then he bends Nell's arm up her back so that for days it hangs useless. She hides the fact: she eats and opens doors and pets the cat with her other hand. Mummy is busy with baby Stella.

Mummy tries – how dare she! – to burn Mousey. Nell spies his bobbly head leaking tangled wool and sawdust atop the pile being sent to the incinerator with Mrs Black. Nell waits until Mrs Black is struggling in the porch with her boots, then she scoots past and snatches Mousey away. She crouches on her bed and tumbles him beneath her nostrils, taking in his sharp, yeasty smell, and the comforting gag at the back of her throat. Then she plunges him into her pillowcase.

Four: being four feels important. Nell notices what else four is about. Legs. Tables and beds, all have four legs so they won't fall over. Horses: four legs for strength and agility: how else can you run a farm or go anywhere? For a while, she envies the dogs their four springy legs and practises running dog-wise over the lawn, up and down the passage and taking a dog's eye view at the yards, but then, bowled over by a bolting sheep, she reconsiders. Her new lace-up boots have pretty leather curlicues on the sides and underneath, *hobnails.* Nell utters the word with each clatter-stomp across the cobbled stable yard. She stands with her feet apart and feels how strong and sufficient her two legs are. She is finding her place: up on the rails when sheep are in the yards; kneeling on her two knees beside Daddy when he asks her to strike the match and hold it to the paper in the drawing room fireplace; standing beside the big table in the kitchen where she's not in the way, but she might be asked to stir a mixture, or pick walnuts from their shells or put jam and honey into little dishes. She might be given a wooden spoon to lick clean.

1902

Nanny and the governess have talking fights about the children. Nell feels vaguely naughty as she climbs to sit with Hamish at the nursery table, as she picks up the sharpened pencil to mark her very own exercise book. Each fresh page, she puts her nose to the centre crease and takes in the papery smell.

An old pony comes to live in the orchard; Monty scrapes her off under the pear tree, but she hangs onto a branch and laughs. She gets the better of him and soon they can go out into the paddocks.

Another baby turns up called William. Billiam. Bill.

Great-grandmama comes to stay for a long time at the summer house, mostly in bed. And then she is gone. Daddy in the doorway says, 'Nellie-noo, it's a sad mercy, that's what it is.'

Easter and her birthday are mixed together: the hunt for painted eggs; the gift of a doll with cold china face and blinking eyelids. Nell names her Paste.

Outside the wash house where Mrs Black is churning clothes, Nell makes patterns on the path with the wooden clothes pegs. She looks up to see a rat watching her from the nearby shrubbery. It sits on its haunches with front paws bloodied and torn. Daddy hates rats so Nell is surprised by its bright eyes with a question in them and its twitching nose. It might be asking for help. Nell creeps closer, but the rat leaps away. She worries for a long time about its poor shredded feet.

1904

There are things Nell wants very badly: a sun bonnet like her cousin Sarah's. A proper pony to ride, not fat and stubborn. A set of five tiny story books in a floral box (like cousin Sarah's). Wanting is an ache from belly to throat. The bonnet when it arrives is in the wrong fabric: too shiny. The new pony won't let her catch him.

After storms at the winter house you can hear the sea breaking on the headland. Nell wonders where the seals go at night when the tide is high. When it's fine, from the verandah you can see the far hills. If you stood on the very top of the very highest far hill, you'd be able to see the next highest far hill which is a mountain, and from the top of that mountain, after the next far-off mountain, is summer home. Where Daddy is.

Nell rides Bertie further and further from the house. When Daddy lets her ride to meet the muster, her range is expanded by miles and miles. The hills across the valley have joined the set of things she longs for but, when she reaches them, she is puzzled because they're not as they were. Nevertheless, she goes out again and again, drawn by their blue mystery, sometimes not returning until dusk. Mother gets Stella to find her with the binoculars as she rides home over the flats with the last sun in her eyes.

Nell learns one night on the dark verandah – the children allowed to stay up and watch the moon turn a little bit red – that Stella means 'star'. She is indignant because Nell sounds like nothing: like nil, Hamish has told her. 'Hamish is wrong,' Daddy says. 'Eleanor, and Nell too, mean "shining one"'. She is content with that, especially when they learn that Hamish means 'holder of the heel' and, hearing this, he stamps away inside with his hands plunged into his pockets. Nell takes Stella's hand so that together they can shine up at the moon.

1906

'You'll find that certain things are expected of a young lady.'

Nell doesn't need her father to tell her so (although in this case he is referring to his own expectation that she stop tapping the heel plates of her new riding boots on the floor under the lunch table). Each time visitors come, she notices afresh that men and boys are lords, and that women and girls look after them.

Except at haymaking. Then they all go out together. Everyone has a pitchfork and they toss hay with all their might for hours and hours until the children can't stop laughing and falling over. Everyone cuts their own fresh-made bread and cheese when they need it, and helps themselves to tomatoes, slabs of fruitcake, apples, and lemon barley water which goes down with a cool shudder in the oesophagus (hand slapped to sternum, Hamish supplies the word) and will ever after conjure that sense of gold-and-lingering joy.

The hill rises sheer behind the low-slung homestead. There is an actual moment of stepping off the flat and onto the slope. It invites, then holds Nell as she climbs. It is so steep she has to monkey-walk, hands pressed to cropped tussock and grass. So steep that the sheep tracks criss-crossing it are sometimes only a stride apart.

Nell used to go to Bertie for comfort, but he died. Dad found him tangled in washed-up trees on the river-bank after the storm and said he must have lost his way and his footing and been washed down. Who ever heard of a horse drowning? When she'd taken him into the river on hot days, he'd swum like a dog while she clung on.

The early afternoon sun beats down and she's done it again: gone too far to the left and plunged into the matagouri thicket. The mood she's in, she won't retreat. On hands and knees, chin tucked in, she forges through the vicious spikes. Barbs comb her hair and blood stripes her bare arms. She doesn't care. There's something heroic about scratches and she's not a sissy.

Out the other side, she half-runs to the crest and rolls onto her back. A light breeze courses up from the south and fans her face in delicious contrast to the sting and burn of limbs. Up here, who cares about Hamish and the stupid argument over who owns the barometer Uncle Joe left them? Hamish stormed off with it and she heard him banging a nail into his bedroom wall. She shouted that she'd bang one into hers and take it back. But why couldn't it stay in the hallway where Mother hung it, midway between their rooms? Up here she doesn't care, but she'll probably have to have another go at him later.

Far below, in the kitchen garden, Mr Baruch is wheeling a barrow between the newly pruned raspberry canes, stopping to shovel horse manure around them. They ate the last serving of late raspberries last night, picked from the prunings. Mr Baruch's nephew Robert had come and he was amazed by the pile of berries, by the thick cream they dolloped on with icing sugar.

Nell has seen the ordinary become extraordinary. Not only the cream she wrung from the separator while Robert watched, but almost everything impressed the young man from the city. As she showed him around the garden, the sheds and home paddocks, he kept exclaiming: how quaint the house is! what an expanse of lawn, oh, and even a tennis net! the size of the sheds! so many horses! He went right up and put his face into the roses cascading over the stone wall. 'And the farm goes all the way into those hills?'

As he took it all in, she eyed him back: the fine-wool jersey slung over his shoulders; the ironed shirt, pressed trousers and gleaming leather belt; city shoes that slid as they went down the lawn. The face and hair: close-shaven, neat and smooth. He was out of place, enchanting – like a new book turning up in the mail bag amongst the riff-raff of ordinary letters, parcels of fabric or spare parts, all opened amongst the detritus of lunch. Such a book arrived yesterday, late for her birthday: *Anne of Green Gables* in its engraved blush-pink cover with Anne in a green frame the exact colour of Robert's jersey. Sophisticated, he and the book, and Nell wants as much of that as she can have. Before lunch today, she washed her face and brushed her hair back into a tortoiseshell clip. She pulled on the blue gingham and sneaked into Mother's top drawer for a dusting of Anne-coloured blusher. All Mother said when she noticed her sidling back into the kitchen was, 'Eleanor, you're ten.'

Too bad Robert had to leave after lunch. As the trap trundled away to meet the coach, the air grew empty and Nell's entire future simply gaped. Back inside, she supposed she'd better run through her piano scales, just once, but carefully. Imagine Robert was listening. She slid her back along the hallway and stopped to stare into the barometer, tapping the glass as her father did. The needle quivered and settled between *Fine* and *Change*.

That was when Hamish clamped his stinking hands over her eyes and nose, and her elbow punched back into his belly.

As she works her way down the hill, Nell raises a wrist and sniffs. Mother's Lily-of-the-valley. Oh! Nell longs, she long, long, *longs*, for something else she doesn't yet have. It has to do with Robert and his smooth jersey, with kindly Mr Baruch and his peculiar green eyes, with cream and the smash of raspberries, with holding the little silver spoon *aloft* and catching Robert's eye…

It has nothing to do with a stupid brother called Hamish. It's the … what's that new word … it's the *antithesis* of brother.

1908

'Try these ones.' Daddy lifts a pair of skates from their nail on the wall of the little shed.

Nell's dreams for this winter have seen her in tan skating boots. These are brown and scuffed, with odd laces. She sits on the low bench in the frosty air and wrestles her double bows undone, wrestles her boots off, wrestles the skating boots open, wails when her heel won't enter the lace-bound ankle...

Daddy is all patience today. The pipe clamped at the corner of his mouth glows like a tiny bonfire as he kneels to take her socked feet in his lap and gives them a rub. He works the boots open, sees her feet in and tugs gently at the laces, this side that side this side...

Hands tucked into her armpits, Nell boils with *im*patience: Hamish is stepping onto the ice and Stella is up and stamping her blades on the frozen earth. Nell feels a yell building in her as the laces are wound twice around her ankles and tied in their own double bows.

She leaps up and stumps towards the pond.

'Nell, I need a hand please.' Mother, with Billiam.

Hamish is already halfway across the pond and, look, he's remembered how to turn with that stylish lean. His hands go into his pockets. It's unendurable.

'What?'

'Not that tone, thank you. Go and help Aunt Jane with the little ones, or take Bill with you. Just until I have my skates on.'

Nell looks away and rolls her eyes at the pale blue sky. Mercy.

'When I was five, I didn't need anyone holding my hand on the pond,' she tells Bill as they step sideways down the bank.

He looks up at her, huge blue eyes under a too-big pompom hat, and she wants to squeeze and kiss him. It's not *fair*.

Hamish comes scorching past and Stella's not far behind, stepping her skates tap tap tap because she doesn't trust them yet.

The sun bursts above the far hill and lights the frosty poplars spanning the valley. Bill laughs as he and Nell slide together onto the ice, clutching one another with both hands.

The whole day suddenly opens to her: skating, cocoa, grown-ups curling, hot thick pea and bacon soup, kids chasing the hockey puck, egg and bacon pie, and when the sun's fallen behind the hill, the last circuits, when she and Hamish have their hand in and won't stop, can't stop, circling, swerving and swooping over the ice…

Nell has gone down-country with her mother and the younger two by the time the snows fall. And fall and fall. Dump upon dump. Word comes of nine-foot drifts. Of sheep frozen in the hundreds, then the thousands, tens of thousands across the high country. As soon as there are signs of melt, and horses can be sent up the track from Kurow dragging logs to crush the snow, Mother takes

Nell with her, riding for two days into the whitening landscape, by blue-shadowed cuttings through banks and hummocks of snow, back to the station where all hands are needed to keep the fires stoked and the stew pots filled. All day the men look for sheep. Most are frozen dead. On the outgoing journey, they skin the upmost side then flip the animal over. On the way home, when it's thawed, they skin the other side – up to a hundred and fifty skins per man per day. As soon as the ground softens, pits will be dug for the carcasses. And new stock sought from who knows where. Thinking of the men slogging and bending and hauling day after day, Nell tutors herself to learn everything about running the kitchen, and by full spring, when Mother needs a day in bed, she can manage a whole meal for twelve all by herself.

Dear Eleanor,

Thank you for the pretty card. It pleases me to learn that you will go away for further schooling. Not too much, I hope, but enough to make home all the sweeter. A woman with a few small accomplishments and a taste for reading is to be admired and will always make decent company.

Your grandfather, as I write, is out repairing and cleaning up the bird bath for me. This afternoon we watched a very fat and inebriated wood pigeon fly, or rather flop, from the plum tree onto the edge of the bath, which tipped onto the lawn, upside down, on top of the bird. Evidently it bears a charmed life for it sprang wetly and drunkenly away when your grandfather turned the bath right side up, and seemed none the worse for wear.

Are you coming for Easter? Please ask your mother who seems unable to find the time to write to her mother.

Fondly,
your Granny

'Nell, come down.'

She is crouched on the windowsill in socked feet with her back to the drawing-cum-school room and her face to the valley which is half-eclipsed by the rush of green on the English trees. Trudy their governess is only three years older than Hamish, who has absconded this last day of term to help with crutching. Bill with a sore tooth has gone to town with Mother for the dentist and the Christmas shop.

'Come down. You won't be allowed to do *that* at school.'

'Exactly. That's the point. Do you realise this is my last opportunity to wear only socks to school? My last chance to perch with my heart in the hills and my derrière in the classroom?' Nell swivels and drops to the floor. She tugs the sash window closed.

'I do realise, and it's also your last chance to perfect your long division, and finish reading *Ivanhoe*. I'm taking it with me tomorrow.'

'Can't I mail it to you? I'll make up a lovely parcel, with slabs of ginger crunch in it too.'

'No, because as you know you're to write a paragraph – today – about the plausibility and satisfactoriness of the ending.'

'Satisfactoriness?' Stella flops to the floor from the sofa she's been lying on. 'Is that a word, truly?'

'Truthfully, I'm not sure, but it's self-explanatory.'

'Ah yes, I mean oui, Mam'selle. Sous le sofa j'ai vu un chenille.'

'*Une* chenille. Viens, assieds-toi.' Trudy pats the place beside her at the long table.

Nell stands a moment at one end. Everything *sur la table* is painfully familiar: Trudy's Mexican pencil case; the never-ending *Ivanhoe*; the glass vase with the 'daily biology sprig'; the ink tray; the jar of pencils and the ashtray mounded with the year's sharpenings ('No!

Don't throw any away!' Stella has insisted); her own exercise book in its wallpaper cover, smudged, and fat with written pages. Sensations thicken her throat, she could almost bite on them: love and weariness; disdain and sorrow. Soon she will be thirteen and, as she told Mother melodramatically at breakfast, 'My childhood ends today.'

1910

In the bedroom (she thought it would look more like a *dormitory*) is the crushed pink and white scent of stocks crammed into a vase on the washstand. Nell sits on the bed beside Mother's cake tin and oranges and runs her hand over the rust-red coverlet. The other two mustard-covered beds are against the wall. As first to arrive at the boarding house, she was encouraged to take the bed with window and view; she hopes her roommates won't hold it against her. Mother has gone downstairs to talk with the Misses Shaw while Nell puts away her things: unders, cardigans, stockings and swimming trunks in the bedside drawers; tunics (in serge, cotton, tussore silk), blazer, raincoat and mufti dress hung at one end of the enormous mahogany wardrobe. She tries out the calico curtain that screens her bed from the others.

Nell looks at everything; she wants to capture details as a camera does. Start as you mean to go on, Father has often said. She intends to make the most of every opportunity and encounter; to be curious about everyone and kind to all, and to put her feelers out for a friend. She means to keep alive the small flame of excitement burning in her chest, which has something to do with freedom. 'Freedom to blaze my own path' are the words that come to mind ... but probably she read them in a book where they pertained to some more vivid soul. 'Blaze' might be overstating it. At least she will try to keep the flame alight.

The window looks out over a handful of rooftops to the western hills, and through the small pane above her bedhead is a glimpse of sea to the north. Eyeing that grey glimmer, she feels suddenly tiny and inconsequential. Fright pulses through her: what if she gets homesick, overwhelmed by all that will be expected of her. Her arithmetic is shaky, her memory for dates and capital cities appalling.

She turns and walks over to the stocks, nips a few pink buds from the bunch and drops them on each of the others' pillows.

'And that,' the rabbit sighed, 'is that.' Miss Diane closes the book on her lap and snaps her eyeglasses into their case.

On the sofa and armchairs nobody moves. A log in the fireplace implodes with a muffled whump.

'I don't know if I feel sadder or gladder, about the fox,' Dora says.

'Well, with a good story, one can feel both, and more,' Miss Diane says.

Nell nestles back into the cushions and stretches her feet over Meg's lap. *Evenings are lovely*, she wrote home earlier in the year. *With only 12 of us, when we've finished our homework, we go to the drawing room for reading and music.* And now that the evenings are cool, the fire is a glowing link in their circle.

Adele arrives from the kitchen with the tray of mugs for cocoa, followed by Jinny and the steaming jug.

'Are you all right, Madeleine?' Miss Diane asks.

All heads turn towards the pink chesterfield closest to the fire. Maddie holds a hanky to her nose and her chin is tucked into her collar. It juts a moment as she says, 'Someone was unkind to me today.'

'Oh?'

All eyes follow Maddie's, back to Nell.

Miss Diane lifts her eyebrows. 'Eleanor?'

Nell frowns. A sick feeling steals over her. What on earth?

'At drill.'

Oh, that…

'You called me a lump.'

Nell thinks. 'I said, don't *be* one. I was trying to get our team moving.'

'Was it kind?' Miss Diane asks.

'It was … impatient. I was impatient because—'

'Because you are quick, Eleanor, and have little tolerance for other modes. Here, we make allowances for one another.'

Quick, hot anger rushes up from Nell's belly. Why did Maddie wait to bring it up here? 'You should have told *me*.' Nell glances at Maddie then stares at the fire, flame to flame.

'I just did.'

Cinders wink on the sooty bricks.

'Then *sorry*.' It comes out like spit, a sneer.

'Eleanor, you will go upstairs now, without cocoa, and when you are ready, before school starts tomorrow, make a proper apology to Madeleine.'

Public disgrace! she writes in her diary. *So VERY unfair. The whole team was ready to start, but Maddie was still flopping about on the grass.*

She's not sure, though, which burns deeper, anger at the injustice or contempt for that anger. Why get so riled, when it's only Maddie, whose nickname (unknown to her, hopefully) is Maddening?

'Let not the sun go down on your anger.' She can hear Dad saying it, usually to Hamish who gets contentious when he's tired. The sun went down hours ago. She's doomed for the night. Nell pulls off her gym frock and stockings, and then hears shuffling: Meg is at the curtain with a mug. 'Here, I managed to nip out. Silly old Maddie is lapping it up.'

'Poor thing.' It comes without thought and pouf! the anger is gone. Poor old, silly Mads, who doesn't have a friend like Meg. And pity feels like higher moral ground than anger.

Dear Nellie,

Your mother asked me to write while she seals up the fruit cake in haste because Hamish is battening the hatches on his suitcase as he wolfs down a last plate of mutton sandwiches, in order to be on time for Wilson the new farrier who is taking him back to school – from where he'll deliver this missive and cake to you when he can. Might be astute of you to make your way to Boys' High before the latter becomes barter. Mind you, your good mother seems to have done one for him as well. (Like the home owner who says 'We built

*it ourselves' without ever laying a hand to brick or timber,
your mother's 'I've made cakes' implies the full complicity of
Mrs B or the latest young Sadie.)*

*I heard both good cheer and a forlorn note in the letter
your mother read aloud the other night. You're surprised
by your enjoyment of arithmetic, charmed by French and
dismayed by Latin. Your father, at school, was considered
too dense to be taught the technicalities of a dead language,
but hears not infrequently from a Certain (m)Other that it
can come in handy for hazarding a guess as to the meaning
of the occasional obscure word. In order to make such
demonstrations of superiority it is surely worth persisting,
daughter of mine. Chin up. And now your mother is giving
me darkly significant and hurrying looks so I sign this note
with a loving flourish,*

Nell's Pa

*p.s. (she's got chatting to Mrs Wilson) you do paint a cosy
scene of wintry nights in bed with rain bashing at the panes
and the piano tinkling up from below. I say, those Miss
Shaws are good sticks, and tonight I'm going to put that
Chopin on the gramophone. Raindrop prelude, I think you
wrote.*

'Wait, wait. Meg and Lenora are coming,' Nell calls to Mr Dawson the wagoner. She catches the carpet bag Meg tosses through the opening. Lenora clumps up the steps and plonks herself down beside Nell. As usual, Meg has climbed directly up the wheel and slipped down on Nell's other side. Miss Faroe shakes her head and frowns, also as usual.

'Everyone got their lifebelts and shark whistles?' Mr Dawson jests, as always.

At least the swim itself is ever-changing: in blue sea under a blue sky; in rain that flattens the bay to chipped steel; or in waves that dash and churn but never pull your feet from under you.

The air is close and by the time they've clopped down to the bay, Nell's arms are damp from contact with Meg and Lenora's.

The nor'west clouds droop, peculiarly stippled, and the sea, in shades of green and grey, laps at dark sand far down the beach.

The girls climb down, break into their clusters and spread out.

'I hate low tide.' Lenora swings her swimming bag around her shoulders as they walk.

'You should have left your things up on the dry sand,' Meg says.

Lenora stops, flat-footed and looks at her and Meg. 'You're in your togs already.'

'We had them on underneath,' Nell says.

'Didn't you notice us dropping our skirts et cetera up the beach?' Meg is pushing her plaits into her bathing cap.

'Too busy talking, wasn't I. Oh well.' Lenora bends to take off her shoes. 'I'll sit everything on top of these.'

As Nell watches, Lenora thins out – as she'll describe it to herself later. Her inverted face turns transparent grey and the sand can be seen right through it. Doused in sudden alarm, Nell glances at Meg, but she hasn't noticed.

And it's only for a moment or two. Meg springs away and Lenora becomes substantial and laughs as she flails and swivels in her efforts to pull costume on and clothing off with decorum.

Nell waits for her. Meg is her closer friend, but Lenora is *vulnerable*. That was her mother's summary, when they all met for that afternoon tea in the botanic gardens. 'A child like that is a liability,' she said, and Nell has since wondered what it is precisely that makes her so. Her lack of coordination, she supposes, and her dreaminess, tardiness…

Once in the sea, though, Nell forgets them all. She leaves Lenora equivocating at the water's edge, wades out to her thighs and dives under. Cold courses over her and she comes up with a whoop of pleasure. She lies back, feet to the oncoming swells and surveys the weird sky, the black-backed gulls bobbing a little further out, and the line of ships and port bustle to one side of the bay. Her swimming costume balloons and she stands to tuck tunic top into shorts.

After a few minutes of free swimming, Miss Faroe will make them practise strokes.

Before that can happen, there's a commotion. Cries. Girls milling and diving by turns in chest-deep water. As Nell wades over, Lenora's head and shoulders come up, followed by Meg's, who has evidently pushed her from underneath and now gasps for breath.

Lenora is not gasping, or even looking. Two girls take her under the arms and tow her in. Hair covers her eyes and mouth.

Miss Faroe runs down the beach, everything joggling in her swimsuit, and kneels with the others around Lenora.

Nell runs for a towel to wrap around Meg who is shuddering and castigating herself. 'She tried to copy me. Doing handstands.'

The teacher's fingers delve between Lenora's blue lips. 'Help me,' she instructs the nearest girl and they roll Lenora onto her front.

'She was lying on the bottom and I couldn't get her head up,' Meg says.

'You mustn't blame yourself. You were the one to pull her out.'

'But if she's dead…' Meg's fearful eyes search Nell's.

A *liability*. Nell looks it up later, after Lenora has been pumped by Miss Faroe's capable hands, has spewed, coughed, and been taken to hospital where she is said to be in a serious condition but likely to recover; after they have put their clothes on and jogged rather than ridden back to the boarding house, because Miss Faroe believes in giving shock an outlet. *Someone whose presence or behaviour is likely to put one at a disadvantage.* There is that, Nell thinks. You know you don't want to go adventuring – or swimming now – with a Lenora. But what about Mother's other word, *vulnerable: in need of special care or protection?*

Lenora was vulnerable and although Nell was given an inkling (her transparent face!) of the danger she was in, she turned away for the sake of her own pleasure. Meg has the high ground: she *saved* Lenora, while Nell abandoned her friend on the brink.

She herself was answerable, *liable. A liability.*

Two things happened today, Nell writes into her new birthday diary with the gold-edged leaves, *besides turning fifteen. Well, one happened yesterday. My monthly arrived at last. Today it hurts badly. Who wants forty years of this!*

The other thing: she was released from school at lunchtime to be taken home for the Easter holiday. First, though, Mother took her to lunch at the brand-new Hydro Grand. As they waited for their macaroni cheese to arrive, Mother opened a letter from her friend Mrs Walker. Nell looked absently at the deckle-edged pages in her mother's hand, then out through the window to the blue-green bay.

I leaned my forehead to the window and heard the crickle that hair makes...

The pen halts as she tries to capture the moment, but its genesis eludes her. Alarm simply welled up and she turned straight to her mother.

'What's happened to Mrs Walker?'

'What do you mean?' Mother looked over her spectacles.

'Something terrible.'

Mother looked all over Nell's face. 'She says she's very well, playing a lot of golf, can you believe it. There's nothing in her letter to indicate...'

By the time they reached home, a telegram had arrived from Mother's other close friend: REGRET MARION DIED ELECTRIC SHOCK. STOP. SHALL WRITE.

I told Mother about Lenora, too. She says it might be 'the gift of second sight'. Granny had it. She was not pleased and said I should try to forget all about it. Some gift. I <u>much</u> prefer the leather riding gloves from Aunt Liz.

'Gosh, your little sister's a bit of a card.' Meg takes Nell's arm as they exit the stationer's, each with a fresh supply of writing paper, and Nell has at last spent her birthday token, on a couple of *Argosy* magazines she can read aloud or share around the dorm, and a bottle of the most delicious deep-green ink.

Nell gives her a dubious look. Having Stella at school this year, in the boarding house, has brought both comfort and tensions.

'Did you see how she managed to farm out her mending?' Meg asks. 'She had Vivienne hemming her nightie, someone fixing her ripped stocking, and someone else doing her cross-stitch. What's her knack, do you reckon?' Meg stops suddenly to look at the array of autumn hats in Campbells' shop front. 'Swanky, the rose one.'

'Isn't it just?'

While Meg goes in to buy ribbon, Nell waits out in the puddle of sunshine. She conjures Stella as she saw her last night, lolled on a chair, legs over one rolled arm, head hanging from the other. Imitating the new groundsman's clipped tones, her bearing in hilarious contrast with his brisk, upright posture. The other girls were drinking it up. Stella's gifts, her charisma, haven't been so unstintingly admired by the family at home.

As for 'farming out' her chores: 'Stella knows how to please,' Nell tells Meg when she comes out of the shop. She won't use the terms *flatter*, or *manipulate*. 'She will have praised Vivienne as the neatest stitcher in the world, and whoever darns her socks will be showered with praise, or kisses.'

Meg laughs. 'She's dinky.'

'I'm probably to blame. At home, she gets in terrible pickles and I'm so impatient it's easier to sort them out myself. Simpler to wash a grease stain out of her best jumper, say, or plait her hair myself, than watch her dawdle around, or tie herself in knots. She's quick in some ways, and perfectly capable in the end, but somehow she's learned to … to be looked after, I suppose.'

'Well anyway, I gather she got "best hanky" in sewing this week.'

Clever old Stella.

1913

'Mother says you're finishing up this year.' It's the first May holiday afternoon and Hamish is at the other end of the verandah sofa. Their socked feet are sole to sole. 'Coming home to dance attendance.'

Nell pulls the cushion out from behind her and wallops him. 'That's not funny.'

'It's not a joke. All said and done, according to her.'

'No.' Nell jumps up. 'Where is she?'

She finds her mother in her bedroom, kneeling at the low drawer beneath the ornate standing mirror. Around her are the small lidded boxes and bowls of trinkets and jewellery. Seeing Nell, she stands and holds out a triple strand of pearls. 'Yours, my dear, if you'd like them.'

Nell's legs tense all the way to the floor. 'You mean, if I don't go back to school next year?'

Mother looks over the tops of her glasses. 'Why would you go back? It was meant to furnish you with the fundamentals, and three years have surely taken care of that.' She drapes the pearls along her sleeve. 'Just a bent clasp, easily fixed. Besides, it's only a tiny school, limited in its scope.'

The jewellery boxes kaleidoscope. Nell snatches the pearls into both hands. '*Home* is limited in scope!' One sharp yank snaps two of the strings. Pearls fly across the rug and chatter over the wooden floor. 'Just because you never had any kind of proper education!' She flings the remnant necklace away and flees the room.

'Eighty-five seconds.'

'Is that respectable?'

'I should say so, if you've never run it before.'

'Well, not on a track.' Nell is thinking of the driveway, twice the length of this flat, grassed circuit on the school playing field. She and Hamish have spurred each other up and down the length of it since they could both run.

'When you've caught your breath, try a pair of these.' Miss Faroe the drill teacher indicates the basket of running spikes. 'Here comes Virginia. See if you can keep up with her.'

The school's senior champ rolls her shoulders and jumps on the spot while Nell finds her size and laces the lightweight shoes. To a barefoot runner they feel awkward, throwing her back on her heels.

'Take your marks, get set…'

From the first leap forwards, Nell senses vitality coursing up through the spikes. Their grip on the earth triggers springs in her legs. Her feet are barely touching the ground. Some unusual power is in her, and not only for the run. Joy coils up. Nell is opening out, she feels it: the joy of life! Halfway around the circuit, with Virginia just off her shoulder, Nell is as fresh as when she started. She only begins to labour in the last twenty yards, as Virginia pushes up beside her and they thump together over the finish line.

'Golly,' Nell grins at Virginia, 'is it legal to race in these things?'

Virginia laughs. 'I remember the first time. Like graduating from a trike to a bike, isn't it?'

'Seventy-eight,' Miss Foster says. 'I want you out here training every afternoon, Miss Preston. Three and a half weeks until athletics day.' Miss Faroe holds out the basket for the shoes, and walks away over the field.

'Looks like you're in.' Virginia sinks into a lunge.

'In what?'

'The team. Unofficial, but understood.' Virginia lifts her chin towards the far fence where Jane is raking the long-jump pit, Lorraine and Binks warming up at the high jump beside it, a couple of girls jogging along the edge of the playground.

'Ah.' These girls win the ribbons and are as much a part of the sports ground as the walnut tree and the white painted lines on the grass. The team. Why hasn't she put two and two together? 'It's not really my thing. I was just humouring Faroe.'

'It obviously is your thing, Nell. You're two years younger than me, and almost as fast. And that's before training. It's a talent.'

Hardly, Nell thinks, when all but the lame or elderly can do it.

'Plan ahead for sports day in Feb.'

'But I won't be here.'

'What?'

'I'm leaving.' This thought brings on, again, the swoop and the plunge.

'What a waste.'

Nell draws a circle in the grass with her toe.

It's too hard to talk about.

She's been bought, but she smells freedom, too.

There is to be a car.

My dear Nell,

I read your mother's letter to your Uncle Joe as we were having afternoon tea just now. 'Well, that's a rum thing,' woofed he, through a cocoa-nut and cream confection called a Lamington, at the news of your exchanging school for home and car. He rather thought you were Head P. material. He regrets that we didn't encourage Sarah to go beyond the fifth form.

Here, we are pausing for breath between undertakings. The spate of spring deaths seems to have ebbed and apart from an unfortunate child later in the week we have no body on the near horizon. That means time for cleaning, for putting new tyres on the hearse and going through the accounts. You wouldn't believe how many families think it beneath their consideration to pay for the burial of a loved one whilst in mourning. Mourning amongst the close-fisted can go on for years.

I gather you are uncertain as to your future direction. I know that the injunction to 'Marry well, young lady' is out of favour these days, which is foolish, because what could be better than to find a man who adores you and wishes to pamper and support you in your personal endeavours forevermore? Of course, that is what your uncle promised me before he sank all his money into the dead-end profession in which we are now equally interred.

Shall I touch on the wretched war? Best not perhaps. That way lies real grief. I began planting a rose in the home garden each time a young man of our acquaintance was killed, but soon saw that I was creating an impossibly vast thorn-thicket of heartbreak. Surely it will be over soon.

As will your deliberations. You would have made a splendid teacher, I dare say, or a doctor, a lawyer or — they say young women will be all of these on an equal footing with men ten or fifty years hence. I suppose the only advice I dare give is to 'Choose for yourself, dear Nell.' And visit us when you can.

Your aunt,
Elizabeth

Nell is perched on the forge high stool, holding the big gelding's halter, one foot on the ground in case he throws his head up.

George Wilson, the farrier's son, strokes a hand down the foreleg, pulls the knee onto his leather apron and leans into Major's chest.

'When do you leave?' Nell asks.

'End of the month we go up to training camp. Three of us from the district.'

Nell won't ask who else. The war looks set to gobble up the best of them. She looks at George's substantial back, the spine ribs muscles straining under his shirt as he scrapes packed earth and dung from the sole, releasing that sharp, foetid smell. Major's ears flick back as the file rasps across the toe. Nell puts her palm to his cheek.

'Will you be going over to the dance on Friday?' George drops the hoof and straightens.

Nell presses her head to Major's and goes still. She knew the question was coming. It's never the boy who interests her who shows interest back. George is nice enough, but if she goes to the woolshed dance on Friday, it will be in hopes of Harry or Jim being there. And what if Harry, too, has enlisted?

'Probably,' she says, 'but it depends.'

'On your mother's say-so?'

'That and … other factors.' She looks pointedly at his tool box.

George takes the hint and picks up a shoe. 'Might be the last dance I ever go to. You can't help thinking that. The last horse I ever shoe.'

Nell bites back the impulse to laugh at the melodramatic statement. Because it's true. It might be so. Therefore, she must go to the dance. It's actually the car that complicates matters. It arrived a month ago and Nell finds herself both thrilled and embarrassed to be in possession of such a prize.

Driving comes easily; as Dad says, she makes ready co-ordination of limbs, eye and distance. But the Singer comes with strings attached: Mother expects to be taken here and there. Nell is to go each month or two for pantry supplies, to Timaru or even Dunedin, sometimes with a parent in attendance. She is expected to be frugal, considering carefully each mile she travels and seeing if it can be made to accomplish more than one objective. For example, as she set out for Simons Pass yesterday to deliver a load of rabbit skins to the couple who are curing them by the hundreds, Mother put a date loaf for old Mrs Gilmore on the passenger seat, and a gallon of vege and mutton soup on the floor, to be taken to the head shepherd's family. If she drives to the dance, she'll be made to take mountains of cake and sandwiches just because she can, and the car itself will draw unwanted attention.

As George rasps and hammers and swears quietly, Major falls into a stupor. His head and bottom lip droop. Nell amuses herself plaiting his forelock.

The year has gone quickly, lambing well past, the

ewes taken onto the hills and the wethers mustered for shearing – she's been out twice on Major to chase rogues down from far slopes and gullies. Hamish took over management of the station three years ago, although he's only twenty now. He consults with their father, but Dad is away three weeks of the month, travelling between runs and seeing to their productivity. Soon enough, Hamish will find a wife, Mother will move down-country and this won't really be Nell's home.

The letters that flew back and forth between those who stayed on at school and those who left have dwindled as interests diverge. Lenora has been sent to look after a grandmother in the North Island (*Pity Gran*, Lenora wrote with insight). Meg wants to go to university and has her head down, studying. Without an actual plan, Nell is determined to put her best foot forward this year, to do all as willingly as she can, to keep her secret hopes alive and see how it goes.

George stands up straight and stretches his arms. 'Tell you what, I'll treat you like a princess on Friday night, hang your coat, fetch your supper – lots of cream, I know – fill any gaps on your dance card, if you'll come by and fetch me in that car of yours.' He winks at Nell. 'My old man won't believe his eyes.'

'The Barley boy has gone.'

'Charles? You know he's Charles. And why *gone*? You mean he was killed.'

'You needn't be coarse, Nell.'

'You mean the truth is coarse?'

'And don't take that tone with me.'

Nell reaches to unclasp and push open the steel window beside the table. 'I can't stand it. We should all be banging pots on the street, tearing out our hair. *Boys* are being killed. Slaughtered! But it's, oh, another one is lost, or *gone*. All the propaganda makes us dumb.'

Her mother stares at her knitting needles. 'It behoves us to hold the fabric together, Nell. To keep our composure and sustain hope for our men. By whatever means we have at our disposal. Besides which, *we* are unspeakably fortunate.'

She is referring to the minor ankle defect that has disqualified Hamish thus far from army service and kept him on the station, to his vexation. To the bounty of butter, eggs and meat; carrots, spuds, silver beet if it comes to that. To wool; at the other window her mother is knitting a sock for a soldier.

Silenced by reasonableness, Nell presses her pen into the page. Her finger goes white before the nib snaps off backwards. The tiny blue crash releases a tiny sob.

Her mother is oblivious. 'What are you going to do this month, have you decided?'

'VAD don't want me yet, so I thought I'd go to Bea.'
Bea is her motherless cousin, mother herself to two small
children.

'I thought I might go up myself.'

Nell and her mother stare at one another.

'Mrs Black will be here to do for Hamish and the
men. We can travel up together.'

'That's not...' She can't say it: the joy of having a
car is to drive it alone, or with a friend. Or it's to go to
her cousin's and get stuck in, helping and chatting with
Bea, yet with the means of escape at the time of her
own deciding. With Mother along for the ride, Mother
in residence at Bea's ... Nell gets overwhelmed by both
of them together. What they want, what they need
(quite besides the baby's demands) looms large and she
becomes to herself a cipher who scuttles about doing
their bidding. She'll be expected to mind the baby while
'the poor little mother' is taken away for treats, and Bea
will overlook Nell since Mother will eclipse her.

Mother thinks she's going up to help, but Bea has
confided to Nell that she finds her aunt hard going. She
expresses her opinions about child-rearing without ever
putting her hand to the housework or baby-minding.
Mother thinks that her presence alone is a boon to her
niece.

Nell takes a pencil and begins to write, possibly to
Meg, but saying it is what matters: *I always thought my
mother the hardest working of women. She's always there,
everywhere in the picture, giving her opinion, ordering this
or that, but in fact she does very little!! She has house-help or*

helps (Susanne, Tess and Jane for starters), cook, gardener, or 'my little Croatian friend', wife of the head shepherd, decades older than Mother, who can nevertheless be plied to mend socks or do the ironing.

'I wonder if the tea is far off,' her mother says, but Nell keeps her head bent over the writing pad.

Mother knits for charitable projects and once in a blue moon for her own family; she snips at this or that in the garden, according to her whims, and she wears three changes of clothing in a day (all laundered in due course & ironed by Jane or Tess…) the third after a long bath, which is taken while the rest of the household buzzes like a hive in prep for dinner. Mother knows how to avoid hard work – the work of holding a contrary opinion about the ghastly slaughter of war or the work of getting up and looking after her things, let alone her people.

This is a revelation. I have no memory of being 'looked after' by my mother. I see that I am one of her skivvies (odd word!) as long as I'm in her domain, alert to her expectations, and even more so to her moods, which are easy enough to read, much harder to influence. For instance, as I write, tension builds. Mother has mentioned 'tea' and is accustomed to having someone (the ever-obliging Nell, in this case, since it's Tess's afternoon off) jump up to fetch it. It gives me a strange feeling because I don't think or act that way. I am not like her and until this very hour I've assumed that in more or less every way that matters, I am. How terrible to write this. I might cross it all out. For now, I'll hide this away and see if it still seems true a week from now.

Well then, we go to Bea's and I go on paying my dues as owner of the car.

Nell rolls up the pages, flattens the roll and tucks it into her pencil case. She mustn't leave it lying around like any old half-written letter, inviting the curious.

After all that, she wonders if she might go for a ride. She goes along the sunny hallway and stands at the open door. A brown form is coming up the road, at speed. Horse and rider, growing larger by the second, galloping like the clappers. Head shepherd, Mr Babich.

'Is your mother here?' The old man is wheezing with exertion.

Nell opens the garden gate to him.

Mother has heard the wallop of hooves and she's coming off the verandah. 'What is it?' Face white, hand to throat.

Nell holds the horse while Mr Babich slides off and removes his hat.

'The boss.'

Father and Hamish headed away with the musterers this morning. Mr Babich relates how they all met for lunch on a favourite overhang amongst the bluffs, known for its splendid view, and the great chunk of rock gave way, taking Father with it.

'Is breathing, but we cannot ... rouse him before I leave. We think best thing, take him to Kurow. They on their way.'

'Was anyone else hurt?'

'What are his injuries?'

'Come in at once and have a drink and something to eat. You've covered miles.'

In a trance, Nell takes the overheated horse around to the saddlery shed. She tries not to think of blood, of her father's skull, of possible awful outcomes as she unsaddles, waters, wipes down and lets the horse into the home paddock. And to think, Hamish was there, that he heard the dreadful crack, and had been sitting so close that his heels were left hanging over the gorge.

Nell later admits that Mother is magnificent in a crisis. She meets immediate need, obtains pertinent information, rallies those who'll step up in her and Father's absence, and within the hour has packed overnight bags and a box of food supplies, has issued orders, written lists and is climbing into the car beside Nell, who had only to fill the petrol tank and put together a few clothes and yet feels utterly confounded, capable of only her single duty: to drive the long roads between here and wherever it is that Father has been taken.

There is a long summer at home, with precious little time for swanning about. Besides raking and turning hay in the front paddocks, which means all hands on deck once it's been cut, Nell helps in the household with guests, smokos and meals for shearers, harvesting and bottling fruit and, one rare autumn weekend, with the house all but empty and her parents away to a wedding (Father has recovered, though not entirely; he is forgetful, and prone to frustrated anger), something very other.

'Turns out we've left a bunch up in Lofty's Gully.' Hamish reaches for the marmalade and dollops it onto his toast. 'Dobbs's shepherd saw them yesterday from the tops. About eighty of the buggers.' Hamish enjoys unleashing his vocabulary when Mother is out of the house. 'It'll be a whole bloody day's labour to get them out of there.'

'Besides the hours riding up and back,' Nell agrees. 'Why don't I take a couple of the dogs and do it?'

'On your own? Not a hope.'

Nell, then Hamish, glances at the new boy. Man. Simon, about Hamish's age and here to work for the summer before agricultural college. A distinguishing feature is the still-red scar running from mouth to jaw.

'It'd introduce him to the place.'

Across the table, Simon lifts his eyebrows.

'Mother and Dad wouldn't…'

'They needn't know.' With summer dwindling, Nell

feels reckless. Polite, Simon has hardly said boo since he arrived yesterday. She can see Hamish reckoning the risks. He shrugs and addresses Nell. 'Put him on Chester. Take Stark and Fizz. You'll have to try and pull the bunch together this afternoon, camp out, then push them down through the bluffs in the morning. You know where?'

'I watched you go up last year. South of the creek.'

'Yeah, figure it out on your way up. The dogs know it.'

Nell tells Simon to get what he needs for a night away. She's already milked the house cow; while cranking the separator handle, she compiles a mental list. Inside, she throws the dishes through the sink, then bundles food into saddle bags. Blankets, canvas, billies.

Out in the home paddock, she finds Simon sitting deep and easy in the saddle as he puts Chester through his paces.

'That'll surprise the old dobbin,' Nell tells him as he comes by.

Simon snaps Chester to a halt. 'Can't stand a plodder.'

His face has livened up. Last night's sleepy politeness has gone and he holds her eye in a clinch that discomfits as much as it thrills her.

'Mind if I run the dogs?' It's more command than question.

Nell was looking forward to that, and to showing off just a little. 'I thought you were a townie.'

'Only when it suits me to say so. I've spent every holiday since I was this high on my uncle's farm.'

Nell tightens Pele's girth and tugs at the saddle. 'Did you think of the cavalry?' She tightens it another hole.

'Naturally.' He lifts his chin. It's a sore point with any young man still at home. 'I was turned away on grounds – which I dare say I could sell for thousands were it my choice – of a hernia.'

'Sell?'

'To a conchy, a coward.'

Nell puts her toe into the stirrup and pulls herself up. 'A conscientious objector wouldn't buy your deformity. He'd make a stand in his own sound body.' She gathers the reins. 'We'll take the far gate.'

'Have you actually met one?'

'I know of a local man. Have you?'

Simon shrugs. 'I've heard plenty about them.'

'So have I. And read. And been impressed by a degree of thoughtfulness that seems to be entirely absent from the average soldier's idea of war.'

'It's probably a subject we ought to avoid then.'

Stars crowd overhead in a moonless sky, as the fire dies down. Between Nell and Simon is a pile of old matagouri to toss on in the night, should either of them wake. Fizz has crept up to Nell's back and her warmth makes for a quick slide into sleep.

Nell becomes aware of a warm hand on hers, of a digit travelling softly, softly around her palm. In the calm of new-waking she recognises that this is a novel kind of touch: not the loving, perfunctory touch of a mother, not a father's solid hand on the shoulder, not the nudge-pinch-pull of a sibling, but something entirely other, gentle, but purposeful. She'll wait a moment and see, giving no indication yet that she's awake. The finger strays onto her wrist and drifts back and forth across the veins until it finds one to ascend. Another finger or two join it and the sensation is ... delirious, is the word that comes to mind. Mildly delirious. Up the inner arm, until it meets the resistance of the shirt she's slept in. The hand encircles her arm and flows back to her hand. There's the crackle of grass, body shifting on canvas, and she senses rather than sees him close beside her. His fingers find her face and trace its outline: the shivery edges of her hair, of ears, eyes and finally lips. Swat him away, says her good sense. Yield, says her skin, her arm, her throat where his hand drifts while something unbelievably soft strays over her mouth and makes her mouth back. Under her blankets, his warm, gentle hand begins to pour over her, like hot syrup, she'll later think. It's unthinkable to pull back; home is a thousand miles away and this moment has nothing to do with anything known.

Hand on her breast! His fingers tug and tweak a nerve that connects directly with down below. How extra-ordinary. This is the kind of thing that other people must know. That she hasn't known before now. Husbands and wives must have this knowledge, and who is this man, boy, demonstrating it to her? The tussle begins.

Nell swipes his hand from her front, then she has to take his wrist and remove it more forcefully. The hand flies back to her belly and shoots downwards, under the waist of her underpants. That tricky, torturing finger is suddenly inside her – outside, inside, out, in and mayhem is the next word that grasps her. Sweet mayhem.

She cries, 'No!'

The tussle grows monstrous because some swelling urge is overwhelming every rational thought. She doesn't even know this person; she'll have to marry him if this goes on; her life is about to be ruined.

She wrenches at his hand and goes to roll away, but her name is being breathed onto her face: Nell, Hell, sweet Hellabore, let me love you. His weight covers her and the fingers are back, cajoling and terrorising.

'You mustn't,' Nell yelps as her hips rise to his.

First Church in Dunedin is huge and unaccommodating. She should have worn her long coat; the pew and the air are cold. Mother passes hymn and prayer books from the pile beside her. Nell shares with her ten-year-old cousin Jean. As they wait for the service to start, Jean's eyes flick up at the hymn board, her slim hands dart through the pages. She bookmarks them with strips of paper she evidently keeps in her Sunday purse. A smile twitches at her mouth. Little does she know. As they walked here together from her parents' house, Jean chattered on about her cat, her teacher, her intention to become a laboratory scientist. The organ strikes a chord and the sustained note goes through Nell as a raking strand of nausea. Life is a raw grey morning spent trapped like an insect in the setting amber of family convention. *The incident* has stained everything the colour of cynicism. That is, when she's not actively alarmed, as she was for the week or two after the event when a rash developed and she had to contrive a trip to town and find a doctor (why can it only ever be a man?) who made her show what no man, not even her seducer, had seen. Tinea, he decided, which meant a vile and tacky greenish paste smeared in the creases of her legs, a burning torment that made walking hell and quiet sitting near impossible.

Alarm, shame and shrinking away. Nell has virtually stopped talking to her family.

'And now, let us turn to page thirty-five of the Morning Liturgy. *Great is the Lord and greatly to be praised.*'

On their way back up the hill, Mother says, 'Let's walk together,' as she takes Nell's arm. 'I'm concerned about you, dear. You've not been yourself lately. Are you feeling unwell?'

'I'm not unwell.'

'You have something on your mind then.'

'Yes. Something.'

They halt and look at one another, but Nell shakes her head. 'Nothing. It will pass. I just need to find what I'm going to do.'

'It's not easy, the in-between time. But you know we'll keep you…'

The rest of the sentence is never spoken, but is understood: *as long as you remain at my right hand, doing what it suits me to have you do.*

Whenever she can, Nell goes out on horseback, to move sheep or carry fencing materials around the station; to help with lambing or painting a shed. The men expect little of her, therefore she is free to choose, and she does a good job, clearing a hill of sheep or wielding a paintbrush on a corrugated iron expanse. There's nothing fussy or refined about these days; they expand; the weather is foe or ally; she knows herself outdoors to be strong and level-headed. In short, she is happy.

More often, though, her mother decides the day. A group of ladies is coming from Christchurch on a high country tour, Nell learns one week in early spring, and the next finds herself in charge of preparing three bedrooms, each with a camp cot as well as the bed (Stella has to be turfed out of hers for the duration, and Hamish's rugby boots/pictures/smells must be expunged from his) and of the meals, since they are (as so often these days, with Nell in situ) between cooks.

Two ladies have asked if they might be taken for a ride, so the morning before their departure, Nell is up at dawn, bringing three horses down from the ridge pad-dock into the yard, combing loose the dried mud and brushing them down. Chester's tail is so tangled with matagouri that, in frustration, she cuts off a length. Then she finds that the saddle girths are muddy, so she swaps and wipes and grumbles about those who don't clean up after themselves, and those who expect everything to be just so.

It is refreshing, though, to ride away from the farmhouse with the competent two who, although twenty years older than Nell, have caught her interest and show interest in return. On the river track, the woman called Simone comes alongside. Nell comments on the brooch on her blazer lapel.

'Minerva.' Simone touches the silver owl. 'Five of us wear the same brooch, made by one of us. Only the stones for the eyes differ. Mine are topaz.'

'Is it to mark your friendship?'

'Partly, and yes, we are friends.' She laughs. 'And sometimes foes. Our bond lies in the fostering of best intentions.'

They have pulled up at the first gate and Nell prepares to slide off her horse. 'Isn't the road to hell paved…'

'…with good intentions? So they say. But also the road to heaven. As we state in our brief manifesto, intention precedes action. If an intention is honourable, we look for ways to foster it.'

Nell lifts the chain and hauls the gate over the long grass that's grown along the centre of the track. She feels avid for whatever it is the owls endeavour. She has so many fine thoughts and intentions – to understand, to do good, to improve matters – and most of them seem to evaporate somewhere out in the hills or slip down the kitchen drain with the dishwater.

Frost lies in pockets of grass under the matagouri bushes. Young willows line the river, which wends close and then departs from the dray track. They ride for a while in silence but for the creak of saddlery, clank of bits and hoof-thud on turf.

'Are you a member?' Nell asks Fiona, the other woman, when their horses come adjacent.

Fiona smiles. 'Membership pending. One of them is going overseas. They reckon five is the optimum number. Isn't that so, Si-si?'

'Oui-oui.' Chester jostles up between their two horses. Simone takes a small jar from her pocket and offers it. 'Lip salve, anyone? The thing is, Nell, we acknowledge that, alone, each of us flounders in our intentions. Simply put, we tell one another what they are, and, whether lofty or rudimentary, we encourage one another in their pursuit. For example, two of our number have organised for enormous numbers of letters to be written to the boys overseas, especially to those who receive few. They intended to help, we fostered their best idea, and they acted.'

'It sounds simple. Obviously it's the action that takes the effort.'

'Actually,' Simone taps her riding crop on the pommel, 'the real effort lies in finding the true intention. Often we think we want something, but underneath the desire lies a deeper longing.

'Let's say Jane has fallen for a hat and her intention is to obtain it. We ask her why, and what satisfaction it will bring her. She has several decent hats already, but she imagines that this next is the one that will bring her real pleasure, attention … perhaps even love. So, love is the motive! By careful questioning we learn that Jane is interested in a particular man, but lacks the courage to act. We help her formulate steps for action – a little frightening, understandably, but each one is manageable and measurable. Most importantly, she is not allowed to give up on her plan. The owls are watching.'

Nell turns Major off the track. 'We'll cross here.' She presses him into the hock-deep stream. The horses all stop to wet their noses and paw at the water. 'And what became of Jane and this man?'

'The real Jane? Precisely nothing! She met him as desired and realised at once that he wasn't the fellow she'd dreamed up. There was no kinship. How much of her life might she have wasted in dreaming and diversion if she'd stuck only with her pursuit of the perfect hat?'

On the other side of the river lies a broad flat paddock between creek and river. The women are keen for a gallop, so they urge the horses into a canter, then give them their heads. Simone swings one arm and lets out a wild holler. Fiona clings to the pommel, but she's grinning. Mud flies from hooves and Nell's eyes stream in the rush of cool air.

They arrive laughing and panting at the far gate.

'I'll be looking out for mine,' Nell tells Simone as she dismounts. 'For my owls.'

'Even one is a treasure.'

Feathers arrive in the post, every month or two. White feathers in envelopes addressed to Hamish, the first few with *Conchie!* or *Coward!* scrawled on them. For three years he has made serial applications to the military service board, and has each time been turned down. They cite a weakened ankle following a childhood tendon injury, in spite of the fact that he scrambles all day around the hills on foot or on horseback, handling mobs of sheep, hay, oats and heavy machinery. And so the feathers keep coming. But then, in what will prove to be the last year of the war, when even the flawed are accepted, Hamish marries his friend Florence and packs his kitbag for military camp.

Dear Miss Preston,

In answer to your query, yes! The sooner you can come, the better! We may have sufficient soup-makers, but need automobile drivers to deliver it – from the hall adjacent to the church. Our single driver cannot complete the 'lunch' round before 5 or 6 in the evening. Help! You will have a boy scout to run messages and carry pots and what-have-you. You will have no contact with the residents, or enter their homes unless there is no choice. The boy must <u>not</u> be allowed to do so! Let us know at once if you are coming. Or simply turn up any morning from 11.30 – you will be pressed into service on the spot!!

In haste!
Beverley Watts

'Weeping, Nellie?' Vernon says.

Nell is in the makeshift soup kitchen of Dunedin's city hall and Vernon is her helper. The others haven't turned up. 'You'd weep if you'd done what I've just done.' Nell's shoes clip across the cavernous space. She scrapes the last pile of chopped onions into the soup pot and slides it onto the electric stove.

'A veritable massacre. Let the tears fall, my dear. Balm for the soul.' Vernon wipes his hands on his apron and comes to stand beside her. 'I want to watch you stir this monster to life.'

'It's complicated.' Nell grins at him and turns the dial to 7.

'I see. Women, never divulge your mysteries.' Vernon chuckles and goes back to his cack-handed peeling. 'These knobbly carrots aren't much fun. I start to appreciate my mother's daily labours fifty years too late. It takes a pandemic to enlighten me.'

'Were you a large family?'

'Fifteen of us. I shudder to recall it.' Vernon does shudder, and reaches for the cigarette he keeps smouldering in a saucer.

'Shall I do the leeks next?' Nell says.

'I defer to you. I know only that all these ingredients must go into the vats and be boiled until subdued.'

Nell shakes her head and takes the leeks to the sink. 'Sautéing them first brings out the flavour. Especially of onions and other members of the allium family.'

'You're a smart young thing, Miss Nellie. Do you mind me calling you that? I'm thinking of course of the great Dame Melba. And I heard you singing when I arrived. A sweet sound indeed.' He coughs, and takes another tug on the cigarette.

'Did you ever hear her?'

'In the flesh? Indeed. She toured the country when you were, I dare say, knee-high to a pup. My word, that's already smelling more like something I'd want to partake of.'

'That's the sauté effect. The effect of butter. Now you know. And the bacon ends will help too. Do we have a colander for washing the split peas?'

'Open up your bonnet, boot, whatever and I'll heave the pots out there, shall I?' Vernon presses his fag end into the bowl of veggie scraps.

'We'll do it together. No, wait…' Nell rushes to the open door of the meeting hall. 'Excuse me!'

The youth pushing his bicycle along the footpath is startled, but happy to be enlisted, swinging each pot onto the doorstep as though it were empty, and from there into the boot of the Singer. Nell wraps and buffers the pots with the sacks she brought down from the farm.

Vernon lights another cigarette in the doorway while Nell pulls on her coat, takes her handbag and the crank handle.

'All right then, Nellie? Where's your little helper?'

'I'm collecting him on the way.'

'You take care now and don't be lingering with the afflicted. See you again on Friday, is it?'

'I'll be in again tomorrow, but yes, Friday too.'

The bacony smell of soup seeps from the trunk and in the cold air, the windshield keeps fogging. Nell's second stop to wipe it down is outside the small square cottage where a uniformed boy scout waits on the front step.

He comes and climbs in beside her. 'Hello.'

'Matthew?'

He nods.

'And I'm Nell. Not your first time? Good. You'll want to pull that rug around you. And you can tell me the routine.'

Matthew tells her, adding, 'I'm not supposed to go inside.'

'No, that's right.'

The soup run begins at the top of the south road. They creep down, looking at letterboxes for number 407.

Matthew is all legs and eagerness. He runs up a path lined with flowering azaleas to snatch the saucepan from the doorstep, raps at the door, then runs back to the car. Nell opens the trunk and the vat, fills the saucepan and carries it briskly to the door. Just inside, an old man in slippers waits with an oven mitt.

'Hello, Mr Weatherill, is it? And who else lives with you?'

'Mrs Weatherill. But she won't be having any. She's too crook with the 'flu.'

'Has the doctor seen her?'

'Only the nurse, yesterday. Doctor took ill himself.'

Nell tuts. 'Is there anything I can…'

'No, lass. Mrs Weatherill and I agreed before she went downhill that we'd tackle this alone. No one need catch the plague from us.' He takes the handle and holds the oven mitt under the pot. 'She gave me instructions for all eventualities, and I'm following them. Thank you, lass.'

Nell blinks hard. She looks along the dim passageway behind him. Are there really instructions to be had for all eventualities, even for a man whose wife might be dying while he too is falling ill, and soon neither will be able to get up and unlock the door?

A gust of wind shakes raindrops from the birch tree onto the bruised azaleas. They thud onto the car bonnet and Nell's felt hat as she gets back into the Singer.

Matthew is waiting with the list. 'Next is three hundred and twenty-nine,' he says.

Dear Miss Preston,

I was pleased to receive your question about the society, which is presently experiencing an upsurge in membership, with some of the city's finest minds joining us in enquiry after the Eternal Verities.

Your interest indicates to me that you are upon, or are being inwardly urged onto, The Path. I encourage you to follow interest with action – come and find out if our meetings are to your liking.

A session is held for both guided and silent meditation on Wednesday evenings at 7 o'clock, and each second Monday we enjoy an enlivening talk at the same hour, from a variety of speakers. Sundry other activities take place in the course of the month and, if you would care to receive it, we can mail to you our monthly newsletter.

We are starting to build up a library of illuminating reading. Anyone may join up and borrow books, just as anyone with interest may attend our meetings.

Yours on the Way,
Mary Bedwell

As Nell takes a brisk left onto Dowling Street, the street lights sputter and come on. Dusk is falling early. It's only seven o'clock ... she consults her watch: no, three or four minutes past. Bother. She should have resisted dessert with her grandparents and left herself time to stroll down. Two steps above the street, the big double door stands ajar and the burble of voices comes from inside. She is about to enter when she hears running feet behind her. A young woman leaps up the steps and halts, tearing off her hat.

'Have they started?' Blonde curly hair, pink cheeks, a merry dimple.

'I don't know. I'm not sure I should be here anyway.'

'Your first time too? Hurrah. I'm Peggy.'

Her smile is irresistible. 'Nell.'

Already Peggy has taken her arm and is propelling them both along the wood-lined passage. She insists that they squeeze side-by-side through the doorway, so that they arrive giggling behind a throng of citizens seated in horseshoe rows. A woman points out two vacant chairs in the back row, and two men shuffle along so that they can sit together.

'Why did you come?' Peggy asks in a low murmur.

Her unguarded look draws out the answer quick as a thistle: 'The 'flu. I couldn't bear it.'

Peggy lays a hand on her arm as the president of the local Theosophical Society goes up to stand beside a pile of books (several adjacent piles) almost his own height. All two thousand have been donated to the society's library. 'Take home a handful tonight; just write the titles and authors in this notebook, along with your name and address, and that way we'll have fewer to contend with when we start to catalogue and shelve them this weekend. Volunteers are welcomed for the task.

'And now I'll hand over to our guest speaker, Mrs Montgomery.'

A tall woman with plaited, greying hair wound into a bun comes to take his place on the small platform.

She remains there, still and silent except for her eyes, which scan the faces before her. The *eyes* before her, Nell realises. Her quiet gaze searches, and elicits in Nell an answering spark.

'Before I give my talk, let us turn our attention inward.'

Mrs Montgomery lowers her eyes and suggests that the posture be upright, legs uncrossed and eyes lightly closed. Nell keeps hers open and looks around at the heads, both grey and glossy, the snug-fitting hats. There's a full range of adults, most quite interesting to look at and several distinguished-looking. Peggy's eyes are shut, but her lips twitch humorously.

'Allow your interest to rest on the rise and fall of the trunk…' Nell closes her eyes, and has her first taste of 'meditation'.

As soon as the talk is over, Peggy stands and says into Nell's ear. 'If we're quick, we can get a hot cocoa at Wains. Want to?'

'You don't want to have supper here?'

Outside, Peggy says no, she doesn't want stewed tea and half a dried-out scone. And at the hotel, where they sit each in a deep leather chair waiting for their drinks, she says, 'Truth to tell, Mrs M. is my great aunt, or second cousin or something, and I thought it time I heard what the old trout had to say. My parents call it a load of cobblers, so of course I was bound to investigate sooner or later. But I didn't want to hang around. I'll go and visit her later in the week.'

'And what did you make of it?' Nell slides her shoes off and tucks her feet into the capacious seat. She leans over the high rolled arm towards Peggy who has all but disappeared into her chair.

'I come with a certain bias, so I'd like to hear you first.'

Nell looks beyond Peggy, seeing without seeing the row of indoor plants screening the bar. 'What she called the path ... I have a feeling for that, but I don't actually know what it constitutes in my life, or whether I could say I'm on it.'

Peggy laughs. 'If you attend a theosophical meeting, you're on the path, believe me. Or rather, don't believe. Test everything!'

'Yes, that seemed to be her catch-cry. But what does *the path* mean to you?'

Peggy's eyes gleam. 'Don't you love this? Here we are. I had a feeling I'd meet you tonight.'

'Me? You know me already?'

'Not in the details, but ... don't you sense it? I knew I'd meet *someone*.'

Nell draws back a little. It's anathema to her – certainly to her family – to grasp for quick intimacy, to prattle and tell on first meeting. But she knows what Peggy means. They spilled into the room tonight as if by assignment and yes, she recognises already more ease and amity with Peggy than she has enjoyed with any adult friend.

'I'm pulling your leg,' says Peggy. 'Just a little tug. I believe you're Nell Preston, and you were at the ladies' emporium the year or so behind my sister Virginia.'

'Ah, and you went to the local high school instead. I remember her telling me.'

'Ever the dissenter. As for *the path*...' As Peggy's mercurial face quietens, the hot cocoas arrive. Her eyes acknowledge the waiter, and Nell sees a likeness with Mrs Montgomery's own formidable self-possession.

'For me, it's the tug and draw on your ... your being. Knowing that there's always something to be grasped beyond the obvious, beyond the much our senses convey to us.'

'And sometimes...' Peggy pushes herself back into the chair, 'sometimes that's just a bloody nuisance. Sometimes you just want to plod plainly and do the ordinary, obvious thing, without thinking about it, or trying to extract more. Which is probably *the path* too.'

She lurches forward again, grinning. 'And what else do you think about, Miss Nell?'

'Well,' Nell sips, and licks her upper lip, 'I'm currently taking in the news that I've been accepted to train as a nurse in the new year.'

It's only later, as she enters the gate to her grandparents' house, that Nell realises: she has found an owl.

'Nurse Preston, you take beds twenty-five to thirty-three.'

'Ooh, Nell, you've got the handsome end.'

'Excuse me, Probationer Harris, that is hardly the attitude.' Sister writes their surnames in purple ink across the day's ward plan. 'All of you are to have your first three bed baths completed by a quarter past eight.'

Nell's charges in the busy surgical ward include three officers returned together from a military convalescent hospital in England. Amidst the men who slump and lounge or are bowed by age, the three, in spite of their injuries, are upright, well-presented and watchful. Even now, at the end of the bed-lined corridor, they can be seen sitting to attention, heads turned towards the nurses gathered around Sister's desk. Nell's belly tightens. She will not be cowed. They are patients, nothing more. And she is their nurse for the day.

She starts with the two elderly men in her charge, cutting off any curious looks from the officers with savage sweeps of the curtains about the beds. She's aware of them though, listening through the yellow fabric, and her conversation is stilted and minimal. 'How have you slept? Have you had a bowel motion since yesterday morning? Will you lift your tail-end while I slide the towel underneath? Here's the cloth for you to finish off with.' She hears the snicker.

'You have a professional way about you, nurse,' Sister says later, 'and I see you're no stranger to hard work, but don't be afraid to prattle a bit. The men like to have a breath of life from the world outside the ward.'

'Prattle?'

'You don't want to be thought a prig, do you, Nurse Preston?'

I love it, Peg, she writes at the end of her first month. *It's unlikely I'll ever master the womanly art of prattle, but daily I feel the privilege of being with patients in their undefended state, of offering a steadying arm or listening ear, or some encouragement regarding the facts of their case. I find our lessons simplistic, but there's nothing to stop us reading up in the medical library. Of course, there are grim and disgusting elements to the work, but most of it is plain interesting and the worst moments are soon forgotten.*

There's a boy of 12 in the ward currently, who had a stake driven into his leg, and developed a dreadful sepsis. He's become like a little brother to us nurses. We all wept when he hovered near death, then wept again when he came out the other side. Two or three of my fellow nurses are terrific girls and we have a lot of fun.

What worries me are Mother's letters. She has developed some vague, debilitating condition since I left. The doctor is baffled, and Mother fears the worst.

Nell drives into the shed and switches off the engine. The iron roof ticks above her. Birds are skittering in the eaves. She stares ahead at the harvester with its gleaming teeth, at the rows of dusty harness unused for five years or more, at her own hands on the steering wheel, fingertips peeling from the constant application of lysol. She can hear the tractor up on the terrace and, closer at hand, one of the dogs is barking acknowledgement of her arrival.

Back where she started.

She leaves her suitcase and boxes in the car and walks

across the lawn to the house. Yellow wisteria leaves have drifted across the verandah and the door is wide open. There's no one in the kitchen. Silence in the living rooms. She listens. Nothing.

Nell runs upstairs two at a time. 'Mother?' She has tried hard to keep alarm at bay in recent days, but her heart is banging as she pushes gently at her mother's bedroom door and follows it on soft feet.

Empty. The bed made. Flowers on the dresser.

Through the open window she hears women's voices, and laughter.

She has an inkling.

She hardly dares go down.

Nell goes to wash and change her blouse. She kicks off her shoes and throws the stockings into the corner of her room.

Outside, she follows the voices to the raspberry grove. Mother and Mrs Black have an end each of a large net and are flicking it high to free it from the bushes. Mother's movements are vigorous and easy. Seeing Nell, she pushes her end of the net into Mrs Black's hands —'Just tug it away onto the wall' – and walks over to Nell. 'You came, dear. And none too soon, I must say. We've been hard-pressed.' Pausing to examine Nell's face: 'Are you quite all right?'

What Nell experiences, and will never forget, is the rush of heat, up from her belly, down from her head, that clashes and roils beneath her breast. The voice that comes out of her is clear, deep and forceful. She seems to be hearing it from a step or two away.

'No. I'm not all right, although you evidently are, in spite of what you wrote. It's been a hellish ten days.' Nell snatches at a raspberry wand and tears off leaves and berries. 'I wrestled with my conscience. I wrangled with the matron. The hospital board berated me. I wrote my painful letter of withdrawal, then completed all my appointed duties in shame, knowing that my short career as a nurse was over.' She looks at her hand and shakes off crushed leaves. The juice remains. 'Yesterday morning I said goodbye to my friends as they went on duty without me, then I scoured my bed, floor, locker, window.' She rubs at her palm. 'All this was eased, though, just the tiniest bit, by knowing that the cause was just: according to the daily letters and – was it three, or four? – telegrams, my mother was very ill, disabled, and I was indispensable to her care.'

Nell stoops to wipe her hand on the grass and when she stands again her head is swimming. 'How could you be so selfish!'

For days, Nell won't speak to her mother. She takes her meals to the verandah and simply shakes her head at her father when he urges forgiveness. 'That won't happen,' she tells him. 'I'll speak to her when I'm ready and not before.'

Dearest Nell,

We can't know the wider, broader sweep of purpose in such very difficult circumstances, however you must believe that there is such, and that it is working itself out. You acted from filial duty for which there can be no blame or shame. Your intentions are noble, so that whether you are nursing or helping your family, visiting friends or riding in the hills, the prow of your ship stays pointed true north. Believe in this.

I find that when I forgive, it is done (in due course, when the cause of anger has been looked at and the matter felt in all its aspects) for my own sake, so that I grow not bitter.

Do let's go skating again this winter. I was just getting the hang of it by the end of the last season and sometimes, particularly while sitting to meditate, I find myself tensed and exhilarated, only to realise that my toes are clenched in the boots, with ice speeding beneath them and cold air burning my cheeks…

Your friend,
Peg

Nell heads away from the station in her little Singer later than intended, and is further held up by a chain of men restoring the road. They won't let her over the new stretch until it has been pounded and rolled – time she spends eating a late lunch of egg sandwiches and reading from the pile of library books on the seat beside her. It is full dark by the time she reaches the main road, and for some reason her headlights keep fading. She creeps through Oamaru, and finally books herself reluctantly into the Millhouse Hotel. She telephones her grandmother to say she'll arrive in the morning.

The narrow bedroom is dank, the bedding clammy. Nell is glad to be out of it at the first sign of dawn. She throws her suitcase into the Singer's trunk, then goes back inside for tea and toast. A freight train roars by across the road and moments later the maid setting out jam and butter gives a shriek.

From the window beside her, Nell sees the inexplicable sight of a bay horse, saddled and bridled, on its side and thrashing on the grass verge between rails and road. By the time she has run out, the horse is still, with only a hind leg raised and moving in a slow gallop. Blood has pooled and spread beneath its shoulder. The train is screaming to a slow halt, the end carriage already a hundred yards away.

'Where's the rider?' someone shouts.

'Carried on by the train, do you think?' There's a man beside Nell, along with two hotel maids and the boy who showed her the room last night.

They scan the empty verge.

'We'd better search the bank on the other side.' Nell is aware at last of her pounding heart and shaking legs.

She and the man step onto the rail tracks. While he scans about on the far side, Nell walks in brisk, truncated steps over the sleepers to the north, towards the train, peering into the bracken, left and right.

A lad has jumped from the guard's van and is running towards her when she hears a *cooee* and turns. A figure in riding attire is limping from the hotel's yard.

'A bolter,' the rider tells them when they've gathered beside the horse. 'I thought he'd got over it. I was only halfway on when he took off, out the gate and across the road.'

Into the train's path. The horse's eye is half closed and its leg has slowed to a quiver. Nell blinks at tears. The sight takes her to other horse deaths: beloved Bertie drowned in the river; a musterer's hack tangled and torn in a fence before being shot.

The train driver, the policeman and the grocer all arrive and the man who searched the tracks with Nell touches her arm.

'Are you all right?' He is tall and might be a year or two younger than she, with dark, quiet eyes unlike any she knows.

'Shaken,' she confesses. If there were no one else around, she would fall on the horse's neck, and breathe while it is still warm the inimitable smell, and release the sobs pent up in her.

'Will you let me take you in for a cup of tea?'

'I'm not sure I need taking, but tea would be welcome.'

She goes to the car to retrieve her coat since the accident has turned her cold. A step or two behind, her companion whistles. 'This is yours?' He touches the amber bonnet. 'What's it like to drive?'

Nell has seldom had the chance to sit alone with a good-looking man whose attention is entirely in her service. Daniel is a law clerk from Christchurch on his way to visit grandparents in the south. They will be surprised by the frequency of his visits over the next eight months as he seeks opportunity to see Nell.

'This is the way Mummy did it and we came to no harm, Nell. Come away outside and you'll see, it will end soon.' In spite of Lucy's shrieks, Stella waves Nell towards the door to the garden.

Married at nineteen to a parson, with a second child already on the way, Stella is the object of Nell's admiration and pity. The latter because, although she might look homely, she isn't truly domesticated, the way she dithers and dashes and loses interest in tasks. She should have married into wealth, not penury; the family all agree on that.

'But Lucy was trying to help,' Nell protests. 'She didn't mean to spill the milk.'

In the bedroom, the shrieks are lengthening to wails.

'She knows how I feel about her interfering in the kitchen, and then when I told her off ... I won't tolerate tantrums.'

'But there's a reason for a tantrum.'

'Naughtiness. It was your method. Under the pear tree that time. I remember thinking I wouldn't dare make that noise, that display of rage, in front of Mother.' Stella ducks into the outside wash house and pulls out a basket of washing.

Nell takes the other handle. 'I don't remember. I dare say I was shut in my room for it, and I dare say I harbour the injustice still.'

'Well, you stopped behaving that way. Peace in the household.'

Nell gives the basket a shake. '"Woe to those who say, peace, peace, when there is no peace."'

Stella gives her a strange look. 'Just wait until you're a mother, then you'll find yourself doing the thing that comes to you, following an instinct.'

Nell has been reading Freud. 'What you call instinct might be a habit, and not necessarily a helpful one. Surely it's important to understand what compels a child's behaviour. Mother didn't understand us. Not really. She applied one method to all.'

'Depending on her mood, you must admit.'

'Method *or* mood, agreed.'

From the clothesline, where they peg a dozen shirts, Lucy's yelling is fainter, and has taken on a weary, drawn-out quality. When they reach the tangle of socks at the bottom of the basket, Nell glides away and goes back inside.

She hurries along the hallway to the nursery door. 'Lucy?' she says, when the tot pauses for breath.

'Mamaaaaa…'

'No, Lucy, it's Aunty Nell. Listen, lovey, I know you wanted to fetch a drink for Mummy, and Mummy didn't realise.'

Hiccups come from the other side of the door.

'She got cross and that's because she's tired—'

'Mama!' Lucy's voice is tremulous with sobs. 'Where's Mama?'

Nell presses her head to the door, speaks melodiously: 'It's also because her own needs for patient attentiveness were cut short by the arrival of her brother...' She's speaking into a crescendo of wails. 'And as Freud would explain...' The distress is intolerable. Stella must be held accountable. Nell spins away to fetch her, and bumps straight into her.

'Get away from there,' her sister hisses. 'How dare you undermine me. I'll handle my own child my own way.'

'As a farmer says of his dog,' Nell retorts. 'Let her out and comfort her, for God's sake.' She darts back and turns the key to the door, pushes it open.

'Hellooo. Anyone home?' The woman's voice comes from the kitchen. 'Mrs Thomas, had you forgotten the rag collection?'

The fire goes from Stella's eyes, replaced by desperation as Lucy comes and clings to her leg and the parish lady bustles from the kitchen into the hallway.

'Oh, my word,' says Nell. 'I'm sorry, Stell. Let me take Lucy out to feed the chooks.'

Stella nods, tight-lipped. Nell hoists her niece, tearing her hands from her mother's skirt and carries her, wailing, out to the garden.

My dearest Nell,

I hardly know what to write, I am so happy. As I carry papers and files here and there across the city, I am in a daze of wonder after our second precious weekend. I see you striding along the golden hillside at Karitane, and standing in the sea with the sun glinting on your hair. I recall the (you surely agree, rather dreadful) plum wine, with which we washed down our sandwiches, and the (you surely agree, utterly delectable) x's that followed. No wonder I delivered the wrong envelope to an important barrister yesterday. No wonder I forgot to take my lunch to work two days running. My mother took note and said, 'Really, Daniel, are you in love?' as she galloped out the door with her herb cutters, not waiting for my answer.

'Yes,' I told the kitchen clock. 'Yes, I believe I am.'

Does that alarm you? I trust not. I trust that four and a half weeks hence you will gladly contrive, again, as I shall, to be in Dunedin with only a passing obligation to dance attendance on our dear, generous elders, and with great – ever greater – liberty to be together. Dear, dear, Nell, I am, most affectionately, yours,

Daniel

Nell glances at her watch and shifts around the corner, out of the wind that's snaking along George Street. Five minutes until he'll be here, which gives her time to look at her unease. She didn't enjoy letting her grandparents know just now that they aren't the only reason for her being in town. Of course, they expect her to have errands to do and friends to see, but she found herself unable to deflect the questions about the 'friend' she was having supper with tonight. So, they know it's a man and she knows they won't go to bed until she's safely home. And then tomorrow's picnic, also with Daniel, will have to be negotiated with them. She hates them suddenly, with their quiet concern, their tweedy clothes, shelves of old books, heavy furniture and ancient moral code. And they are such dears. She loves them. Why the unease? Is something skew-whiff when it comes to Daniel? The last two weekends spent thus (for the first, he was included in outings with her cousin, so that was easy to arrange; and last time her grandparents were preoccupied with a church conference all weekend) have been light-hearted, conversationally easy, and their patting and kissing thrilled her ... although he did become a little intense that last afternoon.

And yet, a certain intensity is called for, surely. At church and in school divinity lessons, reinforced by parental expectation, the one path was outlined: of chaperoned outings (stilted conversation and longing looks) before semi-chaperoned engagement (aunt leaves room to make a cup of tea so that brief kisses might be exchanged), before marriage and consummation. There has been scant mention of the sex urge, which tears at moorings and for which the one path gives little room to manoeuvre.

Of course, there are other ways to live: with abandon, or at least without the church's moral voice in one's ears. Of the girls Nell knows, a handful have swung into action and are known to have had men and experience far exceeding her own. She met Selma in town while out with Daniel and couldn't help comparing their own cautious innocence with Selma and her beau; the stroking and the fiery glances, their overt, alarming animality.

And here is Daniel, coming along St Andrew Street. He is 'a fine figure of a man', as Mother might say, with his well-cut jacket and well-pressed pants, polished shoes. And Nell has taken extra care with her dress, new stockings, and shoes borrowed from Peggy that offer more garnish than comfort. She hopes they won't be walking far. She touches her hair; extra care with hair too often results in a shambles, like over-fiddling with a flower arrangement, so she has simply washed and clipped it up.

Nell looks down at her coat, tapered toes, gloved hands and wonders at herself. Who is she, away from the hills of home, without horse and riding boots or a job to do? She suffers a moment of blank fear, and then Daniel's hand slides across the small of her back and he presses his cheek to hers.

'Hello. You got away without any trouble?'

She nods and smiles at his smooth face and kind eyes. 'No trouble.' She takes his proffered elbow and falls in step with him.

He takes them up York Place and her heels are complaining by the time they turn in and climb a set of stone steps to the home of an acquaintance of his. He refuses to say more as they knock on the door of the imposing brick house, and are led by a man wearing tails across the atrium. In a large room, guests are quietly taking to chairs placed around the room's perimeter. She and Daniel are seated directly across from the two young men and two women perched and leaning together to tune their two violins, viola and cello.

She murmurs to Daniel, 'How perfect.' Whatever they play, no matter how newfangled, she is eager for it, and mightily relieved not to find herself in a candle-lit nook having her soul searched and her knees nudged by Daniel.

'Mostly Mozart, I gather. I hope you enjoy it.' He looks calmly around the room, while keeping a hand on her arm a fraction too long.

Dear Sis,

Don't give yourself a hard time about that Daniel. I gather Mater thought him the bee's knees (without actually meeting him – a lawyer in the family and all that bunkum) but you will've had your reasons. You wrote that you found it easy enough to call off, but hard to relinquish. The old what-if anguish, eh? Trust your instincts, sis. Something warned you off and fifty-odd years is a long time to live with a mistake. No flies on you. Daniel in the Lions' Den comes to mind. Remember that governess, who ended every lesson by enacting a Bible story? She was a corker actress, I'll give her that much. Anyway, you are my lion-hearted sister and you'll find a man to match you, I'll be bound.

Grass is coming through here. What a relief. I thought the cold was never going to let up this year. Just as the first lambs are popping up like spring mushrooms. My new trick is to stand on the water tank each morning with the binoculars and scan the Corriedales on the river flats. If I see nothing untoward, I can eat my porridge in peace. Otherwise, I'll grab a crust, saddle the nearest dobbin and fly off to play midwife. Thank God the merinos look after themselves, although there are the bloody keas, of course. They start on the after-birth and move on to the lamb if the ewe doesn't clean it up quick.

Hamish

'Women must find their own vocations.' Peggy has the other side of the dinghy they're hauling down the Vauxhall slipway.

'Must choose from the limited choices available, you mean.' Nell slides her sandshoes over the green algae.

'There's no end to the number of choices. What's required is courage.'

They've reached the water's edge where Peggy steps back to take off her shoes.

Nell follows suit. 'Courage to live on crusts or charity?'

'Come along, Nell. Neither of us will ever be reduced to begging. And with the privilege of comfort comes the responsibility to do one's utmost.'

Shoes thrown into the dinghy, they shove its bow into the water.

Peggy, with her facility for European languages, has taken up translation of texts for the Theosophical Society. She's paid a pittance for her elegant renderings of talks delivered in Berlin or Nantes, and substantially she lives on an allowance from her parents. Nell relies similarly on hers, but it is understood that in exchange she will work when she's home, or will go and assist her sister or grandparents; that she will do women's work.

'What my utmost might be, I have little idea. I thought I would find it in nursing, but now…'

Peggy is sitting amidships. Putting one foot over the

stern, Nell pushes them off and scrambles aboard.

'Cold!' she says. 'Shall we take an oar each?'

'And head straight up the harbour until the beastly east'ly gets up to blow us home?'

While the water is placid they set up an easy rhythm rowing into the early sun. Nell closes her eyes for a while and enjoys the sensations, the dip and pull, the splash and swash of oars and hull.

'How can it possibly have come up so fast?' Nell asks. 'It was flat twenty minutes ago.'

Above the bow, low clouds crown the hills and daub the blue over the harbour. The first few are scudding overhead.

'Perishing, too. Time to turn back?'

Even pulling about feels perilous with the sudden appearance of waves and troughs, and wind whipping spume from the crests. Nell's oar catches, is lifted out of the rowlock and flipped from her grasp.

'Quick!' is all she can say.

Peggy hauls on her oar but this turns the dinghy side-on to the sea and the wind-blown oar is well beyond reach.

'One of us'll have to paddle over the bow. I'll go up front.'

'No, let me. I was the careless one.' Nell creeps to the forward thwart and wedges her knees beneath it while Peggy shuffles aft.

'I don't have much control,' Nell calls back. 'But at least we're headed for town.'

Within moments the boat is swept broadside to wallow in the succession of troughs. Nell hauls them straight, then around they go again.

The fourth or fifth time it happens, Peggy starts to laugh, and laughs and laughs, until Nell collapses too with tears and saltwater sheeting her face.

'Hand me the paddle,' Peggy says at last. She digs it in deep over the stern and the bow swings around to run ahead of the wind. 'That's probably the best we can do to keep on a straightish course.'

'And end up half a mile from the slipway.'

'We'll tie up to a rock and I'll retrieve the boat when the wind drops.'

The waves shove them on for an hour, while they become drenched and cold. Two oranges peeled and segmented offer distraction but no warmth. Every little while they swap places at the stern.

'I feel no need to go to sea again in a hurry,' Nell says. 'I'll marry a nice man on a nice piece of dry land.'

'And give up on your dreams?' Peggy lets Nell take the oar.

'My dreams are hazy, but I have the capacity for hard work, for care-taking, and at least if I have my own family I won't be at the beck and call of others.'

Holding the oar perpendicular in the wake takes all her strength and parts of her are juddering with cold, and yet she sees that her answer is unsatisfactory because it fails to address what Peggy and the theosophists might call her personal vocation – the singular undertaking that only she can fulfil.

Seeing the grip of her hands on the shaft, she says suddenly, 'It must be like this.' She looks around at Peggy.

And Peggy, bless her, gets it. 'Planting your intention. Thus giving the boat its direction.'

But intention is elusive. If Nell can only attain a certain freedom from the family influence, a certain freedom to act according to her own values. She recalls her untried boarding-school self, who intended to make the most of all that happened, and to keep her feelers out. It's imprecise, but it remains some kind of guide. Nell thrusts the oar deep, tightens her belly and holds on.

'Look, who's that?' There's a woman on shore, waving. Peggy waves back. The woman cups her hands to her mouth.

The wind is driving them closer, and while the water is still thigh-deep, Nell jumps out – she can't get wetter than she already is – and wades, pulling the boat with her. The woman is scrambling down the embankment.

'It's Pat Hamilton,' says Peggy. 'She's in our theatre group. Ahoy! Pat, meet my friend Nell.'

The woman grins and takes their painter. 'I was out looking for the spoonbills.' She pats the binoculars hanging on her front. 'Delighted to recognise one of you wild women. Here, let me take that side. Will we pull it above the tide?'

Although Pat offers to 'triple' them on her bike, one on the handlebars, one on the carrier, the attempt is a failure and they walk together instead, up the hill to Pat's little house for hot tea and toast.

It is riotous spring when Nell and Herb meet, though not exactly a season of green and dewy wonder. Nell will muse that in fact they're a bit jaded by life, blowsy already and frayed at the edges: Herb still gnawing on the disillusion and questions thrown up by the war: why were the chaps who were spared spared, and in what is it still worth planting one's energies? Also, in the men's absence, the women altered; they're no longer the innocent sweets they promised their untried hearts to. As for Nell, she's put in almost ten years of hard work at home and away, for half of those volunteering in the city every sixth week, with one seduction and one attempted love affair behind her. Since then, a couple of tentative liaisons, one ultimately too flimsy, the other bewildering.

One Saturday in early October, Pat Hamilton and Peggy take the train to Clyde while Nell drives from the station over the Lindis Pass to collect them in the Singer. On they go to the Fruitlands Valley with the late afternoon sun gilding their heads and the greening willows.

'Turn off just after the poplar,' Pat tells Nell.

She and Peggy hoot and grab at the doors as the car tilts off the road and onto two mud ruts that run away through the tussocks. They bounce and lurch for a mile between low hills, then drive straight at the cluster of green around a white, low-slung house, its three adjoining gables seeming to sink toward the ground.

As they approach, three men rise from the sunny

doorstep to greet them. Herbert's smile approximates his sister Pat's, but whereas she is small and animated, he is well built and firm. He squeezes Pat around the shoulders as his steady eyes take in her friends. Nell, brushing down her blue skirt, is rewarded with an evident flare of interest, a small nod of approval. She finds herself returning both.

The friends, Hunter and Ken, have to head away soon, but they're keen to show the women the scope of their shared farm as visible from the garden, and have evidently tidied up the house in anticipation of the visit. In the kitchen is a square wooden table and four chairs, and in the adjacent room, a hard horse-hair sofa and matching chairs, with stacked apple boxes for bookshelves.

Pat turns in a circle and her hands go to her hips. 'Brother of mine! What a Spartan you've become.' She whistles.

'We don't need much clobber. We work all the daylight hours.'

Hunter and Ken bring tea to the table: pot, cups, milk in a jar, then they leave with thermos flask, dinners packed in canvas bags, and lingering looks at the women. 'Come again soon!' one of them calls from outside.

Nell and Peggy sit. Pat snatches a cloth from the cord above the fireplace and swipes it over the table. 'So, how goes it?' she asks her brother.

Herb outlines for Peggy and Nell the gist of things. Each granted a smallholding under the soldier settlement scheme, the three men have amalgamated their land and efforts, the rough ground to be turned into orchard.

Pat opens the shoe box of baking she's brought, and sets it on the table as Herb goes on. 'The government speaks in high-falutin' terms of growing us men along with our trees. But the fact is, there's a burgeoning demand for stone fruit, which excel in the hot-and-cold climate of Central Otago.'

The men are also raising chickens in order to provide an early income from eggs and fattened cockerels while the tree-planting goes ahead.

'In a couple of years, we'll build a fruit-processing plant and then we'll be away laughing.'

'Just you three?' Peggy asks.

Herb rubs his chin. 'That remains to be seen. There are a dozen or so blocks of land. We enjoy a more-or-less competitive element amongst the chaps who've taken them up. It never hurts to have a goad.'

'A man's world,' says Peggy.

'None of us wish it to remain so.' Herb smiles. 'It's not every woman's ideal, but for one who's enterprising and strong-minded, able-bodied...'

Pat tosses the cleaning cloth back onto the cord. '*One* of those adjectives might touch on Isobel, I suppose.'

Herb shrugs uneasily. 'This is hardly her medium.' He gives his sister a cautioning look and no more is said about 'Isobel'.

Nell sips at the tarry brew. 'I know almost everything about the farming my family does, and nothing of the kind you mean to do.' She looks out through the doorway where a blackbird pecks at a heel of bread scavenged from the henhouse. 'I wish you every success.'

'Thank you.' Herb gulps at his tea and asks Pat for news of their sister Ilona, who is currently painting somewhere in Europe.

'And what of you, Nell?' he then asks. 'What's your pursuit?'

Nell glances at Peggy and Pat, who are paying close attention. 'I hardly know. My help is always welcomed at home, but my brother Hamish manages the station now and since he married I feel more guest than resident. I'll go next week to my younger sister in Christchurch to mind her children while she has the third.'

Nell looks at her friends who are waiting for her to say more. 'I started training as a nurse, but … well, I was needed elsewhere.' She shrugs off her irritation with that tale, and gives Peggy a sideways smile. 'Occasionally I please myself, as I'm encouraged to do.'

Watching her, Herbert slides his heels beneath the table and leans into his chair.

They have each delivered the other a tidy platter of information. His frank look tells Nell that his interest is sustained.

'We've brought an egg and bacon pie.' Pat wipes tea leaves from her tongue and pushes away the enamel mug. 'Shall we have that for dinner tonight?'

Nell, Peggy and Pat go out and haul the canvas tent from the Singer's trunk. With much hilarity, they drag and position, raise and peg it between creek and house. 'Three tussocks,' Peg calls from inside, where she's propping the corner poles. 'One each for a pillow.'

'It's not too bad a slope.' Nell ties open the door flap. 'Heads uphill, we'll be fine.'

When they've thrown their oilskin sheets, blankets and bags into the tent, Peggy says, 'Broad beans,' and takes the bucketful from her garden down to the creek. They sit and pinch beans into their skirts, tossing the pods into the stream.

Peggy gives Nell a look.

'What is it?' Nell asks.

'You know. Inklings?'

Nell glances at Pat.

Pat is smiling. 'He likes you.'

Nell pulls a face. 'You schemers.'

'Not really.' Peggy shakes small beans in her open hand. 'Merely sensing correspondences and possibilities. As fellow fire signs – Aries and Leo – you'd understand each other and have the power to make things happen.'

Nell pouts. 'What's this then – astrology?'

'I've been reading. As we do. You know the Society seeks to penetrate the old teachings.'

'Which are frowned upon by the church,' Pat adds.

'Which are all about finding what corresponds with one's own experience and makes deepest sense.'

'Anyway, whatever your credo,' says Pat, 'you've met my brother…'

'An hour ago!' Nell protests.

'…and you seem to like one another.'

'Who is Isobel?'

Pat purses her mouth and rolls her eyes. 'Not the love of Herb's life, you can be sure of that.'

'But they have an understanding.'

'She will be interested in him if he can manage her upkeep.'

'Glamorous then.'

Pat's head waggles. 'As far as I know they're not engaged to be married, and neither appears to take the other seriously.'

Still, Isobel is a factor, and Nell will tread with caution even though her heart and head have united already in interest. As Herb serves them 'French' toast for dessert that night, smothered in golden syrup and cream, she observes in herself a calm sense of fatedness.

Nell is late finishing, but it's glorious up here, with the wind combing her hair and lifting the shirt from her damp skin. Once she'd seen the Herefords down into the middle paddock, she sent the dogs home while she turned Major to the hill and they wound on up to the ridge, from where she can see away to the west the ranks of blue-hazed mountains. The wild west, the west of freedom. To the east lies constraint: first there was boarding school, then volunteer duties, with too many starchy women seizing the opportunity to boss their youngers – along with the conventions of town behaviour and dress: stockings, gloves, lipstick and hat, shoes to trim the feet. Nell can't stay here at the station much longer (and anyway, Hamish is restless and talking of a larger block), but nor does she enjoy town for more than a few days at a stretch. Once she's seen a film or play, taken in a recital or two and caught up with Peggy, she's raring to leave.

She has heard nothing of, or from, Herbert since their visit six months ago, and has concluded that 'Isobel' has gained her rightful ascendancy in his firmament.

'Good work, Major,' she murmurs. The horse is almost on his haunches, picking his way down the tussock ridge. Better if she walked, but her big toe has turned blue since he stood on it two days ago.

One other thing in town recently caught her interest, though. When she went with Peggy to the Theosophical rooms for the weekly meeting, she felt a peculiar thrill listening to a Miss Fairweather relate her travels in India, 'as much an inward journey as an outward one', the tiny woman said, that 'chimed with some ancient rhythm in the blood'. Nell found herself leaning sideways on the hard chair in order not to miss a word or a subtle change in the speaker's expressive face. She borrowed from the library a copy of *The Leaves of Morya's Garden* from which Miss Fairweather quoted liberally to articulate the longing that drew her to Darjeeling and beyond.

Major is throwing up his head, fearful of pitching Nell over the pommel, so she slides down and scrambles ahead through the chest-high tussocks, yelping now and then as the toe is forced onto leather. The wind, the lowering sun and billowing tussocks fill her with happiness – and to think there might be a purpose to it all! A path beneath her feet that will grow ever more apparent as she applies herself to the scientific techniques the yogis have promised lead to 'illumination'. And illumination was surely the state attained by Jesus, via a similar approach, of 'communion with the Father', which equipped him for his years of ministry. And thus she deals, for now, with doctrinal unease.

At the bottom gate, she mounts and lets Major reach into gallop (as long as it's not every time, as long as he doesn't get into the headlong homeward habit) around the base of the hill and onto the gravel driveway. He springs over the cattle stop and she pulls him back into the showy, splaying trot that pushes out his chest and makes him snort with the effort of restraint. Nell laughs and pats his lathered neck. She makes him stop in the dead centre of Mother's rose lawn, then take three steps in reverse. And bow, nose to knee for her amusement.

'Bravo!' comes a cheer and the stamp of feet. Hamish and two others are on the verandah, as it happens, glasses and pipes in hand. One is very still and upright at the rail. His eyes catch and hold hers. It's Herb.

Dear Nell,

This letter might surprise you, or perhaps not entirely. To go straight to the point, I hope I might take you out to tea when next we coincide in Dunedin. I will certainly be there for a day or two in April: Easter obligations, parental birthdays and what-not.

I recalled the other day your handling of that chestnut brute (the cavalry used mainly geldings; we had 300, and 50 mares, on the ship out with us). Hamish had told me that his sister was a skilled horsewoman, but a performance has to be seen to be appreciated in its finer points. Not that you were performing, exactly, but anyone accomplished in an art artlessly makes a fine demonstration for those with eyes to see it.

Your mother put on a splendid meal, but the breakfast eggs you prepared for us were poached to perfection. I did enjoy talking with you in the kitchen before the chaps came hurtling in to coarsen the atmosphere.

Please write and tell me that you'll see me again.

With kind regards,
Herbert

'I detect a very different kind of affection,' Peggy tells Nell as they walk along the lakeside.

'Different from?'

'Oh, I'm harking back to Daniel. You always seemed a little uneasy about him.'

'We weren't a fit. With Herb, I feel settled. I can't imagine not marrying him. If he, or I, were to walk away now, life would seem gaping and pointless.

'Look.' Nell points out the floating grebe. 'Look closely.'

'What's that on its back ... chicks! Adorable. And that's usual? How sensible. I hate seeing ducklings dangle their tiny feet where eels lurk.'

'Fated. What do you think of that term, Peg?'

'Well...' Peggy crouches and turns over a stone at the water's edge. She peers at the wriggling larval form on its underside. 'Only so much of life can be chosen or controlled. Reason often proves a weak force against passion. Or folly.'

Passion. Does Nell have that with Herb? She has felt exhilarated at his side, especially in company where he cuts a dash, and can be commanding and persuasive. Then when they're alone, he becomes more ... well, more comfortable. Companionable. Yes, she is looking forward to the marriage bed, to the full initiations of sex, and she senses that although Herb has hinted at previous experience, he will be kind as well as vigorous. 'We're not like Selma and her man,' she tells Peggy. 'Remember I told you about meeting that friend? Teasing and tearing at one another.'

Peggy laughs. 'You'll show more decorum in public.'

'Indeed we shall. Decorum matters to Herb. And somewhat to me. But really, I'm pretty happy, Peg. I sense that the events carrying me along are the right events. Heaven preserve me, I want to live in that tiny shack he's fixing up, and make a go of things with him. The parents approve well enough, my siblings are glad to see me settling. I'm ready to apply myself to a project that's lifelong.'

'As far as you know.'

'Quite. And I'll have you to tell me if I look as if I'm growing complacent or forgetting my higher calling.'

'Marriage and family are high callings.'

'To which ninety percent of humanity answer yes.'

Peggy makes a wry face. 'But how many answer with the intention and the capacity to make it a sacred institution?'

Nell senses in herself a division. Peggy's question might have a facetious edge, but in her own mind's eye a golden ideal exists of man, woman and children growing together in vivifying curiosity and a tenderly wrought harmony.

On the other hand, her soul is tired, with the tiredness of all humankind in the years following the war and the flu, with their griefs, privations and slow recoveries.

The little grebes have slid from their parent's back and hover like bumblebees on the water.

Might it not be sufficient to walk on with Herb, one foot in front of the other, learning from him (and he from her), working hard and practising kindness when she can?

1925

Outside the big house, music and light spill from the doors and windows. On the broad front path, Nell's elegant shoes disappear into golden leaves. It's been someone's idea of romance, to let them lie in golden swathes around the house. She presses her cheek to her mother's. She takes her father's hand. She flings at them thanks, praise, the promise to write soon.

Herb hovers, conscientious in his thanks but magnetised towards the new Ford auto which is his father's wedding present to them both. He's been twitching for the last hour to leave, but Nell pleaded with him, in what might have been their first overt difference of opinion, to relax, to let her enjoy their guests, who have come from all over the island and some from further north. Apart from this, she has felt cherished and lovely as she glided, first in her simple cream bridal gown, now in the Wedgwood-blue drop-waister and fur-edged shawl, from group to group, friend to friend, amongst cousins and siblings, elderly aunts and uncles, farmers, merchants and their wives.

At last, she lets Herb seize her hand and hurry her, both kicking up leaves and laughing, to the car. Hunter and Ken each hold open a door and see them off with a cascade of rose petals and leaves tossed into the open chassis. Something rattles along behind and as soon as they're away from the big house, Herb stops under a streetlight to cut off the trailing tangle of tin-cans, old

billies and holed enamel mugs, before driving on to the
hotel for the night.

A night in which what occurs between them is made up
of oddly familiar and even comforting sights and sensations. Some manoeuvres surprise Nell by the adroitness
of their execution, one or two by the feelings of alarm
and revulsion they arouse in her. More surprising still
is that the whole bundle of experience that sex turns
out to be, including and perhaps especially the iffy
or the perturbing, cleave her to him. She senses this:
she might be a tender pea shoot clinging to stake or
stalk, knowing in her marrow what's needed for her to
toughen, to reach for the sun, and produce her own best
flowers and fruit.

'Here's the turn-off.' The Ford straddles the two dirt
ruts that run away through the tussocks. The pipe stem
between his teeth gives Herb a fixed grin as they bounce
and lurch for the couple of miles she remembers, through
low hills, past the house where she first met him, and on
another half mile. She glimpses the sod hut before he
swings the car in a wide arc to face the way they've come,
and switches off the engine. 'Wait,' he tells her, and he
bounds around to open her door. 'Mrs Hamilton.' He
bows deeply and puts his palm out for her own.

Herb leads her into the recently planted ring of yellow-
leaved willow cuttings and squeezes her upper arm.

'This is us.'

The three little words so apt, Nell will later think.

Bare bones. With all the work yet required to put flesh on them.

They approach Herb's whare, the tiny, iron-roofed miner's hut he's restored in haste since he met her. Before winter, they plan to move to the three-gabled house with Hunter and Ken, but for now, privacy is called for. Herb insists on lifting Nell over the half-buried spar that constitutes a doorstep, and lets her down on the patchwork of jute sacks pinned direct to the earth. Their smell, mingled with the soil, permeates the single room. At least the weather is fine and it's only midday: Nell counters a flare of panic. There's time to make something almost plausible of the set-up, which is a broad shelf for their two adjacent ticking mattresses, a single, smeared window, a wobbling table and open fireplace. Anything else they need she has to hope will be found beneath the canvas tarpaulin roped onto the little trailer behind the Ford with its red leather upholstery. It's a shame they can't live in the car. She returns Herb's embrace in the middle of the room, and his kiss.

'Let's be happy here,' she says. Let's play make-believe.

And Nell finds in herself a primitive joy at the thought of fixing up the whare, as if it were a playhouse. After lunch out on the grass – sandwiches from the hotel in Clyde, and throat-catching lemon barley water – Herb obliges her in her plan for unpacking: 'This is your territory,' he concedes. He rolls up the tarpaulin and exposes everything in the trailer, opens boxes and stands them in a circle outside the door. Gets a fire going, to heat their four pots filled with water from the creek in the nearby gully, while Nell cleans the window panes, scrubs the table and sweeps what she can from the nooks and cracks of the bed shelf. The floor is going to be a nightmare. Already sacks have loosened and catch underfoot. A rug will have to be obtained, pronto. Still, double sheets and blankets have been made to cover most of the mattresses, with the embroidered bedspread quaint against the mud walls.

Once Herb has finished unloading, she begs him for another shelf or two. He drives down the track and returns over an hour later, having obviously had a drink (Ken and a friend were at the house). He has planks in the trailer, though, weathered and muddy but able to be sawn and propped on apple boxes, two-deep, to make a kind of pantry space between table and fire. She'll need more jars and bins. More of many things.

'I have a kitchen sink lined up,' he tells her. 'We'll have a rainwater tank.'

Nell glances at her watch. Almost four o'clock. They've been married for twenty-four hours. She wants to tell Herb, but can't bear it if he simply lifts his chin and goes on with his efforts to attach one of the planks to the wall above the fireplace: a mantel shelf, balanced on three slim wooden pegs hammered into the clay.

'Did you mean it when you said you'd make our meal tonight?' she asks.

'I did. As long as you're not expecting a banquet.'

She presses his arm and smiles wryly at their little kitchen. 'Simple and hearty is all we'll need.'

They head outside then, and without discussing it, walk. First to the tiny creek wending down through a split in the green hill. Herb has dug a kind of landing stage in the gravel, where they can crouch and hold a billy into the flow that curves against the bank. Across the creek, they make for the ridge that soon gives them a fine view of the valley, of the whare with its coiling smoke, the car and trailer and the faint trail of their footsteps circling the hut.

After half an hour, Herb turns and cuts down a gully to get on with the meal, while Nell meanders back along the ridge. She arrives at dusk. The heavy enamelled frying pan lies out on the grass, blackened and glistening. Inside, the mud and hessian smell has been overwhelmed by that of mutton. 'Signs of industry,' she manages with a smile.

Herb has pushed a pile of clobber to one end of the table and set two heavy white china plates at the other. Salt on a saucer, and he's pounding peppercorns with a hammer onto paper laid on the hearthstone. He tips the fragments into his palm and thence to the saucer. He commands her to sit (at least they brought two chairs with them; most of the wedding gifts will stay in town until they're in the proper house) while he spoons mashed potato from a billy and slides two mutton chops onto each plate.

Herb pulls his chair close to the table. Without looking at Nell, he rattles off: 'Bless, O Lord, this food to our use, and us to thy service, and keep us ever mindful of the needs of others, Jesus' Name, Amen.'

'Amen.' Nell raises her head.

'Fingers, don't you think?' Herb sprinkles salt and pepper over his meal and takes a chop in one hand, a forkful of potato in the other.

Nell feels the prick of tears and chides herself. He's being practical. He's done more than most men even know how to.

Herb's attention is on his food. He was famished and now he's eating. Nell tackles a chop with knife and fork, but can scarcely saw through the band of gristle. She eats the potato slowly, plays with the chop and offers the second to Herb. 'I'm not as hungry as I thought.'

If she'd wanted a sprig of flowers on the table, a cloth, a candle, a dash of colour on their plates, she should have come and quietly done it, instead of expecting Herb to have a clue.

At least he doesn't expect praise for the meal. He performed a task and she will perform others for him. It will all balance out.

Dear Nell,

Enclosed are a few clippings from the daily paper for your entertainment, since I gather you are economising to the extent of foregoing the daily delivery. Herbert's father and I would be glad to pay the subscription should you allow us to.

I did enjoy your description of the hens – their establishment of a 'pecking order' and their befuddlement when the frosts set in. I do hope you are keeping warm and that Herbert is wearing the woollen combination sets we sent.

Here in Dunedin the last of the dahlias have toppled in the cold and I've been busy cutting all the perennials down to the quick. The aspect is a bleak one, I admit, especially when the clouds sit so heavy on the hills and the neighbour's chimney pots belch black with the filthy coal they burn over there.

Daily help is increasingly hard to find to and keep – a refrain your mother, too, made in a recent letter. This week we are between helps and managing entirely on our own. The baker has seen rather more of me than usual while I don't have anyone to knead bread or make a pie for lunch guests.

Now, to a matter of some delicacy since we have not spoken directly of our hopes for a grandchild sooner or later: I have received word of a consignment of goods: a pram, bassinet, blankets and large number of tiny garments and napkins, all in good wool or linen, which could be had at a very reasonable price were I to act now. Let me know if this raises your interest, or if indeed it would meet a necessity in your household. It would give me great pleasure to obtain these items.

With affection,
Louise and Thomas

p.s. we were surprised to hear that you're still living in the hutch, 'for privacy', Herbert wrote, but I must urge you back to the proper house before long, for a baby's sake. And for yours.

'Fifty-five.' Herb throws the last white hen into the coop and rolls up the sack.

She fluffs her feathers and blinks in the light of an autumn afternoon. Her comrades are in various states between dazed and deliberate – enquiring and stabbing around the base of the tussocks, looking askance at the looming henhouse. It's a reassembled car-case, painted with an 'end' of lemon yellow. Nell has claimed that inside it looks cosier than the whare, with its twelve inches of straw and mānuka roosting poles. (Herb took the hint and put a pole across the corner above the bed, for clothes on hangers.) The hens were cheap this end of the season, going off the lay, but, come spring, they'll be back in business. Herb goes to the car and brings out the tea box with Charlie crammed inside. When the lid is opened, the rooster springs out like a jack. He instantly forgets the abasement of the journey and goes to croon and strut amongst the girls.

Nell leans on the fence. 'He's a striking fellow. What will the chickens be, I wonder. Look at all the colours in him.'

Herb steps back to join her. 'More to the point, what about our little chick? Blue eyes, or greenish like yours? Dry wisps like mine, or golden curls.' Hands in pockets, he regards the swell of her belly. It happened quickly. She took in the sixth month of the marriage.

When he looks up, she holds his eye. 'I want to be in town for the birth. I want Doctor Avery. We need to plan ahead for that.'

'I don't understand this insistence. Everyone says the local man is worth his salt. And his midwife.'

'This is my wish. I have no feeling for Chapman. And you wouldn't consult him yourself when your foot was inflamed. I need to be able to trust…'

'It's three months off, so let's talk about it closer to the time. Things change. No, please don't set your mouth at me that way. I'm the one you ought to trust. That way we grow closer, in an event such as this.'

'Do you think that what I feel myself as the child grows inside me is unreliable?'

Herb gathers up the sacks, and sighs. 'You know what you've been like. Tears one day. Smiles the next. It's a delicate time and the more matters you can leave to me, the better.'

Nell puts a staying hand on his arm. 'You know why my feelings have been changeable. I'm still adjusting…' She looks up at the hill, at the whare, at the ten rows of cabbages. 'To being so alone with my thoughts.'

'But you grew up in a place even more remote.'

'It was never like this. Every night there was a table full of family, guests, workers. Things were talked about – well, matters pertaining to the farm and news from beyond.'

'As we talk. I share everything I'm doing, or intend to do, with you.'

She looks at him with a small shake of the head. 'You

do. But my opinion, my thoughts, make scarcely a dent on yours.'

'Don't talk nonsense. I listen to every word you say.'

'You might hear every word, but you dismiss them as readily. The birth is a case in point. You're always right.'

'You say so. I think things out carefully. I could simply go ahead without telling you anything. Talking it all out with you is costly, timewise, but it's a way of including you, of letting you know what's important to me.

'I say, are you all right?'

Nell's chest and shoulders heave. Feeling wells up and overwhelms her. She utters a strangled scream and hurls herself at the sacks in Herb's arms, pushing him over and rolling right past him, onto the ground. She gets up onto hands and knees and sobs, one foot flailing at him.

Herb stands and dusts off his trousers, his shirt. 'I'll put the sacks away and get the hens' mash. When you've composed yourself, I suggest we both tidy up. I saw the chaps down at the road earlier. They're likely to call in fiveish.' He holds out a hand to her.

'What? You didn't tell me. More to the point, you didn't ask if it would suit me.' Reluctantly, she takes his wrist and pulls herself up.

'I knew you'd made a big pot of stew. I didn't want you to get flustered.'

'Flustered!' She stares wildly at him, at her wrist watch. 'It's five now. Dig me some potatoes.' Nell's eyes fill and she wipes them harshly with the back of her hand. She shakes out her pinny and marches into the hut.

Winter sets in early: the first frost before mid-March, a white scuff appearing on the grass in the half hour before sunrise, the chooks stepping high over the cold mud of their run, and fluffing their feathers as they ask for their morning mash. The dog (Herb brought home a nuggety terrier called Toss, to keep the rabbits at bay) leaps in alarm at sensations underfoot, then charges around bouncing and swerving over the crunchy ground.

In the next month, the cabbages not yet harvested for sale freeze and split open. The kitchen garden greens have to be eaten regardless, along with the cabbages – boiled, fried with leftover potato, or roasted in slabs. The holes Herb has dug all over the hillside stand empty – it's too late, too cold now, to put in the young trees. It's all on hold: the eggs and cockerels, the vegetables, the fruit business. Herb asks around at the pub, ten miles down the road, and gets work: painting, building yards and cutting wood, jobs that dry up as winter deepens. By mid-May the ground is set hard and the mornings are white – grass, hills, willow branches – beneath brilliant blue sky.

In June the sun disappears behind a billow of cloud that creeps up the valley one afternoon and settles, unmoving, for the next six weeks. Each day the frost is whiter, spikier, heavier on the fences and posts. The tussocks near the house are crystalline explosions; the willows have sprouted leaves of ice and wire barbs on the fences put forth frosted shoots.

Nell and Herb have hung on in the whare. Again, the thought of living with Hunter and Ken through the flimsy walls is distasteful to them both. Inside the hut, it's cosy as long as three logs or more are burning at any given moment. The walls are thick and hold warmth, but cold seeps through the window panes and the wooden door. It comes up through the sacks on the floor.

Nell is heavy with child. She agreed when they married to leave the Singer in town for occasional use there, but now she sees that it was a mistake. She keeps her small suitcase packed in hopes that Herb will relent one day and let her take the Ford away into town, but of course the dangers increase daily: her size and the baby's imminence; the coating of frost on the road, black ice on the corners. The doctor goes about with chains permanently wrapped around his tyres, headlights probing the fog.

She has allowed Doctor Chapman to assess her, in case she can't get away. Towards the end, he brings with him Mrs Dench the midwife, a woman twice Nell's age. She appears kindly, but her face hardens when Nell mentions what she's been reading: that peasant women the world over fare well by remaining ambulant in labour.

'We are not peasants. Our women have a different constitution,' she says, when Herb and the doctor have put on their coats and gone outside to smoke. 'Doctor and I will guide you through. I'll come at the first call, and he'll come when I call him.'

The event is expected this month. Unless a miraculous thaw occurs, allowing Nell to leave, when signs of labour begin Herb will go to tell Ken and Hunter, who will go and telephone from the neighbour's five miles along the road. A month ago, Nell's parents visited from town, bringing a hamper lined with tissue paper and filled with the requested items to supplement those she has clumsily knitted herself: there are tiny singlets and nightgowns, booties, mitts and hats, soft blankets, napkins and pins. The midwife looks through them. 'Are you not expecting your baby to grow bigger than a bedbug?' she asks. 'You'll be surprised at how quickly he'll need the next size, and then the next.'

Nell is dismayed. She can barely imagine the baby that will fill this unlikely array of garments, let alone larger ones, let alone a child who will need leather shoes, a coat and trousers. Events have overtaken her. Marriage, Herb, the whare, the frost, and a baby. This frightful woman, the arrogant doctor. She senses in herself a deep core of numbness that has allowed this to happen, that lets her go on functioning, nonetheless.

She and Herb go silently about inside the tiny house, which itself is cocooned in silence.

Nell makes a pot of tea and sits, hands to the open fire. What she's hankered for since childhood and has convinced herself she is steadily making her way towards, is freedom. Freedom to say yes or no. To speak or not to speak. To know her own mind, her true impulses, and to follow them.

Here she is, though, pledged to Herb for life and living in a hut, enclosed by mud, locked in by frost and fog, and skewered by the needs of this burgeoning baby. Burgeoning? No further growth is possible. Her skin is stretched to splitting point, surely. She's been reduced to wearing Herb's woollen combination underwear beneath a full nightie. Mother promised another dress that she had someone in town run up, but it seems to have been lost in the post. Nell's toenails are in sore need of cutting, but they'll have to wait until she can reach her feet again. Herb did them last time, but insisted on using clippers like wire cutters and there was blood.

Within the week, Doctor Henderson reckons.

Nell wishes she were more in sympathy with the midwife, who is well-meaning but overbearing, and fiercely opinionated about how Nell should conduct herself during the labour – which is to say, passively, like a cast sheep, letting the midwife assess, instruct and aid as she sees fit. Nell will keep matters to herself as long as possible, only calling for her when momentum has built up.

Mother wanted to be here, but Nell urged her to wait until the initial flurry of support has ebbed away after the birth (Hunter and Ken have promised to bring a meal each day for the first week), and by then spring will be imminent. Mother will have to have a cot bed in the corner, unless Herb puts up a tent for himself, and Mother shares with Nell ... no, that would never do. She can sleep near the fire, and tend it if she wakes. It's unbearable to let it go out, as they did two weeks ago, exhausted as they were by their day's walk. They woke to find frost on the blankets, the window intricately curtained by ice, and the bread, butter, apples, all frozen solid.

Their walk mimicked Herb's of the previous day. While he initially forbade Nell to make the journey, he relented on the proviso that they turn back the moment any change occurred. Muffled like mummies, they set off, sidling up the long zigzags Herb's boots had marked out, with ice cascading around them as they knocked it from tussock and matagouri. Their feet were numb and the rest of them cold despite their wrappings, so slowly were they travelling. They couldn't see more than a few feet in any direction. At least they could follow their tracks home again. After an hour, the fog lightened and they began to warm. When they could see one another at ten yards, Herb began to sing, 'Early one morning, just as the sun was rising…'

Nell's heart was pounding fearsomely in the small space allotted to it, and her lungs were bursting as she stepped out into a dazzle of sunshine, golden tussocks under a deafeningly blue sky. She could have wept. Herb grinned as if he'd conjured the scene himself. Spread out before them was a vast sea of cloud, as flat as if poured and patted into place. They stood on a gilded isthmus, spilled from a golden ridge, beyond which the Old Man Range stood broad and reassuring, snow-streaked under the blue. At their feet the ground steamed as the morning's thaw completed itself, and skylarks thrilled overhead. They caught one another's hands and spun around a little before Herb took out the square of oilskin and thermos flask. They sat – Nell like the great golden

Buddha, legs crossed, smiling and marvelling at her belly
– and peeled off their outer layers. Herb took his shirt
off, as he'd done the day before, to absorb more of the
sun's rays. Nell leaned back and felt them on her face,
throat and hands.

'Won't you lift your … dress,' Herb fingered the
cambric of her nightie, 'and expose your girth, for the
baby's sake?'

'He's safe enough in there. The happier I am, the
safer.' She didn't know if it was true, but it seemed so
in that moment. As if nothing could go wrong. The
accumulated dread of the previous weeks melted away
as if it had been no more than a rime of ice.

They wished they'd brought lunch with them, firewood and a billy, dinner, a tent. They wanted to move
up onto the hillside. But after an hour they grew restless.
Below them, the fire needed stoking, washing had to
be turned on the indoor rack, bread to be baked, ice be
broken on the hens' trough and hot water added (several
times a day they did this) and Herb had to creep away
over the frozen gully road to collect another trailer-load
of macrocarpa wood from a farmer he would drudge for
in exchange. In short, they had to return to their small
prison.

There's a maniac in Nell's body, turning a crank handle,
winding her innards tight, then releasing; winding,
releasing, hour after hour. She started out on her feet,
walking about the whare: to the door, to the bed, the
table, the fire, and back the other way. Herb went off

to call the midwife, who soon put an end to her pacing.

'Up on the bed with you.'

Still, Nell didn't want to be lying. When the midwife went out to her car, she rolled onto hands and knees and rocked herself there, until Mrs Dench pushed her, none too gently, onto her side and told her how to breathe as she put on her rubber gloves and probed inside.

'Less than half an inch. It's going to be a long, slow business.'

Long, slow and every minute or two painful, as if a knife is slicing through the skin between her pelvic bones, or holding to it a burning string. The corners of Nell's pillow grow wet, as she buries her face with each contraction and bites down.

Herb is outside mostly, finding goodness knows what to do with himself in the white and cold. Scraping out the hen-house, he'll tell her later. Replacing the straw. Filling every water receptacle and lining them up at the door (the rain-water tank hasn't yet eventuated, the several steps involved interrupted by ice), and every now and then creeping apologetically inside to stoke the fire and boil water to make another pot of tea for the midwife, then take a thermos flask outside again. Nell is allowed sips of tea only, and after a while only black, although sweetened.

'How is it, lassie?' he asks, timorously on the morning's third visit, using the midwife's own term.

Nell shakes her head at him. She won't grimace in his presence, even though the moment demands it, the fiery knife doing its work while her belly grows taut as a sheep's with bloat.

'You don't need me here then?'

She shakes and nods her head. She wants someone, someone near and dear who knows, who can locate the self sliding in and out of view, the self whose body has been commandeered by an alien force. 'When'll the doctor come?'

'Not for some time yet,' the midwife says. 'We won't want him till you're near fully dilated.'

Hours pass. The day goes. The night. Candle-light; Herb tossing on the cot near the fire, Nell's moans and growls tugging him again and again from all but the heaviest sleep. The midwife dozes on her chair and falls face-first onto the bedding at Nell's feet. She wakes in the blue gloom of dawn.

'No change,' she tells Nell, her voice full of accusation.

All night Nell wanted to get up and walk, but dared not. Now she's too tired, too agonised, too distraught to do anything but follow instruction, or refuse to.

'Is it not time to call him yet?' Herb asks mid-morning. He's completed all the tasks he can without leaving the property. He's scraped the ice from the window, for all the difference it makes.

'Can't you paint it blue?' Nell's voice is harsh and hardly her own. But Herb is cutting bread now, and has no idea what she means. Sun. She aches, aches for it. Or her mother. Or some angelic being who understands where a woman goes to while this thing is happening to her.

'Please,' she begs, 'please go and fetch…' Whom does she mean? The waiting child? For a long time, it has not felt like a child. It has felt like a boulder waiting and refusing to be born.

Mid-afternoon, the midwife agrees to Herb going away to phone for the doctor. She's keeping herself awake with tea alone, and another night is looming. 'Tell him thirty-three hours and one point two inches.'

Mrs Dench says she will take the body away. The body. Nell hates her with every shrunken impulse remaining. The midwife hasn't allowed him for an instant to be a baby. Nell says no. Then she says it louder, with a force that grates in her belly and thighs, and the midwife is taken aback. Nell should have been this way hours ago. Days, weeks ago. She should have found this bruised and savage place within her that brooks no opposition. She takes from the midwife's proffering arms the piece of blanket with its little occupant. 'You can go,' Nell tells her. 'I need to be alone.' She stares until her wish is granted. She unpins the flap of blanket over the baby's head. The little boy's. Herb has followed the midwife outside. Nell pulls the baby into the cave between breasts and thighs, the cave her body forms when she breaks in the middle. She is a sobbing cave, her walls wrenched and wracked by sobs. She opens up the blanket and the swaddling. How quickly he's cooling.

124

Spring comes, sweet and swift. A mild wind rolls the fog away, clears the sky and melts ice from fences windows tussocks trees tracks roads. Nell's numb silences, long silences broken in the end by tears, have the power to get things done: the water tank arrives and is installed before the week is out. Her mother comes and first takes her away to Queenstown for a couple of nights, then ensconces herself on the cot near the fire, by day helping Nell wash bed-clothes and winter woollens. Yes, actually helping, Nell marvels. She sends for a rug, which is delivered the day she leaves, so instead of a mother to make her pots of tea or send her out to walk in the spring afternoon, Nell has a red-patterned carpet that covers most of the floor, is pleasant to sit on and even nicer to lie on. Afternoon sun comes in through the open door where Nell – instructed by the doctor to rest – stretches out for hours on end, losing herself in book after book; she hardly cares what – Westerns, penny romances, gardening manuals or the odd classic or new novel – she asks Herb to raid the shelves of neighbours, hotels, magazine stands wherever he goes.

The baby clothes are bundled, tissue-wrapped, boxed and shoved beneath the bunk. Nell sees them – she makes herself unwrap and look at one or two before the start of every reading session – and she sees the little face hands feet scrotum bottom chest, the knees drawn up like a real child's. She sometimes stares in mute puzzlement, sometimes moans and wails, then she blows her nose and loses herself in a book.

A parcel comes from Peggy, who knows how things

have turned out and who promises to visit before summer. There are two slim books of poetry and the expensive, newly published 'original and unaltered' *Secret Doctrine,* along with a study guide, and Alice Bailey's *The Light of the Soul.*

As with the talks she attended at the Theosophical Society, Nell finds herself strangely drawn by the obtuse lines and impenetrable paragraphs. It seems, nonetheless, that as she reads, a stream of clear water is rinsing through her mind, and she rises from the floor after four pages of the Bailey treatise with her thoughts and purpose lightly disposed, so that she can go out to join Herb on the hillside without rancour or withdrawal.

As the soil thaws, he has been widening the holes he dug last autumn, ready to receive the fruit trees that stand around the hen run, five hundred budding stems striking up from five hundred hessian-wrapped rootballs.

'Is it warm enough for you up here?' Herb asks. There's caution in his voice. She has not been easy to live with.

'Perfectly. So let me know how I can help.'

He indicates the bucket of wood ash and lime that is to be dropped, a spoonful into each hole, before the tree goes in.

'Take a little at a time,' he says, 'in the bowl. You mustn't lug the bucket about.'

Nell feels ready, though, at last, to lug and bend and lift. She wants to carry the trees up the hill and stand them ready in their holes. She asks if she might unwrap the first. The string around the sacking is knotted tight, so Herb's pocket knife is called for. They end up working together: Herb holds the tree on its side, while Nell works the knife and pulls away the wrapping. Herb lowers the tree and scoops earth in around it; Nell presses it down and tidies the surface before cutting the sack wrapping into a kind of poncho to drop over the tree and pin to the ground to repress growth around the base.

While Herb moves on to the next each time, Nell kneels and touches the tender wand with its tight buds and says the word 'Blessings,' putting into it all the meaning she can; she sees the leaves unfurl, twigs and branches sprout, blossoms appear, fruit swell and *become*.

1926

Hard work, congeniality, misunderstandings, fiery exchanges, softening and fun again. A miscarriage, possibly two: lateness, much blood. Then none.

For the last month, Nell has been staying with her parents at their city flat, savouring the warmth and comfort: of the small electric heater to dress beside in the morning, of the living room fire lit early each day by her father, where she can read and muse after her brisk daily walk around the Green Belt. The bone-warming luxury of a hot bath every night before bed.

There's unease too, when she thinks of the impending delivery and the outcome, but the family's doctor has reassured her that with medical care on hand she will have an easier time of it, her body having been seasoned already by one baby.

Herb calls her on the neighbour's phone, asking if there are signs. She has only to think of him hovering near her bed as she labours and she can hardly breathe for the fear that sweeps up through her belly. Tonight, she tells him she's had tea and cake beside the fire with her friend Peggy, and that she spent the afternoon cleaning and ordering the flat's little anteroom. 'So you see, I have the purging instinct. I'm sure it won't be long. Perhaps by tomorrow night I'll have news of activity.' Nell fails to tell him about the regular tightenings and half an hour ago the show of mucous. When she's said goodbye, she goes to her room to lay the waterproof under an old sheet, she takes a fresh nightie to air beside the fire, she asks her mother to phone the doctor, and then she begins to pace the house.

❦

Dear Nellie,

Seeing that your father's money has come through, and since you showed no urgency when we talked last night, I decided there was time today to cast my eye over a piece of land – a mere 70,000 acres – running from the Kyeburn River to the top of the mountain, taking in Mt Buster and the slopes to the west of Dansey's Pass.

It's a grand bit of country and I feel the urge to take it on. The house is scarcely bigger than our Fruitlands hutch, but there's a plan and a foundation in place for a larger house, and plenty of plantings on the flat land around it.

They run merinos, and a few cattle along the river.

We'll talk about it when I see you. I may even precede this letter.

With all affection,
H

'We can make of it what we will,' Herb tells her. 'It's only lines on paper. Look, I'll spread the plan out. Pencil.' He waves one at her. 'Make your adjustments.' He takes three strides into the centre of the concrete slab and unrolls the plan, pegging it with his glasses case and, after casting fruitlessly around, his hat.

Nell stands frozen on the edge of the slab. She eyes the car where baby Adam is, thinks of its warm, leathery fug, out of this cutting wind. They've just visited the tiny roughcast cottage where Herb expects them to live while the building takes place. It's only slightly less primitive than Fruitlands. Now he wants her to walk about her new home, to envisage their future family eating, washing, playing and bedded down a few inches above this square of concrete. And when she has decided – or agreed, and agreement is what he actually wants because changing the plans will cost precious money – on the layout of its rooms, slab will be added to slab and their concrete house will rise on the rabbity expanse of paddock surrounding it.

Her breasts are hard: Adam has been asleep for almost three hours and at the thought of him they tighten further and out the milk spurts, filling the folded handkerchiefs in her brassiere.

The new baby startled her in his first moments with the intensity of his stare. 'That first, adoring gaze', her mother called it, but to Nell it was equally a stare; she was being stared at and found wanting by the ancient being in the form of her son.

Adam is a severe child. How can that be, in a creature so defenceless and dependent? But it has been so from the first day. He drinks with forceful, lengthy sucks, like a small machine. He stares at her (gratefully or appraisingly? was the milk to his satisfaction?) and then he sleeps. Three hours later he wakes and will not be soothed before his napkin is changed. He feeds, he stays awake for three hours, then drinks and sleeps, and this is his regime, day and night (until at ten months he will learn to walk and suddenly, from one day to the next to wean himself and sleep through the night from eight until six with scant variation. And somewhere in the fine-ground tilth of this regime, humour will take root, and gentleness, flowering like morning glories and as swiftly retracting when severity is called for).

Nell pulls her cardigan close and presses with her forearms. He's not awake yet; she'd hear him wailing through the open car window. So, she goes over and uncurls the bottom of the plan with the tips of her shoes. Elbows to knees, she bends close. She sees at once that the kitchen is too small, and why must the laundry's only door be to the outside? She draws another into the adjoining hallway. Her pencil seizes a yard and a half of the generous living room for the kitchen. It enlarges windows to the north and west. Her nose drips in the cold and her finger, on wiping the drop, opens a kitchen wall. Why not? She draws in a door (*sliding*, she writes) and adds a small square onto the large square of the house: a walk-in safe and pantry. Nell arrows the coal range toward an interior wall and adds another kitchen window. She'll tolerate the lavatory being far closer to the children's rooms than to her and Herb's, but she pushes out the corner bathroom's walls so that the bath can stand free, so that there's room for a table, a towel rack, a cupboard and children.

Herb has been pacing out garden fencing and gates. He comes and sketches onto the plan, then peruses Nell's markings.

'Pricey,' he says, 'especially these.' His forefingers press on the pantry, the enlarged bathroom. 'They'll need further foundation.'

A thin wail comes from the car, then the full bellow.

'If you want me living here,' Nell's glance takes in the trampled ground, bulky clouds hiding the hills, her hands chafed and white with cold, '*these* are not for negotiation. Nor the larger kitchen. Nor light from the north.'

Whereas there were quaint elements in the whare's deficiencies, the cottage where they live for months while the farmhouse is being built – while the concrete is being mixed and poured and dried, while the lining and finishing are done – shocks Nell with its utility. Every wall is a harsh greenish yellow, the paint hard and shiny, and all the floors laid with ash-grey lino. The kitchen is small and barely admits a table for two, let alone the paraphernalia needed for keeping a baby safe near the coal range, which over-heats the small space. The living room fire is narrow, and smokes, so she tries to direct the kitchen warmth across the hallway, but until the days are reliably warm (not until January up here at two thousand feet) she and Adam are always moving from heat to chill and back again.

Every day, too, she bundles them both up and trudges with pram or pushchair over the muddy paddocks to inspect the house. She wishes to let the men know that what they do or fail to do is noticed. She also wishes she were more trusting, but twice, then three times, four, finds corners being cut, small and not-so-small attempts to deviate from the plans. She tries to insist that the concrete, mixed by hand in its casings, be confined to those casings; it makes her indignant to find that shovels and trowels have been wiped off on tussocks and 'garden'. At least the cottage is far enough away that she doesn't always hear the trucks of cement arriving, or the engines' roars and men's shouts as the slabs, once set, are hoisted into position as walls.

Herb barely notices any of this, so weary is he by day's end from studying the new farm in all its aspects. After his morning inspection of the building site and a talk with the head builder (Herb is the boss with the right to instruct, whereas Nell is a pest because she finds fault) he takes himself out on the hills and quizzes the manager, whom he plans to let go as soon as he can, hiring instead a young shepherd, inexpensive and experienced but malleable, and he reads late into the night, books and periodicals about sheep breeding, cropping and soil nutrition. He buys dogs and two more horses. So far, Nell has only ridden in the home paddock within sight of Adam asleep in his pram. She finds that her feeling for the horses is dulled, diluted, she supposes, by her preoccupation with Adam's wellbeing.

One Sunday in their second spring, Herb announces for himself a day of doing 'absolutely nothing' (and for her, he hastens to add, without consideration as to who will keep the stove going, make their meals or look after fifteen-month-old Adam). They've been in the new house for a month. The cupboards – in kitchen pantry bedrooms hallway wash house and living room – all await their doors, so nothing put below waist height is safe from an energetic toddler. Nell has managed to treadle up half a dozen curtains for the living room, but on the table in that room yards and yards of linen and lining await her, for all the other rooms. On the floors, pathways of sacks run over cold cement, until the carpet people can come. Unshaded lights glare from the ceilings and every indoor wall and window surround needs paint. Herb has given her a budget to hire a painter, but it will only go halfway. Nell will have to do the rest.

And thus she is kept confined to home base, as she writes to her mother after lunch. Herb in the chair opposite stirs the fire and totes things up in his diary, then he leans back to stare out the window, eyes following the fence-line. Nell turns to look. The far hills tantalise, and for the first time since they arrived, and with Adam asleep, she finds in herself the urge and the energy to saddle a horse and go.

'You'll be back within a couple of hours?' Herb says.

Yes, the only possible reply.

Up on the slopes of Mount Buster, she ties the horse and climbs direct to a steep ridge from where she can look down into a shadowy gully. Remnants of bush cling to the sides of a burn that leaps and races from one rocky basin to the next. Nell straddles a tussock and leans into the hill, sensing the hum of its life around her: insects rustle and flicker; a skylark circles, singing, and is joined by a second. Nell lays her head to the hill. Voices. She looks up through feathered grass at the blue sky and keeps very still. They murmur, rise and fall like wind, impossible to decipher male from female, although she is certain she's hearing a group of adults and children. The exchange grows urgent; all (Nell simply *knows*) have broken into a run, in pursuit of moa. She sits up straight and crawls back to the vantage point from where any person within audible range will be visible, but of course the hillside, the gully, the slopes to windward, all are empty. Did she fall asleep? Certainly she did not. Nell is stricken. These hills she and Herb have claimed with such ease, and worse, heedlessness; whose feet have known them more intimately than theirs ever will, and where have they gone? That this land has been obtained by the flimsy transfer of numbers and papers is suddenly preposterous. And yet, what can be done about it now that they have a house built, a baby, and all their livelihood invested here?

The life of the farm goes on at one remove. Herb tells her of his intentions and the day's achievements and always she has an opinion, but she learns to give approbation, to hold back when she sees flaws in his plans, or to make her suggestions oblique, insouciant. 'James B. said he was surprised by how much bigger their turnips grew when he planted a week or two later last season.' 'I suppose it was this time last year that you had Bruce here…' Trusting he'll recall the visit and its purpose and get a move on: mustering the far blocks before the first snows.

Nell has the Singer still, and a petrol allowance from Herb. She plans each week an outing for duty, and one for pleasure. The shopping trips to Ranfurly, or now and then to Oamaru while Adam sleeps in his basket in the back, include visits.

She seeks a friend and calls for a morning cup of tea with Myrtle up at the hotel, who performs her duties without mirth or complaint, with no emotion evident ever on her broad bland face. Which Nell would over-look were it not for the fact that she has a child a few months younger than Adam, and that child seems like-wise flattened and blank. Her cry is narrow, she feeds without vigour. Her thin pale arm whacks rhythmically at the side of the bottle as she lies on her mother's arm (at her age, Adam drank from a cup while sitting on a chair), as if she derives more comfort from this than from the milk itself. Nell finds it depressing to sit in the parlour with Myrtle, to try and extract something from her that isn't mild surprise, 'I didn't know about that', or

'Did you (Will he/Are they), love?' She calls her love and this makes her seem older than Nell, so Nell is inclined to impute to Myrtle wisdom, as well, except that she can't seem to dig it out.

It feels, she thinks as she winds her way up Dansey's Pass afterwards, like her recent impulse to go and plant sprouted cuttings out on the bank, only to find when she plunged the spade down, that it jarred her wrist, her whole arm, because under the streak of grass were stones and clay. When she told Herb, he said, it depends what she wants to do. She could spend years building up the soil with mulch, manure and compost, or she could simply go and dig somewhere a bit more sympathetic to the spade.

Coming home the other way, Nell takes a box of fruit, vegetables and oddments to one of the families along the Pigroot. 'Oh, they were over-supplied and practically begging us to take them,' she says of the tomatoes and the greengrocer, and, 'Silly me, I forgot we already have a big tin of golden syrup, so you'd be helping me out, truly.' She gives a pie and a string of sausages to the peculiar man who sits on the gate and lives in who-knows-what kind of hovel up in the gully behind.

For pleasure, she drives to the river, to any one of half a dozen spots from where she can carry a basket and guide a toddler over the stones and silt, can let him poke about while she lights a fire and boils the billy. The river burbles by, the sweet smells of damp earth, damp broom and woodsmoke assail her, and, as autumn deepens, the sky above the gold diggings and the riverbed sings in ever sweeter notes of blue. After such an hour, she returns home rinsed and calm.

A picture arrives from Herb's sister Ilona, now back in New Zealand: one of her own oils on a piece of hardboard, 'to warm the house, or perhaps your bedroom'.

'Good lord,' says Herb as they open the parcel on a cleared space of kitchen table.

A naked woman reclines on a green-striped sofa. Uniformly tanned, like Ilona herself last summer. No pale thighs or upper arms for her when they all went into the Kyeburn River one sweltering day. A red shoe lies discarded on the floor.

'That's awkward.' Herb might be referring to the oddly triangular shape of the sofa, to the woman hiding her eyes from the open curtain, to the raised foot seeming to kick a pink cloth (a tiny garment?) off the end. Or to the question of where to hang it. If at all. He flips it around and reads, '*The Lorelei*.' Turns it back. 'She hasn't signed it. What the heck. Just for a laugh, is it?'

They take in the unpunctuated breasts and fingerless hands.

'It's not finished,' Nell says. 'But it is rather fun.'

Rather fun, except that it makes her and Herb lose their bearings; fun in an awkward way, which means it will be relegated to a dark corner in the least-used room of the house, and hung more prominently ('I won't have her saying we're prudes'), temporarily, next time Ilona comes to visit.

Herb reaches for the bundled baby and pulls her close. 'I'll hold her in the back seat,' he says, 'and she might fall asleep.'

Nell considers the sight for a moment, of Herb's work-roughened hands clasping the cream wool blanket, knitted in tiny stitches on slender needles by her mother. He is besotted with his new daughter. Nell feels for Adam toddling ahead of them to the car – although 'toddling' is the wrong word for a boy so steady on his feet and so intentional in all he does – because Herb has always regarded, rather than held, his son. Adam puts his hand to the car door, waiting for it to be opened.

'Daddy's going to sit with you today,' Nell tells him.

His eyes widen at the prospect and once in the car he stares warily at his father's form.

Nell puts her carpet bag on the passenger seat, filled as it is with nappies, spare clothing, sliced apples, drinks, a thermos of hot water in case of spills or poop. 'I'll just run in and fetch the pie.' And the scones, the biscuits, the freshly dug carrots and parsnips for Pat, Adam's teddy, his gumboots and jacket…

Back at the car, 'Oops, one more thing.' She goes inside for the other basket with the other thermos, the mugs, tea, jars of milk and cream.

'Hang on, she's fallen asleep,' Herb says when she reappears, and so Nell has to make way for him in the front of the car, arranging the paraphernalia in the boot, then making Lettie more secure in the back: she tucks another blanket around her and wedges the ends into the crack between seat and back rest.

'I thought you were organised this morning,' Herb says, mildly enough, as she takes her seat at last.

'Believe me, I am, and no child has run amok, so we can be grateful for that. We're still running early.' She shakes her head. 'Joe's birthday present.'

Herb doesn't offer to run in and get it. He says, 'I'll start walking. Pick me up on the roadside,' and he is gone.

'Sorry, lovey,' she tells Adam. 'One last thing.'

The baby wakes as they rattle over the cattle stop. She wrestles and mews and Nell sees in the rear mirror that Adam has put a palm to her forehead, which appears to soothe her. Last night Nell had a team of fencers to feed, and two of them came in and talked until late. Lettie woke her at five. Now they're on their way to picnic in Middlemarch with some of Herb's family from Dunedin, none of whom have met Lettie, or seen Adam since he was a real toddler.

Lettie sleeps again and as Nell slows to cross the Taieri Bridge, she has an overwhelming urge. 'I'm going to get out for a minute.'

'Call of nature?' Herb asks.

'I want to have a look…' She waves at the river. 'I'm only going a little way.'

'Tit for tat, is it?'

'Not that I'm aware. I just … I've been rushed.'

'Can't you take the boy with you?'

'Won't you just keep him?'

'I don't want to be left with both...'

Nell opens the door. 'I'm left with them all the time.'

'As is only right. You wouldn't want me to leave you with a mob of restless cattle.'

Nell looks at him until he turns away. He chose to forget that she, given the chance and the dogs, can manage any kind of animal, in any number. She won't flaunt her capacities, though, nor will he acknowledge them.

She gets out, but Herb's wounded look has spoiled any pleasure she might have felt as she slips down the bank and walks towards the pool that is glimmering gold in the late morning light. The smells of damp river stones and willow are blighted by his 'Be quick then'. Even if the trout is there – and yes, it is, dappled, suspended in green dapple – she is unable to slip her mind beneath the water, or exalt in its undulating beauty. It is mere object and she is beset by haste.

With moonlight seeping around the bedroom curtains, it's hard to tell if dawn is here. Herb is awake, though, and pressing himself to her back. Nell holds onto the corner of her pillow as the rhythm of his pressure grows. Moonlight means a clear sky. She didn't manage to hang the sheets out yesterday and if it's even half fine today, she needs to muck out the henhouse.

'You awake, Ellie-Nellie?' Herb murmurs into her hair.

'Not especially. What's the time?'

'Almost six.' His hand ascends her leg and a well-placed finger sends a jolt of desire through her middle. She wants, she doesn't want … better to get on with it, though, then that will be Herb taken care of for a few days. She covers his hand with her own, a gentle encouragement, and soon she turns to face him. They have become quite proficient at joining on their sides. They call it a toasted sandwich, because a cast-iron clamp was coincidentally delivered to the kitchen the day they first did it.

Afterwards, while Herb goes to stoke the fire and put the kettle on, she reaches into his bedside drawer for a handkerchief, which she tucks between her legs as she sits up … and quickly lies back down.

'Queasy,' she tells Herb coming in with the cup of tea.

'Are you…?'

'What?' Oh. 'Late? No, because I haven't had a monthly since Lettie.'

However, she did stop breast-feeding her a couple of months ago. Good lord, is it possible? 'Just a little tired,' she tells him.

Six weeks later, after several queasy mornings, Nell has a bleed that she recognises as more consequential than a period. She wonders which of the huge clots expelled onto folded, torn-up towelling contains the rudiments of a child. She can't bring herself to flush them away, but gathers the bloodied rags in newspaper, to be buried or burned with some dignity when she has the time – this week she has no household help, so she can't even think of staying in bed.

Fortuitously, her energetic sister-in-law calls on her new telephone, and hearing Nell's coded news, saddles her husband's big gelding and rides the twenty miles up the Kyeburn, arriving late in the afternoon. Sylvia banishes Nell to the sofa in front of a new-lit fire, feeds Adam and Lettie, finishes meal preparation for the adults, bathes the children and brings them sweet-smelling and pyjama'd to the sofa as the light outside fades.

'Do you take any precautions?' Sylvia asks when the children have gone and Herb has not yet come in. 'I mean, I wonder...' Usually unflustered and forthright, Sylvia blushes and picks at the seam of her jodhpurs. She and Jim have been married for six months.

Nell adjusts the hot water bottle over her belly. There are not many topics she'd be in the mood to discuss in these circumstances, least of all this one, but until now Sylvia hasn't shown a hesitant side to her nature.

'Well, I understand that later in the monthly cycle, there's less chance of pregnancy. That we're most fertile about two weeks after the start of the period.' (She won't say that Herb has refused to consider using what he has scathingly referred to as 'rubber goods for gents'. They remind him of the war: 'The chaps vying to get hold of them,' he hastened to add.)

Sylvia looks thoughtful. 'Did you mean to have your children when you did?'

Nell feels at a disadvantage, cast in the huge sofa. These are matters barely discussed with Herb, let alone to be shared with a woman whose propensity for gossip she is uncertain of.

'Are you wondering about planning your own family?'

Sylvia's mouth clamps. She kneels and puts a branch on the fire. 'Promise you won't say anything to Herb?'

'I expect that we'll both keep in confidence anything that we say.'

'Jim is very ... eager, a lot of the time. Not only at night.' Her eyes glitter. 'I didn't think it would be like this. I feel awful when I say no, and awful when I say yes because I just don't want to ... not so much. I feel like ... like the ducks in the creek, half-drowned by the drakes.'

Nell fishes in her pocket for a handkerchief and offers it. 'Is he violent with you?'

'I, I don't think ... I suppose it's what men are like. But I don't know why I'm not pregnant already because he won't use sheaths. I'm frightened at the thought of having a baby growing inside me, *and* Jim being so eager. He tells me it's all right to do it even if I'm expecting.'

Nell closes her eyes as another cramp tightens its fist in her pelvis. She feels the resultant slide of blood into the wad of towelling.

'Have you told Jim how you're finding things?'

Sylvia covers her face with both hands. 'It's too awful to talk about. His need is so overwhelming, how can I say no?'

What might Peggy say? Sometimes this is Nell's recourse.

She'd say, take a wide perspective.

'Is Jim kind? Do you have fun together?' Surely fun is some kind of indicator so early in a marriage.

'He's not unkind. He tells me jokes.'

'Well, perhaps when the mood is lightened by a joke or a kindness, that's a good time to let him know how you're feeling. Rather than in the heat of the moment, or when it's weighing heavily on you. In my experience, a man finds it hard to respond when one of you is heavy-hearted.'

That is as much as Nell will say on the matter. Her own privacy, and Herb's, is sacrosanct. But she will keep an eye out, and if she sees Sylvia growing hard or hectic or remote, she will talk with her again.

Another mid-winter boy is born.

A fortnight later they wake to the hush of snow lying three inches deep on the lawn and the flats. Then soon after, the weather turns dirty: wind, rain and sleet, and Nell feels bleak as she puts David into his bassinet in the corner of the kitchen and turns to breakfast for Adam and Lettie. Her whole being aches to climb back into bed. When Herb comes in an hour later for his morning porridge he finds her struggling. David is hungry and fractious, Lettie fretting and shrieking about her footwear, Adam scowling at all three and telling them how to behave. The coal range is sulking and gusting cinders into the room. Mary, her help, has phoned to say she can't come until the ice on their steep driveway has thawed, and Nell's cheeks are smeared with soot and tears.

'I'll take these two out for chooks and milking.'

'Won't Clarice have milked already?'

'She's down with the flu. Adam, you can help me, can't you?'

Nell hurries to fetch their coats with the mittens sewn onto the cuffs, their hats and thick socks.

'We'll be back in half an hour or so,' Herb says.

An hour later, when she's managed to get the fire burning clean, and David bathed, fed and settled in his pram, there's still no sign of them. Wind bashes at the chimney and rattles the window frames. Hail shatters across the iron roof.

Outside, cold sneaks into every seam and buttonhole. It's not bracing, it's brutal. Nell tugs the blanket up over David's sleeping face and wheels the pram out across the ice and sludge of the back lawn. There are two gates to open and close. Wind snatches the first one wide, and while she runs, heavily in half-tied boots, to haul it back, another gust catches the pram and throws it onto its side. David is rolled onto the snow, his mouth wide in a noiseless scream of shock. Nell gathers him, hat, blanket and all to her front. He gasps and shudders there as she checks the milking stall (empty) and the hen house (the girls scratching about for the last breakfast grains), manoeuvres one-handed the gate to the workshop (nobody there). The woodshed holds only wood and axes. The truck, tractor and cars are all in their corrugated-iron hangar.

Surely he hasn't taken them walking. David is hiccuping into her chest and, along with the exertion and mounting alarm, warming her. She'll try the woolshed. The catch on that gate is too tight for her to move with one hand. That means sliding between wires on the fence that runs through the macrocarpa hedge. Conifer catches in her hair and her knees sink into wet snow as she wrestles through the gap with David bound inside her coat.

The woolshed paddock is fully exposed to the south. Nell leans her head and shoulder into it, mouth to David's woollen cap, arms enclosing him. Her boots slide and grip unreliably on the green and white underfoot. Her mouth is dry with fear. The sheep ramp to the north is clear of snow, so up she goes, and she steps into the vast, dusky stillness of the woolshed, although the great iron walls creak and whump, screech and whistle. It takes a moment to regain her balance, out of the wind. Her heart is pounding against the baby as she scans the empty space. There's a long, groaning crack, the sound of a branch shorn off a pine close by and she flinches at the *whack* and scrape of it against the iron.

'Herb?' Her voice has no substance.

Nell finds them in a pen, nested in wool scraps. Before they've noticed her, she watches them over the wooden wall and leaks tears of relief. Herb is crouched and watching Adam push a huge curved needle through a piece of sacking. Lettie is teasing merino fleece into a fuzzy globe.

Herb has a pipe between his teeth and is patient, his hands hovering but not insistent. Nell is suddenly a girl between her own father's elbows, having her stockings pulled taut on her feet and her boots laced up. Thank God Herb is a kind man. His intention is to be kind. She goes and kneels in the entrance to the pen. Adam's eyes gleam – 'Look, Mother' – as he shows her the stitched and wobbling line marking the seam of a miniature sack.

'And Mama, look Mama.' Hettie holds out her wool.

Nell smiles at them both. She smiles at Herb.

He pulls the pipe from his mouth and empties it onto the boards. He stands and grinds the ash underfoot. 'All right now? I'll get on. I left the milk at the clothesline for you.'

'Wait, Herb, please.' She wants but won't ask for the

scene to be prolonged, for the nest to deepen and hold them all just a little longer. 'At least help us through the gate?' Her voice is brittle.

'All right.' Herb puts the empty pipe back between his teeth. He wraps the needle in the sacking and thrusts it into Adam's pocket, takes Lettie around the waist and strides across the shed, Adam at his heels and Nell with baby David wading in his wake.

'Oh, how dreadful.' Nell looks up from the morning newspaper and pulls her teacup close.

'Are you reading the news from Europe?' Herb asks.

'Not even near. About a young woman who jumped from the H on the Hollywood sign.'

'Why do you read the dross? Scandal-mongering.'

'If you insist.' Nell's twinge of shame is followed by indignation. 'It's a social scandal, that she should have felt the need to end her life.' Why should Nell not read what is 'popular'? The kind of story that arouses feeling in women and is bound to be talked about in local gatherings – more so than the apparently sordid intentions of that Hitler chap (although Herb is 'keeping an open mind' on that, being mildly enchanted by concepts of racial superiority) and the revival of nationalistic fervour in far-off Germany. 'This poor child was lured by the promise of the silver screen, so-called.'

'But why need the world be told of it?'

'Because we all go to feast on the magic.' She and Herb have been to the pictures on each of their last visits to town, have been beguiled by Chaplin, entranced by *The Miracle Woman*. Nell's unmarried friends make a regular practice of going. 'We want beautiful young men and women to entertain us, but that industry, as they call it in the paper, fuels more dreams than it can ever fulfil.'

'Silly girl then, to let herself be lured.'

'Don't we all want to find and follow a dream?' Nell glances around the kitchen, never the place of her dreams, but at least it is humming with her own modest intentions: bread rising at the back of the stove, parsley seedlings greening on the windowsill, barley soaking for cordial, onions stewing in butter for the evening's casserole. 'Where would we be if no one ever extended themselves beyond the circumstances they find themselves in, or defied the odds set against them?'

'I'm just saying that she must have chosen foolishly. She evidently didn't have the talent for it.' Herb is sweeping crumbs together, putting cup and saucer onto his plate.

'But she did. A letter came the day after her death, to say she'd been chosen for the lead role in a play... Oh!'

Herb stands. 'Then she evidently hadn't the fortitude. Her parents, especially her mother, should have kept her from entertaining the notion.' He gathers up his notebook, pencil, woollen hat.

Nell shakes her head. She has read the final line: ... *a play about a woman driven to suicide.*

Cruel tale aside, Nell allows herself a few moments to contemplate the life of a movie actress, one who must live by her wits and her glamour, inherent or projected. Could her own life be further from that strange illusive world? In a minute or two, David will call for milk, and Adam and Lettie will return from the wash house where they have been allowed by Mary to stand and watch their father's filthy farm clothes being swirled soupily in the tub, to poke them with sturdy sticks and warm themselves against the enamel side. Nell will feed David, then bundle them all into the Singer and drive a mile up the farm track. She'll leave the car, and carry and coax baby, able toddler and small boy up towards the old pond. She's sure she saw geese flying in, and if so, Herb has agreed to go and try to shoot one for his own birthday dinner in a few days.

These small industries will involve milk – produced by her, swallowed and sicked up by David onto her shoulder – and nappies, to be removed, scraped and replaced; fussing children and Nell's need to anticipate the effects of hunger, cold, damp, wind and (please, God) sun too, on small bodies. There will be the car, obstinate to start these days, heavy gates to open and close, mud under wheels and then underfoot, gumboots and tricky foot-work. And later, with any luck, there will be hands gored with goose blood and feathers, the horrid stench of the carcass plunged in scalding water, the pernickety pluck and tear of quills from dimpled skin. Nell laughs at herself, at her catalogue of unpleasantness, at how distant this life from glamour, glossy hair on a big screen, a man gazing on a woman's flawless complexion with she at leisure to please and be pleased... Well, what Nell has is raw and vital and right on the wondrous edge of things. And Herb, for all his sharp opinions and inclination to see others as authors of their own misfortunes, he is benign and has promised that later this afternoon they'll go to the village and try out the new asphalt tennis court for as long as the children allow. It's hard to imagine the kind of hope, and the despair, that led the poor girl to the top of the big H.

1933

Men are turning up on the roads, in sheds and at doors. Primarily they need food and nearly all are willing to work for it, whether it be an hour's chopping and ferrying firewood for the kitchen range in exchange for a single meal, or a day or days working on the fences for a sack of provisions. One man did a fine job breaking in a fractious young horse and, being the same size as Herb, went off eventually with a woollen suit, dress shoes and a leg of mutton.

As has happened at intervals since they married, Herb's dreams make him yelp and twitch, rummage and clench, or sit up suddenly beside Nell, eyes straining at the dark. They're activated this time, she supposes, by the presence of the quietly desperate men. A few times she wakes to find him climbing back into bed, frozen. One night she hears him slip out, and when he doesn't return, she pulls on her shawl. In the kitchen she finds him mimicking the motion (as she learns when he wakes, alarmed by her gentle, 'Herb!') of loading and cocking a row of rifles to lay at the ready on the table.

'Back in the war this week, are you?' she asks.

'Damned unsettling.'

In bed with cocoa, she coaxes him to tell, but, 'Best left alone,' is his one solution. 'I have a spell of them, then none for ages,' he says.

'But do they not tell you of something that wants to come to light?' Nell asks.

'I know what they're about and nothing will change the facts. The deaths and the other...' He's shaking his head.

Nell is receptive, but he slides back under the covers.

'I'm ready to sleep,' he says, and the bottle of nightmares is, once again, lightly corked.

A vagrant trudges up the driveway and, finding Nell in the garden, opens his canvas roll on the grass beside her, showing the pitiful collection: tins of salve, a couple of brushes, matches, needles and spools of cheap cotton. There's nothing she needs, but if he wants to sit on the verandah, Nell tells him, she'll fetch a pot of tea and a mutton sandwich.

She watches him walk away later and, as he passes the hawthorn thicket, momentarily the trees are in front and he is a brown, man-shaped mist swimming through them.

Next morning, their neighbour calls in with the book inscribed with their name that Nell gave the man to read.

'Dead on the roadside,' he says.

Later, with Herb: 'He passed through the trees,' she tells him, and hears that it's only a murmur from 'passed away'.

'I don't like having these ... *knowings*,' she tells Peggy on the telephone (Peggy's treat, to pay the toll bill). 'What does it mean? It feels unorthodox and conjures up ... I don't know ... witchiness. Herb can't bear it and says it's one of the dark arts forbidden in the Bible. I think he's inclined to ask the minister to pray against it.'

Peggy has sitar music playing in the background. Her tastes are increasingly South Asian and on her last visit to the farm she wore for dinner a kind of pyjama suit, flattering but outlandish. Nell sometimes wonders if she ought still to be applying to Peggy for wisdom. Her own interests are so caught up now with the concerns of children, household and farm, it's years since she read one of Peggy's theosophy books. If she reads at all, it's afternoon snatches of the newspaper, a gardening magazine or, last thing at night, something light from the local Athenaeum.

'I do pray, in my own way, for protection – from these thoughts and impressions,' she adds.

Peggy moves closer to the music, then the volume is reduced. 'As I deepen my study, I find myself surprised that events from the past or the future don't intrude more than they do on this time we call the present. You have a sensitive nature, Nell, and are, as you know,' – Peggy laughs – '*on the path*. Now and then the veils part, and those with eyes to see are given a glimpse, off to one side, or around the next corner.'

Nell looks at her fingers, twined within the spiral phone cord. 'I've never sought foreknowledge, or wanted it. And I'm seldom in a position to alter the other person's fate. I can pray for them, wish them well, but that's all.'

'And perhaps that *is* your gift to them. It's a mystery, and my advice would be to neither foster nor fear it. Simply allow, and make the best of any knowledge it supplies. What else could you have done for the poor chap? You fed him, showed kindness, but you had no way of knowing if he was going to die that hour, or the following year.'

Nell sighs, glad enough to concur, and asks Peggy about the little theatre company she's involved with. At least this recent 'vision' and its culmination came close together. She wasn't left to fret long about the poor man's fate. Until the next time it happens, if it even does, she'll manage more or less to forget about the awkward capacity.

Dear Nell,

It was so good of you to remember me – again! Lordy, one of these years I'll surprise you by sending a card for your birthday, not simply a letter of thanks written weeks after mine. I do laugh at the antics of your family, although I suppose 'antics' is my interpretation of behavior most vexing. Such as Lettie and Davy plus dog rolling about in the sheep muck! Or you crossing the Rubicon strung about with babies and baskets...

I badly wanted to telephone you earlier this year because I felt that you with your decades of experience in 'man-handling' would surely advise me sanely. As it was, I didn't, but held my nose, shut my eyes and jumped in. Yes, Nell dear, I have hitched my wagon to a solid and big-hearted work-horse called Sol. (Solomon, and half of him comes from those island parts, so you can imagine we make a striking pair – I with my pale transparency and wan locks, he of burnished brown and frizzing on top.) We met and will continue to live in the warm far-north, where we are trying our hand at growing various novel fruits, grains and vegetables. (Yes, I have turned out to be somewhat practical, at least concerning vegetation. My grandmother, rest her soul, would be astounded.) Have you heard of the Chinese Gooseberry yet? Come to think of it, I'll jolly well box some up and have them freighted to you. Ripen them in the airing cupboard until soft, and then in your stark wintry landscape you will have a taste of the tropical sun.

I know we say it every time, but you must come up to visit, and I must come down – perhaps we could meet in the middle – as soon as you can see your way clear of the kiddies for a few days, and as soon as I've tired of the novelty (I'm told I shall) of having a man in my bed-bathroom-kitchen-life!

Your fond friend,
Lenora

Adam instructs her. 'The length of the roots equals the breadth of the crown,' he tells her at six, while staring at the jar with its sprouting bean on a bed of wet cotton wool.

Breadth. Crown. Where does he find the words he needs? He asks Nell no questions and, not being a prattler, she finds herself accompanying him often in silence. His mother is for sustenance, provision, for keeping order in his day and, once in a long while, for comfort. When he is hurt, or outraged by some injustice, momentary or prevailing, he leans into her face-first, hands at his sides, seldom wanting to hold, or be held, until his tank of fortitude is refuelled – by his own thoughts, it seems, since any soothing or instructive words of hers are likely to be hushed. 'No Mummy, I need you to be quiet.' And so she is, until he is done, when he pushes himself upright and walks away. She has come to find it oddly gratifying, to be used so by her son.

She has heard Adam quizzing the men about the place, finding out their specialty and boring in: 'How do you sharpen the blades?' 'Why do you start on the belly?' 'How do you make the sheep keep still?' He tails his father, as long as Herb is in a tolerant mood, and he bides his time, not firing the questions rat-tat-tat as he does to a visitor, but watching for the apposite moment – at the forge: 'How can you tell when the shoe is hot enough?' – in the truck: 'What happens if the oil falls below the line on the dipstick?' 'No, what *exactly* happens?' so that Herb's own thinking is made audible.

The only topic on which he will question Nell is on driving the cars. This is her specialty, the smooth handling and maintenance of the ageing Singer and the Ford. If she and Herb are out together, he prefers her to drive (and depending on their destination she has learned to pull over without argument five minutes short of it and swap places). By eight, Adam will want to know about the interplay of clutch and accelerator, what Nell is listening for that signals time for a gear change and what is happening under the bonnet when she pulls out the choke. He will be only nine when she returns early from the village one day to find him in the home paddock weaving the Singer around a series of barrels, in reverse.

Adam tries to take charge of the little home crowd. 'Mummy, make sure Lettie leaves my stones alone and did you know David's hiding in the living room with a dirty nappy? I'd like to go to the river after that. I'll fetch your basket and put in some apples.'

Sometimes it helps to have a small dictator take a yardstick and measuring string to her days, which so readily fall into no-shape, with the needs of the household and three children tumbling end on end through her hours. She is almost always glad to heed Adam's edict to leave the house for river, gully, woodshed, or the village where he makes a beeline for the tiny museum to interview the day's volunteer guardian and proffer his latest find of insect or geological chip.

She makes him wait, though. She asks for help in exchange: to take the scraps out for the chooks, or a message to his father in the shed.

Lettie is blithe and generous; David silent and secretive, though just as sweet by nature. Except when confounded in his furtiveness. Then he is thunder and lightning combined: an instant, livid rage of bellows and blows to whatever or whomever is at hand. What has made her sons so self-directed and separate? David, at two, tolerates cuddles, but he takes on a faraway look; she is not the object of his thoughts though his hand might sweep the flesh of her arm, or his fingers delve her cardigan's buttonholes.

'All right,' she tells Adam, to his surprise with no

conditions. 'The river it is. Let's take the billy, the bucket and spade ... What else?'

'My bird identification book.'

'Well, fetch it then, and would you like me to bring the opera glasses?'

Adam springs at her, face shining, and hugs her leg with all the awkwardness of a boy overcome. Feeling swells in Nell – and yet the affection is only glancingly for her. He aches to use the ivory binoculars, thus far only ever held indoors over sofa or carpet.

It's hard to imagine life without the Singer, the greatest blessing of her life, Nell sometimes thinks. It has kept her horizons open. Before marriage it took her away during oppressive wintry spells and allowed her to meet with people otherwise kept from her. And now, with the children, the car is her lifeline. She keeps the engine clean and oiled and insists on a yearly overhaul by the mechanic in Palmerston. The children have their allotted places in the back; since Toss the terrier hit the windscreen in a sudden stop, she won't allow children in the front seat.

It's windless down at the river. Nell parks beneath the bridge and asks Adam and Lettie to take an item each besides their own (Adam his book, Lettie her hobby horse). They head away over the boulder-strewn silt, making for the willows, while she potters behind with David who is a game walker, but readily distracted and already sitting to tug at his sandal.

As long as the children are occupied within view and the weather clement, this is Nell's happy place. The river gentles by, pooling into a swimmable hole twenty yards downstream, while here it is narrow enough to be dammed should the children be of a mind for that. Or they might rearrange the riverbank's benign mixture of silt and gravel. Adam is inclined to scoop out hollows for his collections of stones, leaves or twigs of a certain type, while Lettie has several times created a farm, drawing with a stick the layout of buildings and paddocks, giving equal attention to the specifics of house and lands.

David stands and stares at the river. Nell snaps off a piece of willow for him to hold and he is further entranced by the flow of water through leaves. At twenty months, he has yet to utter his first word. This would be worrying if it weren't for the fact that he evidently follows and understands every nuance of the interchanges around him, that his hearing is acute (even now, he is cocking his ear at the water, throwing a glance at Lettie when she shrieks) and that his lips often move, as if he is sounding out words in his head.

Nell steps across the water from the children's play and makes a fire with newspaper and pine cones from the basket, and while they're catching she scoots about collecting twigs and driftwood. Crouched at the flames with the smells of crushed willow, river mud and woodsmoke, she knows a primitive contentment. She is whole, squatting here; bottom brushing the earth, arms around knees and hair flicked by dangling leaves. Mica specks glint on her hands. A benison. She loves her hands and all they can do. Adam and Lettie are murmuring, heads together. Their two enterprises seem to be amalgamating. Nell swells. Tears again.

Tears are scarce, though, when Father is dying. When her mother's telegram arrives, before she can follow her impulse to drive to the city without delay, Nell must arrange for the care of the children and three orphaned lambs; must roster three local women to cook and clean in her absence; must write notes for Herb about dog food, school bus and sundry obligations. When she reaches the hospital a day and a half later, the doctor insists on explaining in painful detail the mechanism of her father's stroke, before finding a nurse to take her to his bedside, where she is dismayed to learn that, in the last few minutes, he has died.

She cannot make it seem real, and in the weeks after the funeral grief is stoppered. In order to cry, she must bring to mind her old pony, or dogs' deaths – most recently their ancient Toss. Or she pulls out her father's cheering letters to her when she was a homesick boarder. She sniffs them, holds a page to the light, sees him at his desk with the silver ink-well and stack of stock-keeping record books.

Nell finds herself looking at Herb with harder eyes, at the way he runs the station. Or perhaps Herb actually has become more rigid, more firmly opinionated; more chivalrous in company and more dismissive at home of her input, her ideas and suggestions concerning the farm. Father was opinionated too, but he had Hamish (son, not daughter) who from childhood, it seemed, was there to challenge and temper any action springing from his conclusions.

After a few months, she stops trying to conjure Father. If a memory appears, or a sense of him arrives with scent off the hills, in a turn of phrase or scrap of advice, she pauses to savour it. She lets Adam take from her dressing table the magnifying glass Father used for all his reading, and – atypical of Adam – in no time at all, it is lost.

The yard is little by little emptied of sheep as they are chuted off to the dipping trough. Nell is perched on the yard railing. Adam stands halfway along the chute, thrashing each passing sheep's woolly back with the kitchen fly swat. Bleating, heat, wool, manure and the pungent odour of dip thicken the air. Lettie stares mesmerised through the fence beside the trough as each shoved animal loses its footing and sinks into the vile grey stuff, then floats up with a cry. She jiggles, her legs cross, her bottom lip goes out in determination, but she can't tear herself away and she finally stamps in disgust as the wee runs into her sandals. At least she's wearing a pinafore. Seeing all, Nell calls, 'Just take your undies off, lovie, and give them here.'

David has climbed up beside Nell and steadies himself with an elbow hooked through her apron bodice. Below them the handful of sheep mill around, or stand and pant. One has a mouthful of grass grabbed on its way in. Receiving a prod on the flank from Herb's crook, it lets out a long, green, indignant bleat. Beside her, David stiffens. His chin juts at the sheep. 'You don't talk with your mouth full!'

Nell shakes her head. She stares at his golden face. So. He has words, and he knows how to use them.

1934

Nell finds there is anger to be reckoned with. Her own. How it swells unpredictably, and yet reliably enough when she realises the time of the month. It has seized on injustices, slights and neglect, Herb's towards her, but also those dealt out in the family or wider community. When municipal workers made a frenzied savaging of old Mrs Davis's treasured roadside hedge without her knowledge, Nell went after them in the Singer, and gave them an earful. Of course, they had their reasons, but carelessness was in the mix, and she told them so. When Lettie, usually so blithe, came home from a four-year-old's birthday party tear-stained and silent, Nell got it out of her. The mother (a teacher, who should know better) had dressed her down in front of the other children for spilling her cocoa on the birthday table, so Nell, in a boil of righteousness, phoned her up to spell out the dangers of unconsidered public shaming.

And closer to home.

A cousin of Herb's, Ava, occasionally calls in unannounced on her way up- or down-country. Nell finds her fresh and fun for the first half hour, then, increasingly, loud and gratingly self-referential. Ava has no qualms about letting Nell turf a child out of their room and make up a fresh bed for her, with the usual trimmings (it is impossible for Nell not to add flowers, an extra pillow and a soft shawl, to banish toys and clear out the top drawer), and then she gambols about with the tots as if she were one herself, eats the evening meal with gusto, then finds reason to go off to bed when the children do. Nell is left, as always, with the cleaning up. Because it is the usual, Nell overlooks it, until one winter Monday night (it is Herb's Hospital Board meeting so he is out the door before pudding).

Ava has had the little ones dancing like dervishes to her new swing records ('swing'! she's only a couple of years younger than Nell) for the hour before dinner. After apple crumble and custard, Ava makes her usual bid to disappear (thankfully, the children have gone already), when Nell lights into her. Nell hasn't seen it coming. She stands in a column of heat and frost as she delivers her accusations: 'You behave like a child. You let me drudge for you. You've never once offered to help, and then you get a headache, or a belly ache, any kind of ache and I'm sick of it. You have simply no idea.'

Clearing the kitchen side by side is a miserable affair. The silence, the shock and indignation, bristle between them, until Nell says, off you go then. And, as if swallowing a walnut: thank you.

Herb raises it over lunch the next day; he'd seen Ava out to her car. 'You must have given her a savaging, Nell. Surely she didn't deserve it. She was distraught.' And, when Nell seeks to defend the anger, not yet settled: 'So you did what you usually do: you cooked and cleaned, and did a fine job of it, I'm sure. But did you not see Ava doing what *she* does best? She kept the children out of your hair; she bathed them, read them stories and frankly delighted them. Do you begrudge her that? And if she didn't want to stay up after dinner, she's probably half scared of you, Nell, of your capacity and unfailing...' (the terrible pause, she will think later) '...dignity. Beneath which, many flounder.'

Dignity. The word will stink ever after.

'Besides that...' Herb reaches into the pocket of his jacket hanging on the chair behind him, 'she had this to give you. In thanks.'

The gift in its rose-sprigged paper and shiny pink ribbon sits on the table between them. Hot coals raining.

It will take Nell a long time to pick through the strands of the event, to locate the implications of her false position as domestic demiurge, to see and feel Ava's point of view, the children's, even Herb's, to dredge up compassion for the harried girl inside her who sometimes takes over the show, and to forgive herself.

In the general store at Ranfurly, Nell is contemplating the cabbages (her own had a late start and won't be ready before New Year) when she notices the woman beside her slip an orange, then another, into her coat pocket. She watches her walk along the aisle: the windburned cheeks on a lean face, crushed shoes under thick, burred stockings. Into the other stained pocket goes a tin of fish, a box of matches. With pounding heart, Nell follows her outside. When she touches the woman's arm, she flinches away, then gives a defiant stare. Nell holds out a pound note. The woman bunches her mouth, interpreting. Or misinterpreting. Nell presses the note at her hand, which twists and takes it.

'You can pay, and get some more things.' Nell despises herself at once for putting conditions on the money. She considers offering a few days' work, but the woman's shrewd and flinty gaze delivers a kick of fear and she doesn't want her nearer than they find themselves at this moment. The woman nods once and walks back into the shop.

Such conflict between mind and heart, she writes later to Peggy, *as I got into the Singer and drove away with a sack of flour and ten pounds of honey. There but for grace...*

1935

'Lock the doors and you know where the gun is.' Herb is off to town for a couple of days. Since the married couple is also away, Nell will be alone on the farm. 'You'll be fine, of course.'

Nevertheless, he insists she keep Fly in the porch at night.

Fly in the porch is soon Fly in the kitchen. Nell hasn't the heart to turn her away before the children have finished smooching her brow and cheeks, probing her ears and warm corners.

'Are they arm pits or leg pits, Mumma?' David asks.

Fly perches, not quite sitting, on the hearth stones. She quivers at every footfall and her eyes beseech Nell.

'Take her out, Adam,' she says finally. 'Let her have the picnic blanket for a nest.'

Nell hauls the big kitchen table closer to the range and when the children have gone to bed, shovels in fresh coal and does what she has itched to do: a page of Adam's colouring book – a jungle scene – with pencils in yellows and greens.

In the morning, Friday, she lets the children eat in pyjamas and dressing gowns, porridge with brown sugar and cream. They sit together across the table from her, backs to the stove, tousled and easy.

'Do we have to go to school today?' Nell asks them.

Their eyes widen.

'You don't go to school, Mummy,' Lettie says.

'I don't go to gool,' David adds.

'Well, let's none of us go today.'

'Hooray, hooray, hooray!' Adam and Lettie wave their spoons and clack them together.

They eat more porridge, they grow warm, and they begin to scratch. Pyjamas peeled off reveal welts in their armpits, leg-pits, elbow and knee pits. Lettie wears a half necklace of red lumps.

Nell fetches the calamine lotion and applies it with liberal dabs of a cotton wool ball. The naked three sit hip to hip and laugh at their spotted limbs.

'All right, kiddies, we're going on a flea hunt.'

When they're dressed – she only has to help David sort front from back of his trousers and do up the top shirt button – they start in Adam's room.

'Quietly now. Adam, you and Lettie go on the other side and David, come on mine.'

Nell pulls the top sheet up hard, then peels it slowly, slowly down the bed. The children hunch and stare at the shifting line where the sheets part ways.

Adam yelps, pounces and slaps. The flea leaps like a spat seed for the dark seam. Nell goes on peeling. Lettie snatches a glass jar from Adam's bedside table and hovers it above the moving sheet.

'Your head's in the way!' Adam complains, but he doesn't thump her, not today.

If they were searching together for tigers on the savannah they could not be more rapt, more common in their purpose. If only the bed were twelve, fifteen, twenty feet long. The top sheet falls off the end and there is the flea. Lettie whams the jar down. 'What now, Mummy?'

Their heads lean close as Nell probes. Her finger presses flea to glass, pinches it against her thumb. They watch its kicking back legs, as her other thumbnail presses. They are close enough to hear the tiny *crack,* and see the little smear of Adam's blood.

'That's that,' says Nell. 'Now Lettie's and David's beds, and then...' she consults the sky outside, their wondering faces and her heart, '...a bonfire and baked potatoes.'

Nell wakes from a dream so vivid that she's startled to find herself in her own bed, heart thudding but safe. It's early, Herb still sleeping. She goes to stir the fire to life and while she waits for the kettle to boil puts the oatmeal on to soak. She takes their tea back to bed where Herb rolls onto his elbow and sits up beside her.

'There were two tramps,' she tells him, 'like those chaps who came last weekend, all strung about with bags and coats. They were sidling across a hill like Buster, not terribly steep. Then one of them yelled, there was a roar and the hill churned up under them. They were tumbled like washing in the copper, in and out of the boulders and each time they reappeared they were bloodier and more lifeless. I ran towards them across the paddocks. I could see them clearly although I was miles away and aware that I was carrying only a spoon and a sheet of writing paper, that my legs were heavy as lead. One man raised a hand, to catch my attention and his fingers ... the flesh had been flayed from the bones.'

Herb is pressed back into the headboard, chin tucked in hard.

Nell makes a long exhale. 'It still feels ... so real. Please don't let anyone go up the hill today.'

Herb gulps at his tea. 'Can't run a farm on superstition.' He looks at her, a quick look. 'But we've no reason to go up today.'

She sips. She puts a hand on his leg. 'I suppose you saw scenes like that. The men, I mean.'

He draws out the word: 'Scenes? You know I did.'

'You say I know, but you've never told me directly of even one.'

'I prefer other *scenes*.'

'Nor of your dreams.' She experiences their effects, though: his shouts in the night, the scrabbling and tensing beside her.

'Well, anyway...' Herb swings his legs out of bed, '...you're probably over-tired. How many nights were you up with the chicken pox?'

Nell frowns. How many nights does she *not* get up to a child? And the chicken pox was weeks ago. *Over-tired* is a dismissal.

Herb is at the tallboy. 'If any out-of-workers turn up today, send them on to Briggs. He has firewood to be cut up.'

Not a comfort exactly, but telling has dissipated fear, and Mount Buster when she looks out the window is broad and solid. It'd take a volcano to shift it.

1936

'Please may I have a saucer?'

The morning of the A&P show, Herb has taken Adam and Lettie out for the morning chores.

David is cradling the tin-can of sand he carried home from the river yesterday. Nell clears one end of the kitchen table and hunts out a yellow saucer whose teacup has long gone. He tips sand onto it and smooths it, then has to be persuaded to stay and eat his porridge before he rushes out to the garden.

Nell is piecing together a too-elaborate cake. One of the cocoa sponges failed to leave the tin in one piece, so she's made a discreet patchwork of the middle layer, which will nevertheless be seen if the judge cuts into it. She is dabbing butter icing over the whole when David returns.

Sitting across from her, he examines the buds and petals he has spilled onto the table. His dimpled hand presses a marigold into the centre of the sand. Cerise and yellow polyanthi follow in a circle.

Nell sorts through sticky maraschino cherries for those still whole and cuts neat halves from the others.

Across the table, wisteria tips are being laid in mauve spokes and marched around the edge of the saucer.

Nell pops the cherries onto the cake at random but pleasing intervals.

David looks up at her, stiff hands like gates either side of the saucer. His eyes plead.

'I like it very much,' Nell tells him.

'But it's not finished.'

'What else, do you think?'

Silence.

Then, 'You'll say no.'

Nell cocks her head.

'The flag.'

'Flag?'

'The little one. Only for a borrow.' Since Nell is still puzzled, he goes to the next room and she hears the sideboard drawer being opened.

Pinched between thumb and finger he has one of those horrid red and white nylon flags on a toothpick. Herb's sister Ilona introduced cocktails on her last visit.

Nell nods, hiding a smile.

David jabs the flag in at a jaunty angle beside the marigold, and beams.

Perfect, they agree.

Shortly after, with the others jostling in the kitchen, David appears in his tidy jersey and school shoes. He takes the saucer from the safety of the table and crosses the kitchen, holding it in both hands. Distracted, Nell opens the door for him. 'I'm going now.' David walks along the path and onto the driveway, eyes fixed on his creation.

Nell watches, then follows. 'You know we're coming too?'

He stops in his tracks.

'In the car.'

He looks up through tears.

'You thought you had to walk all the way?'

'*Lovey.* Come, let's put that here in the shade until we're ready. I have to take my silly cake along, and they want me to judge the daffodils and tulips. We're all going. We'll have fun.'

Nell bends to kiss his head. What has made their youngest so solitary, as if he has already been abandoned to find his own way?

'Mummy!' Stella's youngest daughter Rose puts a hand to her mother's face and pulls it away from her conversation with Nell. 'Do you know, they have *Mary Poppins* at Whitcombe and Tombs? I really need my own copy. I can't keep waiting for the school library one. Everybody wants it.'

Stella gives her a resigned look as she tucks hair under the child's hairband. 'Really and truly?'

'Yes, really, and what's more, they have a book that you'd love. I saw it in the newspaper. A lady in a beautiful dress and there's moonlight in the name.'

'I would, would I? Nell, help yourself to more tea.'

Nell has brought David with her to visit Stella in Christchurch, partly in hopes that he and Rose will get along happily for these few days of the August holidays, which might prime Rose for a return visit over the summer. Thus far, David has been in silent awe of this garrulous girl a month or two younger than him. All of Stella's children talk a lot, which their father Frank has encouraged. Nell is heartened to see, too, that Stella's early insistence on propriety has been somewhat eroded, in keeping with her mildly anarchic and creative personality. Which itself is currently a little eroded by the fact of four children at home for the winter holiday and Frank in bed with his annual bout of bronchitis.

Watching the city cousins, Nell sees how each of her own brood has, by comparison, learned to find their own solace, their own release (or suppression, it is to be supposed) of pent-up feeling, because life is often too busy for them to expect a parent to attend. Stella's are far more insistent on parental attention, and approval if it can be gained; they keep their parents filled in to a remarkable degree on their intentions, friendships, thoughts and wants.

'Perhaps David and I would enjoy a trip to the bookshop with you, Rose.' Nell smiles at Rose with her quick eyes and soft complexion. She has not been sent out in sleet, frost, wind or sun to feed hens and dogs, collect eggs or dig carrots for dinner. Without the need to grapple with gates, horses, firewood or heavy buckets, Rose's hands bear none of the nicks, splinters or chilblains that mark a farm child's. 'We might go there with birthday gifts in mind.'

'Stellata?' Frank's voice comes from upstairs.

Stella has barely risen from her chair when the phone rings, and a woman's face appears at the kitchen window.

'Rosey, go up and see what Daddy wants.' She reaches for the phone and says, 'Hold on a moment, please.' Then, 'Nell, would you take that manila folder out to Mrs Frew and tell her *Friday.*'

Nell is impressed. She and Stella both have learned, from their mother, she supposes – concedes – how to delegate.

Not that Nell hasn't tried to do it all herself, and trained others to believe that she could. There was a day when she frightened herself and Herb. A raft of his family was in the house for a long weekend. Midwinter, they'd come to skate and curl, but nor'west winds in the preceding days meant that by Friday the ice was too soft, then a southerly change threw them all back inside for two days of eating, debating, board games and endless rounds of tea. On Sunday morning, the children took off in a gang for the woolshed, and Nell started later than intended to prepare the lunch (roast dinner) — after which they would all depart. One after the other, Herb's aunt, his mother and cousin came to the kitchen with offers of help. Nell had had enough of them all. The two older women were more inclined to talk than to act, and of course recruiting their help meant guiding them and interrupting her own flow. She said no thanks.

At some point, Nell was alone again in the kitchen when Herb came sniffing in. 'Meat nearly ready to carve? The chaps are getting fidgety. They want to leave by two.'

'Give them another drink then.'

'They've had a couple already. What'll it take to hurry things up?'

'Are you offering to help?'

Herb cast a helpless look back at the living room.

'You could set the table or put the redcurrant jelly and horse-radish into bowls, or find three extra chairs, or call the children home, or drain and mash the carrots and parsnips. Oh, or stir this custard.'

'I can carve,' he persisted.

A hissing red tide rushed up inside of Nell. Her hand dived into the drawer for the knife and hurled it. Not at Herb, but only slightly to one side. The blade pierced the pinex wall, then released.

Nell had already taken off her apron. She opened the door to the porch and fossicked in the big basket for hat and mitts. She pulled on her wool coat, and an oilskin to wear over that. Thick socks. Gumboots. 'Don't wait for me,' she said.

'So, there I was dug into the trench, dead rats lying all around and stinking to high heaven, and the enemy creeping, creeping over the ground towards me. I could hear their grunts and heaving breath.'

'Herb, please.' Nell speaks over the heads of their avidly listening children.

From ten paces above, Herb looks back at her, one hand on a fence post. The children, climbing on all fours, turn their heads, too, rapt expressions turning to irritation.

'Go on, Dad,' Adam instructs, and the others agree.

'I've turned the lads into rats,' Herb tells Nell. He steps on towards the summit and the children follow. 'I burrowed into my kit-bag. What was I looking for, Lettie?'

Why does he tell the children the stories, and never her? He says he wants to forget, but also, evidently, to remember and to brag. Of course, he is to be the hero of this story set amongst his dead comrade-rats. His voice is modulated to reach Lettie, but not Nell climbing behind her, and the children soak up every word. When do they ever listen to her with the same rapture, she who ensures for them food warmth safety clothing beds beauty and calm? Herb remains for them exotic, quixotic. Idiotic? No, he is never that, not even to her. He is deeply averse to idiocy. He is upright, righteous, plain right, in everything.

Nell sidles away from the fence-line – simpler if she can't hear what's being said. She zigs and zags for a while, then realises she's done it again – shut herself outside the family. There are precious few times when all of them are focused on one activity, one theme, one story, and usually these times are instigated by Herb. He commands the troops to gather, and then he has the power to hold them in thrall.

The summit turns out not to be, and by the time they trek up the final ridge of Mt Kyeburn, all are silent, reduced to breath, intention and footsteps. None of their children is a shirker and David at six is determined to keep up, helped just a little by the bits of Christmas chocolate that Nell slips him from time to time.

At the top, the lightest of breezes touch their pink, damp faces and Nell chooses a rock to sit on close to Herb's. She hands enamel mugs of water to the children and adjusts their sunhats, then cuts up the egg and bacon pie. Herb compliments her on it and when she settles, leans his back against hers.

Adam is uninterested in eating. He stands on what he judges to be the highest rock and turns like the second hand of a clock, degree by degree taking in the ranges to the west; the high northern hills, snow-streaked even in summer; the eastern coast obscured by swathes of cloud that race inland and dissipate somewhere above

Green Valley; the Maniototo plains spread blue across the south. Even when he joins them again ('This was the *very* best thing to do in the whole *world*') his attention is taken by grasses, lichens, grasshoppers and bird calls, and he leaves his pie barely eaten on its square of brown paper.

'Plunket tonight, is it?' Herb sips from his cup of tea.

Nell herds papers to one side of the table and pushes the fruit mince tarts to the middle. 'Yes, final one for the year. Hard to believe it's a month since the last meeting. I've only just put the minutes in order.'

'Do you have to read them out as well?'

'Best I do, given the state of my handwriting.'

'Well, as someone adamant they weren't going to join a committee, you've been nicely hooked.'

She looks at him. 'I saw that I could make a small difference.'

'With your eloquent minutes?'

'In that I make a point every meeting of advocating in some small way against rigidity in baby care.' She stacks her papers and taps them flush. 'If even one mother softens her approach and dares to trust her own kindly feelings towards her baby, then I'll consider my efforts worthwhile.'

Herb breaks a tart and holds one half close to his mouth. 'Can't allow children to rule the roost, though. Imagine if every mother obeyed every whim of her tiny despot.'

'I'm talking about babies, not toddlers testing their powers. A baby cannot be a despot. It makes its simple needs known, and a mother's role is simply to meet those needs.' Nell tops up their teacups. 'Do you really believe that our babies were damaged by my responsiveness to them?'

'By my lights, you did a fine job. They were all a bit noisy at times, but you always managed to smooth things out.'

'Not always. But after the first week or two of Adam's unhappiness – remember? – I defied the so-called rules of strict four-hourly feeding, no handling between feeds, leaving him to cry at night.'

Herb swills the leaves in the bottom of his cup. 'As long as these babies don't turn out soft, unable to brace themselves for hard work or respond to duty's call.'

'Babies?'

'The child is father to the man. War's brewing again, Nell. We don't want a nation of absconders.'

'We should raise every child to be a soldier?'

'Those who did all right in war, who didn't give way to nervous exhaustion or, God help us, cowardice, were those who set their faces "like a flint toward Jerusalem", who had the flint in them in the first place.'

'Oh! Please don't quote at me! I want, have always wanted – and I thought you did too – for our children to be kind and sensitive. Strong-spirited, not fighting machines.'

'Well, you'd better face the likelihood of another draft in the coming years. The Hun's not finished with us yet.'

Herb has set his face like a flint toward the possibility. This is how too many conversations end (end, this time, because she has to go), with each of them on divergent tracks of thought or purpose. Nell slides the papers into her slim leather satchel, stuffed with Christmas cards to be dropped in the post box. She picks up the covered platter of mince tarts for the committee's supper.

As she manoeuvres between the shoes and muddied boots in the porch (why won't they use the rack?) desolation swills up in Nell like tepid water. She no longer has babies, or even toddlers, but her ideals have led her into roles that call for relentless determination (flintiness!). The malaise arises each year with the approach of Christmas. She almost drowns in tiredness and expectations, her own, reinforced by those of everyone wanting Christmastide to conform to its precursors. There will be cards sent and received, gatherings, a tree, guests, as much festive food as can be mustered up, sherry, carols, gifts however simple, and *no one* left out or unrewarded, unthanked. It is this last that wakes her in the night. *Great Aunt Beatrice! The farrier's new baby! And what about the mailman?*

It is a shock to learn that number four is well on its way. Three miscarriages since David have led Nell to believe that there would be no more children. Sexual intercourse has become a rarity, negotiated in mutual silence and self-containment and Nell has done her best to avoid it in the fertile period. The trouble is that those few days of the month are also her happiest, her most affectionate. She's seen it in the mirror: her face and eyes grow clear and light. For a day or two she senses the ease that lies at the heart of things. The body makes no calculations into the future; it wants only what it wants.

1939

Nell gives birth in high summer, to a girl, at ten minutes before midnight.

'A well-seasoned womb,' the midwife had told her. 'That's why you're so large this time around. There's more give. You'll have an easy time of it.'

And so it proves – again – at ten minutes after midnight when, following a single half-hearted push, a second girl slips onto the bed. Nell has had her own suspicions about this, but neither doctor not midwife took them seriously.

'Five!' Herb wails. 'Five bairns!' He is standing at the end of the bed in his pyjamas, looking down at the bundled twins. He's been asleep on the living room sofa where he took blanket and pillow. 'Not identical, are they? What happened to this one?'

The midwife strokes the child's left side, from cheek bone to chin. 'A birth stain. It'll fade. Or it should do.'

'A handicap.' Mouth pursed, he peers a little closer at the sleeping face. 'Are you all right here then?' he asks Nell. Shearing is on. He can't sacrifice sleep for babies. He goes to leave, then relents. He comes and kisses the top of her head. 'Clever old thing.' His eyes meet hers. 'We'll make do, won't we.'

Thank goodness the midwife can stay for a couple of days, as long as none of her other mothers go into labour early. It's hard to imagine coordinating the twins' feeds. They've been given a bottle for their first, then the midwife changes the sheet under Nell and tells her to get some sleep. She'll wake her when it's time.

After breakfast in bed, Nell feeds the twins a second time, each one laid on a pillow, latched on and tucked under an arm. Her arm. Arms. Her bosoms, her body, her babies. Her life now for the foreseeable future. Cast like a sheep. Smiling, staring and weeping by turns.

'Pull the curtains wide,' she tells the midwife because she needs to see the hills.

Lettie comes and coos. She reaches to stroke the downy heads, and eyes with interest the blue-veined expanses of breast, the pink mouths moving on wet areolae.

'This one doesn't try as hard as the other one,' she observes.

'She's smaller and sleepier, it's true. Younger too.'

'Keep her awake,' the midwife says. 'Pinch her if you have to.'

Nell rolls her eyes at Lettie who at ten shares the joke.

But then she loses interest. 'I want to ride up to the chalk pit. Can I? I've cleaned up the kitchen.'

'Where's David?'

'Reading a comic book. The shearers gave him a pile.'

'Did he have breakfast?'

'I put some in front of him. Can I?'

'Did Adam go up to the shed?'

'Yes, Dad's making him work until lunch. Mum?'

Lunch, for shearers. Could the timing be worse? The girl Esther is coming from down the road and the midwife has promised to keep her on the job. Nell adjusts the sleepy baby's pillow.

'Yes, go,' she tells Lettie who is hovering at the door. 'Be back by eleven to help Esther.'

Nell is weeping when David comes in.

'Why are you?' he asks, eyes on her face.

'I'm a little tired.' She takes the hanky from her sleeve. 'These girls turned up in the middle of the night so someone had to look after them.'

'Turned up?' From a yard away, he looks sidelong at the white bundles on the pillowy barricade around his mother. He pulls in his chin and his hands are plunged deep in his pockets. 'I just can't,' he finally says.

'I'm not sure I can either,' she says, and regrets it for the flash of fear on his face. 'Dear, do you want to show me one of your comic books?'

'I think they belong in the kitchen.' He is waiting to be dismissed.

She nods. 'You'll find the babies quite interesting when they're awake.'

He gives her an imploring look and she indicates with her head and a smile for him to go, before the tears begin again.

'How did a greyhound get in with the sheepdogs?' Kneeling beside a bundle of sacks in the neighbour's woodshed, Nell holds the squirming grey body in one hand and inspects ears and belly. She strokes the upper palate with her pinky finger and the tiny teeth bite down.

Herb holds up the black and white male. He flies it at Nell's pup with the angry whine of a fighter plane. The airborne pups paddle at one another.

'John's a bit of a softie and brought the sire back from the races. It ran last and the owner was going to shoot it on the spot.'

'Slow then,' Nell replies. 'Relatively speaking. I like this one.'

'The male's got a bit more fire in him.'

'No; this wee dimple. She's steady and brave, I can tell.'

'Tea or home brew?' John is calling from the porch.

Nell and Herb exchange a look. He widens his eyes at her, then says, 'Both?'

Much has been uncharacteristic about this weekend. David and the toddling twins have been taken off by their grandparents while the older two are with cousins. Herb has declared a holiday, a slim pause between lambing and shearing and, in the idleness of a Saturday morning on the verandah with newspapers and late breakfast, he agreed without demur to Nell acquiring a companion-dog for the girls and herself. 'As long as it's a rabbiter,' his only stipulation.

He drives them home while Nell cradles 'Chloe' on a towel on her lap.

'What say we go to a show tonight?' he asks.

'What show? Where?'

'There'll be something on in Oamaru.'

Nell looks at his handsome profile, mouth curved in a smile. He is pleased with this, his generous idea. But his timing doesn't take into account her concerns. Or the three hours driving each way.

'What about little missy?' She cups the chest of the pup who is sitting bolt upright and panting.

'Little missy is a dog and will be treated as such. Put her in the wash house for now if you want, but then she can go in the kennels.'

My dog, thinks Nell, will have a life apart from the farm dogs. And she will not be abandoned on this first night away from her mother. 'Let's go another Saturday, and plan ahead for it. Why don't I cook something special...' (what could it possibly be, besides mutton? macaroni cheese? or she could try the fancy rice dish Mary wrote out for her) '...and we could listen to the new records.'

Herb shoots her a hurt look, then a cross look, and her belly tightens. He shakes his head and wipes a hand over his hair. 'For once, I felt like going off to a show. Don't expect me to offer again in a hurry. After this weekend, the calendar's full.'

The pup's heart is pounding between Nell's hands. Inside herself, she observes the rush towards compensation, over-compensation: she'll light the fire as soon as they're home, unwrap the soft, smelly cheese Mary left for them, and put on the Schubert even though it's the Rachmaninov she wants to hear again.

Then Herb surprises her. He bumps her arm with his and shakes his head. 'Doesn't matter. It's been a good day, doing nothing necessary. I'll be happy by the fire. Game of gin rummy after dinner?'

1941

Everywhere beyond the horizon of hills or the farm gate, there is talk of the war. And further afield, the war itself. Nell wonders how she might counteract the bleakness of assembling facts. And, as if twins were not creation enough, she finds that a flower garden is begging to be made. Not merely the circle of roses around which the driveway runs, but the lawn surrounding the house cries to be relieved of its monotony. While the earth is still in winter's grip, Nell subscribes to a couple of gardening magazines and makes diagrams of borders and banks of flowers. She wants to make some reflection of the hills; the garden's contours will follow those of the 360 degrees surrounding it: the remote, flattened blue of the Maniototo plains, the close green terrace rising to the south, and the east-north-west vista of ranges, peaks and plateaus. She will conjure their bulk and their ethereal quality; their quick changes and their propensity for disappearing under cloud. Is that too much to ask of a garden?

On every trip away from home she calls at roadside stalls, nurseries or seed tables, and she begs friends and neighbours for cuttings, rootings, slips and seeds.

Trips away from home are few though, with the twins. They're easy girls and amuse themselves together, but toddlers can't be left out of sight, so as soon as the spring garden is tillable, on days when the school bus has taken the older three, Nell bundles them into tights, woollens, jackets and rabbitskin booties. She takes outside a collection of small boxes, bowls, enamel cups and a sugar-sack of sawdust from the woodshed. They potter about with those while Nell takes to the earth with grubber and shovel, spade and hoe. She carries the girls in the wheelbarrow over to the woolshed, then coaxes them home, hanging on one each side of the teetering barrow full of ancient woolly droppings. Chloe trots along nearby with her swinging gait, and when they stop for any reason, places herself within sight of both Nell and the twins, Flick and Floss. The girls have all but lost their given names; it was Adam who came up with the nicknames, applying them so relentlessly, they've stuck. Beyond the family walls, Nell makes a point of calling them Isobel and Monica.

When the days warm up, Nell lays rugs and dolls under one of the greening fruit trees scattered about the lawn. Occasionally the girls actually fall asleep on the rug, and then, although she aches to lie down and sleep beside them, Nell redoubles her efforts and ventures further, to lengthen the driveway border and build up the bank where peonies will wag their pink red white and yellow pompoms at the Kakanui Range.

Early summer brings coloured scraps of glory to the garden and Nell is greedy for more. In the evenings, while Herb works with the day's tallies or goes to one of his meetings – for hospital, water catchment or pest management boards – her diagrams spread over the table, expand and blossom, dense with notes and names.

Shearing intervenes, the days being full to the brim

with shepherds and shearers, children home for the holidays, summer visitors. Pots proliferate on the back porch, her rootings and seedlings, bits of this and that gathered and waiting to be planted.

And then Nell's mother takes ill and calls for her. Nell arranges for local woman Mary to step in while she's away. Her mother's ill-defined malaise has vanished by the time Nell arrives. Instead of attending the bedside, she finds herself running her mother into town to replenish her underwear and visit old friends, and helping to invigorate *her* flower garden. By the time Nell returns home, the nor'wester has dried her pots out, shrivelled every last green shoot or sprout into brown strands and flakes. She hadn't thought it necessary to *ask* Mary to water them, and no-one else has noticed.

After dinner, when they've taken to the porch with their tea and biscuits, Nell sketches for Herb her time away, and complains airily about the pots, hoping he'll look out at them gathered on the verandah steps, wet from a last vain watering. Hoping he'll commiserate.

'The first troops sailed today,' Herb tells her. 'People are distracted.'

Troops sailing, mobilisation calls on posters and in newspapers, whatever the cause, Herb's nights are stirred as if by a big paddle. Nell wakes to find his feet on the pillow beside her, his torso shuddering deep under the covers. She wakes to shouts and blanket theft, or to Herb baying at the window, hands slapping the glass, unable to fathom the barrier to escape. Another night, deep sobs and the cracking cry, 'No, no, bastards, not Fred, not Freddie, no, nah, *naaaah…*'

'Who was he?' Nell asks as gently as she can, when they're settling again, she spooned to Herb's back.

'You know. I've been over it enough times.'

'Perhaps. But not with me.'

'It doesn't help.'

'I think you think you've talked about it because it's so much with you. Telling someone else can bring light. Sometimes.'

'My lieutenant, you must know that. Chap from Duntroon. Fine. One of the finest.'

She is holding him, but he is curled into himself and doesn't respond to the hand she puts between his.

'You were with him when…'

'Shouldn't have happened. And that's all.'

And that is all.

That skerrick of information leaked out, like air from a ball, releases the pressure sufficiently. This season's spell of nightmares is over.

1942

'Mum. Mum! What do I do with the apples?' Lettie is shaking the pot of stewed fruit under Nell's nose.

'They go straight into the oven dish – butter the sides first, then pour the batter on top.'

'Batter. What do you mean?'

'The cake mix. Once you've folded in the egg whites.'

Twenty minutes and the men will be in for midday dinner. Nell loosens her apron ties, tugs the damp blouse from her front. She hasn't even started the gravy or chopped the cabbage. Thank goodness Lettie is doing the pudding, and at twelve she needs only the occasional instruction.

'Keep back now while I open the oven.' In the furnace heat Nell grasps the heavy roasting pan and swings it sizzling onto the bench. She flicks the oven door shut with her foot, and Lettie follows up, closing the catch. Good girl. She knows to keep the heat in for her pudding.

There's a rattle of fly screen and Herb's head pokes through. 'All on track?' He's more anxious than she about her performance for the stock agent and his new colleague. Never mind the three musterers, who've come a day early for the autumn round-up. (Workers often eat their first meal at the family table so Herb can get their measure, before being relegated to the cook-house.) Adam and his mates, Lettie – eleven at the table. David can take the twins out under the peach tree with their lunch.

'Mint,' she tells Herb. 'Two big handfuls. Then you could come in to carve.'

She looks away, not to see his face. Mint is a woman's work when there are men about. But he won't risk upsetting her either, at this delicate hour. There was that occasion – only one, but it left its impression – when she threw the carving knife at the kitchen wall.

At least with a roast meal there's so much bustle and passing – of gravy, mint sauce, condiments, crabapple jelly – that the sometime awkwardness is eased. Sheep men might be talkative or silent; these three young ones are the latter, one in a perpetual blush and all are uneasy seated at a table that's set, hardly formally, Nell thinks, but properly, and Herb wouldn't have it any other way. Herb has placed Dick Stocker to her right and the new chap, Arthur someone, to left: so she can jolly them along should either man need it.

She hasn't yet lifted her fork following Herb's curt grace (*Blessthisfoodtoouruse, 'selvestoyourservice, Christ'snameamen*) when a hand lands on and covers her own. She freezes, staring at it.

'Poetry in motion,' says Arthur. 'I saw from out there the way you choreographed those final minutes before we came inside. My mother made sure I understood the attention to detail that's called for in getting a roast dinner onto the table. Thank you.' It takes only a second, but he manages to smile deep into her eyes as he lifts his hand from hers.

Nell swells inside: grateful, warmed. And then she cuts it off. It's only a meal. Ridiculous man, to make so much of it. Ridiculous and over-familiar. How dare he.

She looks up at Herb and he gives her a quick nod. Agreeing with what – the praise or the contempt?

After lunch the musterers troop out and the children scatter. She and Herb are left with Dick and Arthur.

'I'd be glad to take a turn around your flower garden before we get back into the jalopy,' Arthur says.

They start out, all four walking in a wide strand, but soon Herb and Dick have slowed, talking intently about pasture, while she and Arthur find themselves in the middle of her rose circle. The second flush is scrappier than the first, but the specimens are larger and, it seems to Nell, more vivid. The burgundy Munstead Wood is heavy with fragrance, while the crimson moss roses always make her ache for something as yet unattained. The clear, pale skins of Venus are peeling away their shabby coats to the cheers of the red Gallica whose name she can't summon at this moment. Arthur leans close to touch a Persian Yellow bud and releases his own hints of spice. This also affronts Nell: a man seeking to allure. Nonetheless she is allured, in regions deeper than thought, with a sudden urge to sidle against him, to inhale and feel the warmth of his trunk against her own.

'How do you cope with the isolation, Mrs Hamilton? I know it would turn my wife insane, or so she tells me.'

Nell breaks the yellow bud from the stem. She's never felt isolated here. She looks up at the tawny hills. Not lonely or bored. Sometimes broody, sometimes restless, but there's too much of life here for her to feel cut off.

She could count on two hands the number of meals in a year when it's only Herb and her. She doesn't know if she prefers the more usual table full of children and guests, or when it's just the two of them, and whatever hidden knot lies tangled between them is bound to make itself apparent, in her consciousness, at least. One hand would cover the solo meals, alas. She loves to eat alone, slow and savouring.

She looks back at her companion and smiles.

'No, I understand that you are perfectly self-sufficient. How admirable.' He slips his hand beneath her upper arm and guides her back to the path, and gently squeezes.

Again, Nell goes still inside: pleased, baffled, unsettled. Something is off-key, but she doesn't want to change anything. She is shoulder-to-shoulder with a pleasant-smelling man who petals compliments upon her and whose stride as they crunch along the river-gravel pathway perfectly matches her own.

'When you're next in town, come to the store to collect the sack of rose food I'm going to assign to you, gratis, and let me take you for a cup of tea.'

They've arrived back at Dick's car, and the others are approaching.

'That's not necessary,' Nell replies.

'And doesn't that define a pleasure? Something unnecessary.'

His face and smile are so open and warm, she can't turn him down. Not in this moment. 'That's very kind of you,' she says.

Nell says goodbye and leaves the three men talking, Herb through the window of their car.

She takes the scrap bucket from the porch, away past the compost heap in the back garden because she wants to go further, out of sight. The hens are surprised at this early hour to receive the contents on the scraped earth of their run. Pansy, the head hen, and the only one with a name, seizes a gob of fat congealed around an apple core and runs with it, beak held high, away from the mob.

Nell holds herself by the shoulders. She shuts her eyes and feels the lingering warmth in her belly. It is marvellous and painful to be seen, touched, affirmed. And it is wrong. Arthur is the wrong man to do it. Her affections are wrong. They should run direct, always to Herb. But for a long time now, if she's honest – and honesty is not hard to come by in the shit-spattered hen run with the girls scraping and pecking at her feet – maybe since the first baby, or even before then, her feeling for Herb has been, in part, deflected. By his own waterproof coating, or by her waywardness, she can't be sure.

When a note arrives in the mail two weeks later (thank goodness not on a Saturday when Herb is the one to fetch the post and the weekend newspaper) reminding her of the rose food and the cup of tea, she tucks it into her brassiere. As she feeds the unseasonal twin lambs currently living in the wash house, hangs out the sheets, scours the kitchen and lets the dogs off for their run, she ponders the possibilities of such a friendship: the curiosity, the clandestine appointments, the thrill and the fright, the amusement and the consolation. The temptation.

Later in the day she takes out the rubbish to burn and when the scraps of soiled cardboard and newspaper are blazing high above the drum, she throws on the pale blue envelope, and then the note.

'It's tea now, is it?' Herb stares at the cup Nell has poured, beside his porridge bowl. 'Can't we afford a bit more colour than that?"

'It depends if you prefer many weak cups of tea, or fewer and strong.'

'It's the devil's choice. Anyway, haven't you stashed a bit away?'

Of course, Nell has. Five, she checked yesterday, of the square wooden boxes in the storeroom. But who knows how long the war and the rationing will go on. Sugar and tea will make valuable barter, if it comes to that. More likely, though, she'll share what she's collected with those who are struggling. Why should they live more comfortably than their neighbours? Not everyone has the means to buy in bulk. Certainly not the little family who've moved into the old cottage.

Nell wipes honey over her buttered toast. (At least they'll never run short of dairy as long as the cow thrives.) 'I've invited Mrs Solly up for lunch, with her little one,' she tells Herb.

'Meaning you want me out on the verandah.'

She looks at him over her new glasses. 'Knowing that

would be your preference. I'll set the little table for you.'

'You'll have women's business to talk about.' Herb spoons up the last scrap of porridge. 'How are they settling in, anyway? Want me to find them a bit of mutton?'

'Yes please. I gather that Mr Solly is too much at home. He needs more work.'

'He can come up and cut macrocarpa any time. Sell it on if he wants to.'

'I'll let her know.'

When Herb has left the kitchen for the sleety outdoors, Nell squeezes another cup from the teapot (it's time to start drinking it black; milky and weak is too unappealing) and pulls her chair closer to the stove. She thinks of Adam with a squeeze in her middle. He'll be making his way from dorm to classroom at his Dunedin boarding school. Lettie and David are on the bus to their local schools while, warmed by the little gas heater in their bedroom, the twins have embroiled themselves in a game with the peg dolls and tea-box house Lettie spent the autumn holiday variously clothing, painting, glueing, securing and furnishing for them. Nell savours the rare quiet moments and forks open the firebox door so she can watch the flames.

She ponders the problem of Mrs Solly. Susan.

The young couple have been in the cottage since Mr Solly came to help build a neighbour's hay barn, but then he was left scrounging for work. There's plenty of it about, with so many off to the war, but the local men are wary of him. His angry outbursts and a cynical streak have endeared him to no-one. Except for Susan, and Nell suspects that any dew drops have long fallen from her eyes. Nell has twice observed rags of livid bruising, on one side of her throat, and a little later, on the other. Then, they met by chance down at the river where Nell had taken the twins for a chilly picnic lunch. Susan appeared on the riverbed nearby, apparently talking to herself, grasping and tugging mullein seed-heads from their stalks. Seeing them, she gave a small wave and moved away, but Nell went after her.

'Come and join us. I've plenty of sandwiches.'

Susan turned and her two blackened eyes were a shock. 'He needs to find work,' is all she said by way of excuse. 'I'm in the family way again and it's worrying him.'

She sat and ate hungrily before saying she needed to get back. She'd left the little girl with her husband.

'Please phone me any time, for any reason.'

'We're not on the line. Not until there's more coming in.' Seeing Nell's concern, she added, 'It's all right now. He's calm again. Sorry, too.'

Nell has arranged to have the cottage telephone reconnected, calling it a bonus from the phone company. She can scrape together enough for that. The Sollys needn't know she's paying, and it might mean Susan is a fraction safer.

'Oh, bliss.' Peg falls back onto the old verandah sofa and receives a scornful look from the cat at the other end.

Nell takes their mugs from the tray and nudges the cat away before joining her.

'Is it foffee?'

'Is that what you call it? Barley and chicory. I add a cardamon pod.'

'Which smells heavenly. Honestly, everything up here is bliss, Nell. The air, the sofa, the foffee. And seeing you.' Peg pulls up her skirt and holds pale shins to the sun. 'Things have been so austere, so skimpy in town. It has to be over soon, surely. This week, we heard about Peter Munson from the Society, can you believe it? Somewhere in the Pacific, where he'd just gone with the medical team.' Her face contracts and she gives a brave smile.

Nell strokes her arm and they sip for a minute or two and gaze at the slopes, half under snow, and watch finches hopping about on the lawn.

'Crocuses,' Peg points with her toes. 'By the way, where are the infants? I wasn't expecting such quiet.'

'My helper Mary, when she heard you were coming, insisted on scooping up the twins this morning. She'll put them on the school bus with Lettie at three. And Herb has taken his lunch up the gully. To coin your phrase: bliss.'

'How thoughtful of her.'

'Indeed. So let's make the best of it. Although you'll find me creaky in conversation beyond the domestic or agricultural.'

'Try it out and tell me, what's going on for you this year? No, this spring. No, in this very moment.'

Nell gulps at her cup, then balances it on the fat sofa arm. She pushes back into the corner. As her eyes trace the outline of the mountain, she feels Peg watching her. Tears well and spill.

'Let them,' says Peg.

They are quiet together, then Nell says, 'I hardly ever cry these days. Sympathy does it, though. Simple kindness. Or stopping to reflect, as we're doing now.'

'Sadness?'

'I don't know what. The relentlessness of life? The war as backdrop, the deaths – I wrote to you about my cousin Barney. As you say, though, I live in a kind of paradise. We have fresh food and healthy children.

'And yet I have these urges. Fierce, aching. I can be truthful with you, Peg. The ache to enjoy the kind of passionate, transfiguring exchange with a man that we imagined when young. And that man doesn't seem to be Herb.'

'Who then?'

'Oh, no one. *He* is in the abstract. I don't even know if I'm up for it in actuality. But I imagine I could be. Were I not married.'

'Of course you would be.'

Nell smooths the cushion between them. 'So, there we are. I suppose most of us live with intermittent, thwarted longings. And most of the time I'm too busy to be troubled by that side of things.' She looks at her friend and they nod together in understanding.

'You will sooner or later have to reckon with it.' Peg touches her own heart. 'But not this weekend. Not while I'm in residence.'

They laugh, and joy comes to Nell in a burst. 'Come on. Let's go over to the creek before lunch.'

Mary is an enigma. A few years younger than Nell, she came from somewhere in Europe after the first war. The crisp closing off of vowels when she speaks keeps in mind her exotic origins and Nell finds herself alert to the shape of every word. She listens in a way that Peggy would admire. Is this what attention requires? A small deviation from the everyday, to keep the mind focused and curious. Mary's children are away at boarding school and her husband is the local pharmacist. Although she has leave to use his car, she often turns up at the farm shiny-faced and exultant after an hour's steady uphill pedalling on his bicycle.

Nell marvels at the effort.

'But what a thrill it is, going home!' Mary laughs.

They can't pay her much, but she insists she wants to come anyway. She loves the rigour of a day spent hauling sheets in and out of the copper, pegging them onto 'the high wire' as she calls it, hoisting the pole until the sheets snap in the wind or sway against the blue. Sweeping the bedrooms, shaking out the rugs, scouring sinks and linoleum, her work punctuated by the stages of bread-making.

'Come and warm yourself by the range,' Nell tells her one twilit morning in June as Mary comes into the porch, shaking frozen mist from her scarf.

'Oh, I'm warm. Only the outward clothes are chilly.' She swings her canvas bag in front of her as she strides across the kitchen, and extracts from it a small cake tin. 'You will try one of these.' She lifts the lid on slim, perfectly round biscuits with shiny white glaze.

'I'll have one with my tea in a while.'

'All right. Let's get started and I'll stop as usual at ten.'

She pulls on today's apron, a light green canvas embroidered in golds and reds by her husband, with the legend: *Live to create. Create to live.*

'Of course, in his work as a chemist, he must be precise and not so creative, but these words of mine he has heeded and this is one of his creations.' Mary smooths her belly where the words are emblazoned.

While Nell grinds boiled celery, swedes and carrots through the Mouli for soup and dashes out to the wash house to feed the fire under the copper, Mary dumps ten cups of flour onto the scoured table and pours into it the jug of bubbling yeast that's sat overnight at the back of the coal range. Her forearms rock in and out, her hands scoop and dive as she pulls together dry and damp and works them into a ball. She sings a German folk song, then laughs at her cracking top notes. 'You must help me here,' she insists and so Nell la-la's along with her, comfortable in the upper ranges.

'There is goodness in your voice. I hope you sing always. Teach me one of yours.' She worries the dough for a moment, like a dog with a rat, then drops it into the big ceramic bowl and heaves that onto the wire rack above the stove.

'Ye banks and braes o' bonny Doon, how can ye bloom sae fresh and fair...' Nell stops, embarrassed.

'I don't mind when I'm alone,' she says.

'You mustn't be ashamed,' Mary tells her. 'Is a flower ashamed of its petals? Go on. Sing.'

But Nell has seized inside. She wants to be free, but in this moment there's only obstruction and swiftly following anger.

'I won't be told,' she mutters as she rinses the Mouli under a rush of cold water. Later. She'll sing by herself out in the frozen paddock; she's not here to entertain the kitchen help.

Her shame grows and she throws herself into the job she's been deferring, to clear out the ash pan in the stove. She'll end up smutted and over-hot, but that is fitting. As she plies the shovel and scrapes at the iron housing, she can hear Mary in the hallway singing something martial and forceful. She (Nell) has spoiled the morning.

However, by ten o'clock the atmosphere has altered again. Mary has wound the last load of washing through the mangles, the beds are remade, rooms straightened and airing, and Nell has the kitchen in order, the evening's vegetables peeled, chopped and covered in water (with a dash of vinegar – 'Stops them to turn brown' – has been Mary's addition to the routine).

Mary comes and drops the dough onto a scattering of flour while Nell puts out teacups and the glazed biscuits onto a plate. Mary pummels the dough and then as soon as the teacup is filled, rubs her hands free of it and takes off her apron.

She gives Nell such a full, warm smile, Nell is shaken and ashamed. Differently ashamed.

'Were you and Herb friendly for a long time before you married?' Mary asks.

'We knew each other for a few months.' *Friendly.* Had they ever been that, exactly? It was such a brief time, so long ago. 'We exchanged plenty of letters. We went horseback riding on the station where I grew up. We met with his parents in Dunedin, and dined with friends. Mostly we were apart though, until we married.' Mary's look of full sympathy leads her on. 'We were congenial, of course, but I suppose more curious then, than close friends.'

Mary nods. 'Yes, this is what I observe, particularly in the country. That in order to be together, couples marry. Whereas in the city, young people have many friends and more time to explore friendship. I think it is a very brave thing to come and live here under such conditions.'

This is startling. However, Nell sees in a flash the chute that she and Herb entered, almost as soon as they met: they were both getting on; they were not naive ... but neither did they discuss options for how they might behave. The chute whipped them (was it a descent?) from autonomy to ... this other state. 'What about you and Robert?'

'We were in a large group of friends at university in Auckland. We all discussed who should pair up with whom, pragmatical and altruistic. Of course, there were jealousies and how to say ... betrayings, and people made experiments in the group but, at the end, Robert and I knew each other well and had comparisons to make amongst our friends.'

'Heavens.' Nell tries to imagine discussing such matters with a disinterested group. Imagine gathering one's friends and asking them what is to be done with two who never quite became one, but remain two, living under one roof and pitting their efforts towards a common goal (running a farm, raising children, and making ends meet). She reaches for the teapot and refills their cups. 'That sounds like the revolutionary ideal.' She smiles weakly and takes a biscuit, thinking of the many possibilities life has not opened for her, and probably won't now.

David at thirteen looks fearfully slight and small standing on the middle step below the big school building and seeing them off. Shiny face, cap on straight, hands in blazer pockets and staring after them with the look Nell knows so well: apprehensive, bearing up, his thoughts and feelings battened. Two larger boys exit the swing doors above him, chummy, swaggering and David shrinks, imperceptibly to any but a mother, and when Adam says, 'Come on, Ma, we have to keep moving,' the last glance at her younger son is blurred as she turns her head away and squeezes the key.

Herb has insisted that character must be built in adolescence, for which no home is adequate to the task. And besides, the local high school is not adequate to *its* task either, as Herb sees it. David has started boarding school in Timaru, the year after Adam has left it at seventeen.

'Will you let me drive?' Adam asks as they leave the tearoom in Ashburton for the last leg to the Agricultural College.

'If you'll let me see your room.'

'Of course. And I'll be glad of help getting my clobber inside.'

Adam grins and takes the key. In the car, underway, he turns serious. 'And how shall you find it, Mother? With three of us gone?'

'Keep your eyes on the road. As you know, the farm has a way of taking up the slack. I'll go on missing you, of course, but you and Lettie have been coming and going for years now.'

'I mean, the twins will be at school, too.' Adam runs a hand over the steering wheel. 'So what do you want for yourself, that you could conceivably take up now?'

Nell smooths her skirt. She looks out at the fields flashing by: so flat and tidily fenced. 'When you were small, I dreamed of leaving the farm,' she says with a sidelong look. 'But I've made my peace with it, and much more than. I'll go on with the garden, propagating blues, perennials. Improving the compost...' She names these concrete details because what else she means can't be said. She needs her acre of lawn with garden plots to speak for her, to speak back to the hills and sky, whose eloquence she has responded to more deeply with each passing year. The garden, she thinks shyly, is her song of praise.

At the College, she helps Adam with his 'clobber' – books galore, tent, sleeping bag and tramping boots; and then they find themselves a cup of tea to take into the garden where Nell is offered the elm's trunk at her back while Adam sits cross-legged in front of her.

'Of course, numbers are a bit light in the senior years,' Adam is saying, 'with so many chaps called up. Apparently, Jerry's bombing London again.'

'You heard that just now? It's not to be wondered at, the damage we're doing in Europe.' Nell shakes her head involuntarily and clasps her tea in both hands. Surely it will be over by the time Adam turns eighteen.

'And look.' Adam pushes a leaflet at her from the Canterbury Mountaineering Club. 'Port Hills this weekend, Arthur's Pass the next.' His eyes shine. 'And yes, Mother, I'll keep up with my studies. You know that. And this will be my reward.' He flicks at the pamphlet and swallows his tea in a sustained gulp.

A group of sturdy young men has come out under the trees and stand talking, hands in pockets, feet planted. Farmer's sons, ill at ease, with over-loud voices and much guffawing. She looks at her own farmer's son: his fine profile, quick, sensitive eyes, another kind of creature altogether, but he turns and greets one of them by name and makes a quip that sets them all laughing.

1945

'It was a day just like this when you married,' Stella tells Nell on a Sunday afternoon phone call. She lives a hundred and fifty miles away, but evidently it is blue and cloudless all over the south.

'By Jove, she's right,' says Herb later. 'It was what, twenty years ago? Getting on for half of our lives.' Sitting with her out on the verandah, he's in a talkative mood. 'I see my life in chunks. The first was simple, wouldn't you agree? We were children. The next included the war.' He leans, elbow on knees. 'That span of time still a stone in the belly. Indigestible. I don't know what can ever be made of it.' He casts her a beseeching look.

Nell presses a hand to his knee. 'And since then?'

'Busy, benign. And alarming.' He straightens with a grin and rubs his shins. 'Benign because, although I seldom say it to your face, Ellie-Nor, you are my rock. And have borne me five children, ye gods.'

'And alarming?'

'Wool. Prices. Need I say more?'

He need not. When the farm did well during the war, with meat and wool required in large supply, they extended their spending to a new harvester, breeding ewes and boarding school fees. Prices since then have wavered, and threatened to plunge. Herb has the jitters. Coming late to farming, he hasn't weathered decades of fluctuation, as her own family has. His insecurity threatens the enterprise and he needs constant cajolery.

'No need to cook tonight,' Herb tells Nell on Tuesday morning as he brings in a cup of tea and perches on the bed. 'Don't give me that look. I'm taking you out for dinner.'

'You haven't forgotten that we have two men and two children to feed?'

'What I haven't forgotten is that this is our day. I've asked the chaps to make do with what's in the pantry – I had a look and there's plenty – and to mind the girls. Just for a couple of hours. Andrew is a capable young man. And…' he cuts across her protest '…he said yes. Gladly.'

Getting ready that evening, Nell is not in the mood. It's been too long and the required actions feel peculiar and mechanical in the chill of their bedroom. Applying powder, a dab of eye shadow, a deeper, evening lipstick.

When she enters the kitchen, Herb says 'Aah' as he takes in the green silk dress under her navy coat, the pearl earrings, pearl in the hollow of her throat.

He has put out mutton, slabs of cheese and butter, a jar of relish, another of pickled walnuts, cold parsnips and potato from the lunchtime roast – still in the smeared roasting pan. Nell hunts out a serving dish and goes to shake the vegetables into it.

'Damn it, woman. Leave it alone. All they need is here, and they'll be glad of the chance to dig in for once.' He goes to check his tie in the tiny kitchen mirror. 'Without your niceties to consider, without your watchful, moderating eye on them.'

Nell drops the roasting pan onto the table and spins away.

Whose watchful, moderating eye does he mean? He's always been the one to rap the children's knuckles, to upbraid them (or her) if they slouch or reach across.

'Girls,' she tells them in the living room, 'I want you going straight to bed when Andrew tells you. Clean your teeth, one story book, then light out.'

She flinches away from Herb's hand on her elbow as they crunch over the gravel to the car.

'I didn't mean it like that,' he manages to say.

He drives for a change, and for a change he works to keep the gear changes smooth, the accelerations even on the Dansey's Pass road.

Jack at the old hotel shows them the corner table not far from the fire. Herb pulls out a chair that will put Nell's back to the handful of other diners.

Nell puts a staying hand to that chair and claims the one opposite. 'I like to see the room. Otherwise why come out?'

'We came out so you wouldn't have to cook. So we can be alone together at table, for once.'

She stands again and takes the side-on chair, facing the fire. Herb sits in the chair he first pulled out. He asks the waitress when she arrives for two glasses of sherry and she asks if they want beef bourguignon or chicken pie for their meal. Preceded by soup? Mushroom or tomato.

'What exactly is a bourguignon?' Nell asks Herb, having chosen the pie.

'Some sort of rich, gravy thing. I recall eating it on leave in Paris. A darned sight tastier than boeuf en boîte, I can tell you.'

'Bully beef?'

Herb reaches his hand to cover hers. 'Let's not go there, shall we? These are happier years.'

She gives him a small smile and passes her hand over the table mat. 'Are they though? Are you happier with a houseful of children and a farm to run than you were in the company of chaps on the adventure a lifetime?'

Herb pushes back. 'Why must you do this? If you've gained the impression that the war was a corker *Boys' Own* adventure…' he snatches up the small sherry glass that's arrived at his elbow, waits for Nell to lift her glass, and gulps at his '…then it's because I've told only the agreeable stories, the ones that don't cause distress. In case I've left you in any doubt, our war was hell. And this wholesome, hard-working life with you and the children is heaven by comparison.'

Nell shivers. She resolves to be kind. To be the companion he needs in his version of heaven.

The food is also wholesome, although Herb insists that his lacks something Nell would have known to include. It's evidently a far cry from the Parisian meal.

'What have you enjoyed in our years of matrimony?' he asks.

Her eyes cast over his face, shoulders and hands. They linger on the salt and pepper. She looks across the room, behind him. 'Naturally, I'm very fond of our children. And you, that goes without saying. The hills are a great comfort.' Comfort against what, he might wonder. 'The garden. Seeing you engrossed on the run.'

She feels she has disappointed him. She's given

nothing to indicate that she enjoys or admires him. In spite of all he's done, all he does every day, which is all for her, for the children – she knows his thoughts. Why this parsimony? She detests it in herself.

He taps the passing waiter's wrist and orders a glass of claret.

'Did it occur to you that I might like one?' Nell says.

'You never drink with your meal.'

'Nothing is *never*. I like to be asked.'

Nell wakes before Herb (surprisingly, since light is streaming in under the heavy curtains) and goes out to the kitchen to poke and stoke the coal range back to life. Every morning, she is grateful, though, for the electric kettle. The long wait for water to heat is many years past, but the memory of impatience for the morning cuppa remains. She takes the tea tray back to the bedroom and has pulled the curtains wide on the spring morning before she realises that Herb has tucked his head under the covers.

'Are you all right?'

He grunts.

Nell goes around the bed and bends to him. 'Are you coming down with something?'

He shakes his head. 'Leave me for a bit?'

'I'll put your tea on the nightstand. Do you want the curtains closed?'

Hearing no reply, Nell takes herself out to the kitchen porch where she stands in the open doorway to drink her tea. She holds her face to the sun and listens to the sparrows, skittering across the iron roof and chattering, nest-building in the eaves. She'd better be prepared to go out on the lambing run if Herb is sickening for something. It wouldn't surprise her. His spirits have been subdued.

As if in sympathy with the mood of the house, the twins creep out late from their room already dressed for school. They eat porridge and go without fuss to wait for their ride with a neighbour to the bus. Seeing their small backs walking away, Nell hurries after them. 'I'll come to the gate,' she says, and, 'Daddy will be up soon. He just needed a sleep-in. You know it's been about twenty years since he last had one?' Her laugh is forced and the girls look at her solemnly without reply. 'Bring me home a picture each?' she tries. And then they are into the car and away.

Towards lunchtime, Nell comes in from the vegetable garden (she's taken a chance on the weather and planted out a row of lettuce seedlings, put in another of carrot seed) to find Herb on the kitchen sofa, and there's something piteous in his eyes as they track her across the room.

'Coffee?' she asks, 'or do you want breakfast?'

'I don't know.'

She makes toast and coffee, grateful for this rare day with no hangers-on for the midday meal. She and Herb can have cold meat, and later than usual. And if a portion of Herb's whirring brain has calculated this as a good day to cave in, it somehow bespeaks favourably.

She coaxes him outside to the verandah, having observed in herself that clenched feelings are more likely to open to fresh air and greenery than to the fug of warm rooms. 'Sit with your back to the farm,' she instructs. 'Just look at my granny bonnets and cinerarias.' They have thrust up amongst iris shoots in a wide array of pinks, purples and blues, a sort of fantasy and a kinder sight this morning than the low slopes bestrewn with sheep: pregnant ewes and a handful of lambs. How calculating she is. Herb's silence gives her space to realise it, and furthermore that the calculations are made out of her own sense of helplessness.

She takes his hand and squeezes. Herb manages a grateful nod. She won't ask him to tell her again what they both know: the sum of their debt; the number of demands for payment; the cost of borrowing. 'This time next year, or the one after,' she says, 'things will look completely different. It's the law of farming.' A lore she has made up on the wing.

'You'd be exactly right for the job, Mother. You don't get flustered. You'd keep the doctor on track – well, he does like to talk about everything but – and besides, you know the roads and the people. Call him back *now*.'

Lettie at seventeen has clear opinions on most matters and almost always they are sound. She was finished with school, she declared at the end of the spring term, and would stay home to work on the run. It takes Nell back to her own changeable years on the family farm: of bliss, fret, chafe, escape and return. Certainly there's no shortage of work in the house for Lettie, and she's as capable as her brothers with stock, can take a horse anywhere at all, and is training up a young dog.

'I could be called away at any hour.' Nell tests the waters. 'You might have to get the twins off to school, feed the workers – shearing gang even – put on the evening meal.'

'Just say yes, Mum. It'll do you good. Plus, he's nice. Not like old Doctor Hobbs. *Aaaa-eeer.*' Lettie clears her throat and ducks her head in creditable imitation: '*I think you can trust me on this matter, young lady.*'

Nell goes out to bring in the washing. She lowers the pole propping the line the width of the back lawn. The sheets she flaps into halves, snaps into quarters then eighths and drops into the ironing basket, laying the halved pillowslips on top, then tea towels, blouses, hankies. Into the other basket go two dozen socks, underpants, Herb's work shirts and trousers, towels and rags. Everything dried to a crisp in the nor'wester.

Is it not enough to fill her days this way? She might be a sort of wind-up doll, making the rounds of wash house, kitchen, floors, beds, clothesline, dog kennels – and on a day such as this, there's joy in it, when the house is flung open to the mild breeze and her heart, she thinks, likewise. But a wind-up doll's mechanism creaks and seizes when grey days linger, and the question of finances looms like the weather, which means Herb on a short fuse, grim and harried, or (it's happened twice in the past year) immobilised by a kind of grinding panic. Once he stayed in bed for two days; the other, he made it to the kitchen sofa before he sat, staring alternately at her, whatever she was doing, and into his clasped hands.

So, the money. It won't be a great deal, but it will help.

While she waits for the iron to heat in the kitchen, Nell goes out to the hallway and lifts the phone from its cradle.

Herb has granted her a few days away from the farm before her first duty with the doctor ('Granted?' Peggy will say. 'Can you not claim for yourself what you need?'), and although Nell could have simply told him she was going, and left, the apparatus of their marriage works more smoothly if Herb believes that a wish or a whim beyond the regular is his to grant, or otherwise. And if she calls it a game, this failure to insist on what she wants, letting Herb have his say and usually his sway, it seems more a matter of semantics than of survival. It's a game except when it feels too grim to be called so.

Anyway, asking or coercing, coaxing or claiming, none of that matters as soon as the car rattles over the cattle stop and begins its long, bouncing, eager descent two thousand feet towards sea level and city. She's staying with Peggy and hasn't even told her parents yet that she'll be there. If they find out, she'll claim Peggy's need for company, which will sound convincing since her little dog died recently under the wheels of a motorcycle. That the aged mongrel was blind, incontinent and overdue for a merciful blow to the head need not be stated.

Peggy has been anticipating her visit: her cottage is fresh sweet air, flowers and light amongst artfully arranged piles of books and the spare lines of her furniture (Nordic in inspiration). In the little bedroom allotted her – white with blue bedspread and lampshade, jar of grape hyacinths and one of Peggy's comic portraits (her father? a lover?) inked and framed in Prussian blue – Nell's nose and eyes prickle with sudden tears. That life could be simple and beautiful, clean and full of light. What she has chosen, what has chosen her, is brimful and messy; distracting and all-consuming. Except that it hasn't consumed all of her. Here, in this bedroom, she meets her other, single self, slight but intact, with life's other possibilities yet dangling before her, waiting to be plucked; for three days, this is the truth. Nell uses her hanky to pat her face back into form in the oval mirror, in which she sees a woman still youthful and straight, still eager and faintly vulnerable. She pins back straying hair, then pulls the clips out again – all of them. She'll ask for Peggy's opinion on a new style.

Freshly made bread, jam and salads are laid out on the table in the little courtyard where Peggy is peeling and slicing oranges into segmented discs to lay on top of a madeira cake. 'I'll douse it with spiced syrup, then serve it with cream – but that's for later. I've asked a couple of friends for afternoon tea.'

Nell sits across from her and slices bread. 'Have you read the transcript of Mr Barbarella's latest address?' she asks. What pleasure it is, to dive into the very conversation she wants to have. With Peggy she never has to stand on ceremony or wait to see how the land lies.

'I did.' Peggy puts down the paring knife. 'With some reservations, I admit. I felt that his emphasis on personal discipline rather outstripped his … what's the expression I want? His appreciation for grace, or receptivity, which might be states that women find easier to realise than men do.'

'What do you mean?' Nell's pulse quickens; she knew Peggy would put her finger on the unease she experienced herself, reading this exhortation by the city's leading Theosophist.

'Well, say I wake in the morning with the conviction that I must sit in meditation at a quarter to seven for half an hour without fail. And yet out through the window there's an inkling in the sky that a glorious sunrise will span those very minutes. Which is it better to do: sit with eyes closed minding my own prosaic breathing, or pull on a coat and go outside to take in the glories of the morning?'

Nell first quails: her own mornings seldom offer her the choice. There are children to be stirred into action, breakfast to be cooked and served, washing, food preparation, ponies to catch and saddle if the twins are riding to school … And yet it's a question with a vital kernel: how can she find for herself, in her relentless daily round, moments of quiet nourishment, and what is the better means for it – silent inwardness, or engaging her senses in the world around her?

'I wish I knew myself better,' she exclaims. 'What I find most replenishing might not be the same thing you do. And one's circumstances have to be taken into account.'

'The raw materials. Yes! The inner life, and the outer circumstances that constellate to it, are precisely what we have to work with.'

Nell takes a slice of bread, and a knob of butter. It is a shock to see that she has been waiting for an alteration in her 'outer circumstances', that a part of her (the grasp on her own life) has been in abeyance until that occurs. She has waited for Herb to warm and soften, for Lettie or David to confide in her, for life's busyness to abate. In these matters she has burned with the shame of inadequacy (she has not been lovable, not sufficiently receptive), *and* has excused herself from culpability. What if she were to accept that the men children friends farm guests weather and geography held a mirror to her own soul? How then might she respond?

Peggy has pushed a plate in front of Nell, and the salad bowl with its mixture of chopped herbs, tomatoes and cracked wheat. 'Tabooly', she calls it, and like all she produces, there is a story to go with it.

'Will you put on your seat belt?' Nell asks Dr Langer as she feels for the key in the ignition.

'I tend not to.'

'Are those strapped in not safer in the event of an accident?'

'I can't say I've noticed a difference in those I've attended, or heard of. The person or dog thrown clear is at least as likely to walk away as the one held in place by his belt.'

Nell depresses the clutch of the new doctor's Austin and pulls out the choke. The arrangement is that she will drive him on his rounds, so he can leaf through the notes en route, jot notes afterwards – road surface allowing – and ruminate, as he has put it to Nell on the phone. The engine makes a series of bouncing growls.

'Ease off on the pedal ... now try again.'

The first deep shove has flooded the engine. When she glances, the doctor has one finger pressed to a page of writing and is staring straight ahead. His morning shave has been a hasty one and, with his shock of hair, he could be taken for an itinerant. Still, there's humour in his eyes and mouth, and already they've shared a laugh over the platter of congealed breakfast lying under a tea towel on the back seat. His housekeeper insists on producing three meals for him each day, whether or not he's receptive.

Nell tries the car again and this time finds the fine connection called for between foot and starter.

'That's it. Now if you'll make your way to Enigma Road, off Knights, I'll do my best to absorb this family's medical history.' He pats the fat envelope beneath the opened page. 'Do you know anything of them, by the way?'

'Indicator switch?' Nell sees and flicks it on; the indicator thunks out behind her shoulder. 'It could be said that they've needed more help from the community than most. The girl, a little older than our twins, has diabetes.'

'And the mother suffers from melancholia of some kind.'

The gravel road is alternate ruts and corrugations. Nell has to raise her voice. 'A few of us have rallied to help out during bouts when Mrs Able has been ... well, not so.'

The car's fittings judder noisily, so for a while the doctor reads in silence, making notes on a reporter's pad.

'You'll come in with me,' he tells Nell when they reach the farmhouse and she shows no sign of leaving her seat.

Nell gives him a firm look. She has been hired to drive him.

'It will help all around if you're there. Another woman, another person in the district with a grasp of the situation. And I can talk with you afterwards about what needs to be done.'

'I'm not meant to be *doing* anything,' she says coolly, returning her book to the door pocket.

He makes a humorously menacing face. 'It will help me, to discuss the case with you. I know you can keep matters confidential, or I wouldn't have approached you.'

They find that Mrs Able is again disabled and has taken to the spare bed in her daughter's room, although it's the child the doctor has been called to see, by the father who's now out on the farm. They've let themselves in and Nell stands awkwardly in the bedroom doorway while Doctor Langer questions the girl, who is sitting up in her pyjamas seeming not to know why he has come.

Nell retreats to the kitchen they've passed through and – she can't help herself – quietly rinses and stacks the plates and cutlery strewn across kitchen table and bench. She wipes the surfaces, stokes the fire, fills the two stove-top kettles and stows mutton, butter, jam and milk in the wall safe. Outside the door she finds a broom to flick over the sticky lino. She's filling a bucket in the outside laundry when she hears Dr Langer calling for her.

In the bedroom he asks Nell, 'Have you given an injection before?'

'Only to the house cow.'

He hands her a syringe in a kidney dish. 'You might as well give the insulin.'

Nell goes cold at the treachery, but this is not the place or time for a stand-off.

The bedroom needs light and air. Nell sweeps back

the curtains and opens the window a crack. A protest comes from Mrs Able's bed, but inarticulate, her head tucked like a sea anemone's into the covers.

Nell is surprised by the initial resistance of skin to the needle, then by the ease with which it slides into the girl's thigh. In nurse training they practised on oranges; she didn't stay long enough to inject an actual patient.

'Mrs Hamilton, Jendy has been breakfasting, lunching and snacking on bread and jam, pretty much,' the doctor says. 'What would be a more suitable diet, in this case?'

Nell frowns. 'If you're asking me what I noticed in the kitchen, there are eggs in the safe – do you know how to boil an egg?' she addresses Jendy, who nods. 'Two of those each morning, I should think. Then a meat sandwich for lunch. A piece of cheese and an apple.'

'Capital.' The doctor clips his bag shut and picks up a tube of ointment. 'There's plenty of this left, so put it on the sores three times a day and tell us if they're not gone within the week.

'Mrs Able!'

The covers are lowered to beneath her nose.

'I want you out of bed. You must go with Jendy for a walk, at least to the river and back. Both of you. Walk briskly, then telephone my nurse this afternoon to advise her that you've done it. Jendy: back to school tomorrow and make sure you take your own little towel for drying your hands.'

'Don't you go taking my guest towels, missy,' the muffled voice instructs.

As they let themselves out through the kitchen, the doctor gives a low whistle. 'Quick work, Mrs Hamilton.'

In the car Nell holds the wheel and stares straight ahead.

'You'll be paid commensurately,' he tells her.

'For breaching my role as driver?'

'For assisting me.'

Nell snorts and shakes her head. 'It's a dismal situation, though. Jendy's health, or even her life, is in jeopardy, if I understand diabetes at all, which I do a little.' After a year at the agricultural college, Adam is studying biochemistry at Otago and means to make the application of insulin his specialty. 'Besides which, she's probably filling the sink from boiling kettles – there's no hot water on tap – and stoking the fire.' As Nell did herself with ease from the age of seven or eight, but she's seen none of that native coordination or focus in Jendy. The mother's loss of propulsion has bled into the daughter.

At the next farmhouse, Dr Langer asks Nell to make saline – a teaspoon of salt to a cup of boiled water – and once he's finished debriding the old man's ulcerated shin with a pair of forceps (watching it, her face and hands go clammy) to dress the wound.

'My daughter wants me to put honey on it.' The patient takes the jar of dark stuff from the piano stool beside him. 'She swears it works on her horses.'

'Unscientific,' the doctor says. 'We use gauze with paraffin.' He taps the square tin beside the honey.

Nevertheless, when he goes to sit and jot at the

window with his back to Nell, she follows her instinct to oblige the daughter's request, and applies a dollop direct to the wound before adding the obligatory gauze and bandage. 'Do you keep your foot up on the stool whenever you're sitting down?' she asks.

'I'm not much of a one for sitting. Only in the evenings.'

'Well, you must do a little more of it until this is healed. You might stay and read the newspaper from cover to cover, say.'

He laughs. 'They'll think I'm malingering.'

'I imagine they'll be glad to have you looking after yourself.'

'You have a natural and sensible way,' Dr Langer tells her as the car coasts down the drive. 'The young nurse I had was well-meaning, but life is a sounder teacher, I'm inclined to think, than a school of nursing. She couldn't drive, and she certainly wouldn't have touched the housework. I appreciate the breadth of your concern.'

Nell feels for the nurse. Only recently have hospitals begun to employ cleaners. In her day, the nurses started each early morning shift with the purging of wards. It might be said that by going the extra mile she's letting the side down.

The world of others cannot often be put to rights, but nor can Nell stand idly by when there's work to be done that she can do with swift efficiency.

Three more visits are made before lunch: to an elderly woman being nursed through her final decline by a kind and muddling daughter; a middle-aged man with emphysema, and a farmer. Dr Langer instructs Nell in the art of unpacking and repacking his long, tunnelling peri-anal abscess. Again, a certain clamminess comes to her hands and upper lip, but she manages to stay on the job with deep breaths and an occasional glance at the trees outside.

Between visits, as Nell navigates the gravel roads, the doctor makes notes, ponders his patients aloud, and sometimes dozes. Only rarely does he allow his commentary to roam beyond the purview of his work. Well after the projected finishing time of one o'clock, Nell pulls up at the medical room gates where the Singer is parked. Dr Langer reaches around for the files now scattered over the back seat and hugs them to his chest. (He needs a box file for those. She'll bring one tomorrow.)

He gives her a warm look. 'That went splendidly, thank you, Mrs H. Being relieved of the hours of driving is going to be a great boon to me. I feel fresher by far than I usually do.'

Nell nods, too full of sensations and impressions from the day, and questions raised, to formulate a reply.

The doctor lifts a hand. 'See you at the same time tomorrow.'

Nell has three hours to herself. She hasn't told Peggy or Adam that she's in town, nor for once will she go to the library. Mother sent her money last week ('just because') and she is bent on self-indulgence, as she names it to herself with guilty pleasure.

First, she has her hair reshaped, a whole inch shorter than last time, and she feels light and daring as she steps outside, coat over her arm, with the spring air on nape and ears. She can't help smiling and that draws the attention of every man she passes. Her back straightens, her feet claim the footpath.

She allows herself twenty minutes at a tearoom, where she asks for a pot of white China tea and a date scone, which proves passable (her own are light and locally celebrated).

The lingerie department at Bartons takes her into its embrace. Some delicate, deliberately laid scent cushions her senses and makes her believe for the moment something opulent about her life, something unrelated to the reality of their concrete house and muddy garden. It murmurs to a potentiality that in this moment she wants badly to fulfil.

She refuses help from the two young women who offer it, but wanders from row to row of hangers with brassieres of cotton, silk and satin; plain and lacy, vast and petite. Thank goodness girdles have been removed from the list of the necessary. She plucks at a soft green chemise and shivers. Her mother urges, 'Cotton, always cotton next to the skin.' Nell takes a couple of cotton camisoles into the changing cubicle. The lighting is soft and gives her skin a peachy tone. When the girl wonders through the curtain if she can help, Nell hands the cottons back and asks for the satin chemise. It arrives in sage and rose. She puts on the sage and strokes her front. She'll need the matching underpants too with the softly flared legs. Dr Langer, Matthew, is suddenly at her shoulder. She closes her eyes with a shudder, then shakes herself. How dare she. And yet Herb, she suspects, wouldn't notice if she bought grey cotton, rose silk or hessian.

She takes the parcel under her arm and sails down the elevator to take a turn around the frocks. Her eye is caught by a vision in indigo blue with a flame-coloured motif underlined in green, its simple lines dispensing with the draped lapels currently ubiquitous and irritating. Without hesitation she asks to try it on. No looking at the price. She's only playing – just to see her middle-aged self in another, more extravagant life. She allows the assistant to hover outside, then zip her up before she steps out. Even the shop girl's eyes widen gratifyingly behind her as Nell walks towards the wall mirror. Is that really her, the chic and shapely woman turning her head left and right to see the fall of fabric down her back?

'Wait. What size in shoes?'

The girl ducks behind the counter and reappears with high-heeled sandals.

Nell stands and walks and stares, allowing herself to take in this other self. Elegant, assured, alluring. Is she all of those things? As well as the self she brought along here this morning who is uncertain, capable in an ordinary way, and too distracted by domestic concerns to hold for long any fixed sense of her being. She's not sure she can accommodate this proud and stylish persona.

Nevertheless, she buys the dress. The woman she glimpses in it has insisted. It takes the rest of her mother's gift and a quarter of the month's grocery allowance. She'll offer to work extra days for Matthew, and at the thought of him there is a catch and squeeze at her core. For whom is the dress intended?

She hands over the five pound notes and asks for the remainder to go on their account. On impulse, she says, 'I'll put it back on and wear it now, if I may.'

'Of course, madam. What about footwear?'

Naturally, her brogues won't do. She allows the girl to run away and find half a dozen pairs of day heels in her size, three of which might be acceptable. 'They call these Mary Janes in America,' the girl tells her as she slips her feet into the green ones. 'With Cuban heels.'

Nell signs the account again and goes to change into her new lingerie, heels and dress. She touches up her powder and lipstick and flicks her hair at the mirror. The shop assistant steps back in deference as Nell swings aside the curtain.

'Beautiful, madam,' she breathes.

Outside the department store the city's denizens trudge along George Street as they've trudged for decades in their dark weeds. Nell is entering the wrong city. She ought to be somewhere she's never been, never smelt before. A place with music and colour, warm air, sunlight and optimism. Some people must do that: simply walk from an old life into a new. Make an erasure. Not, like Lot's wife, looking back. Why shouldn't she, just for an hour? Instead of making for the grocery store where she is supposed to meet Herb at three with the month's foodstuffs at her feet, Nell goes back into Bartons and asks the man at Enquiries to look after her bags.

She takes only her change purse, wears her coat slung about her shoulders. The plated heels clip on the flagstones as she enters the Octagon. Like a properly independent woman, is the thought that comes. Children and girls go silently on bare feet or rubber soles; housewives scuttle or clomp about, or galumph in gumboots in backyards and paddocks. A woman walking alone in clipping heels has other purposes altogether.

'Are you on your way to the meeting?' The voice comes at her elbow, of a woman almost running to keep up.

Nell turns.

'Housewives' Association. Trades Hall.'

Nell's impulse, always, is to oblige. 'What is it about?'

'Don't you know then? Making money go further. Finding out why things cost so much. School supplies, rentals, meat and that. Keeping our kiddies safe.' The woman is alongside now, in her camelhair coat and brown laced shoes. Her glance takes in Nell's hair, her dress, and travels down to the green sandals. Her neck retracts. 'Anyone can attend. You might come and learn how the other half live.'

'The other half?' Nell could shriek, or laugh. She pulls her coat closed and veers away, away from the ugly trade hall. It would be all too easy to relent and go where she *should* go, amongst the other struggling women with their tight mouths, tight-scraped hair, their sensible shoes and their anger.

Before the woman interrupted her thoughts, Nell had some idea of a bar that would be pleasant and airy, where a woman could sit at a table and a waiter would come and suggest a suitable drink, and bring it to her on a small tray. Where does the notion come from? Only one bar on Princes Street looks even vaguely promising, but the inside, down a few steps, is hazy with cigarette smoke and a hint of cigar. The only other woman inside looks compromised in various ways and Nell swivels in the other direction. She takes a small table, but it's only by chance that an employee ventures near her, to wipe the adjacent one.

'May I order a drink?' she asks the dark-skinned girl with her hair tied back in a kerchief.

The girl lifts her chin. 'Over there.'

Nell is still banishing the frumpy woman in the Octagon, the housewives' meeting, the image of her own galoshes and wash basket tossed aside in the porch at home. She stands and her heels clack on the floor. At the bar, she asks for a sherry, and must pay and wait for the cut-glass thimble to be pushed across the bench. Well, she wanted incognito, and she has it. 'Is there food?'

'Pie or chips?' says the barman.

'A small serving of chips.' She is grateful to sense bubbles of laughter simmering under the fright.

The chips are good, the sherry bad, but she polishes off both, then sits awhile, idly watching the knees of pedestrians cross the narrow window. What will be taking place at the Housewives' Union meeting?

It's to be supposed that the women running it are strong-minded, socially inclined and find reward in it for their labours. Nell recoils to think of being jam-packed into a hall with dozens of women who are smarting under the regime of wife and motherhood – all of them practising frugality in ways they never dreamed of as young women anticipating happy marriage: frugal with money, with food, with electricity and affection. Of course, that is the place for them to air and share it and find hope of redress, but Nell's had her share, two decades of it. She won't be corralled with the disaffected. She could feel guilty, but then, women can feel guilty about anything, everything, if they allow it. She will not be ashamed to sit here in a beautiful dress, alone, with another half hour to run before something is expected of her.

Of course, she does feel uneasy as she clips back along George Street for the rendezvous with Herb. He'll expect her to have the grocery shopping done, will be ready to throw it into the car's boot and set off for home. Quick anger arises, with remorse on its heels, when she sees him outside the shop – hat down, hands in pockets, with the jiggle of a knee betraying impatience. Nell buttons her coat over the dress.

'I was detained,' she tells him. 'I'll only be twenty minutes if you'll go along to the butcher for bacon and a small piece of corned beef.' The monthly treat, and a rest from mutton or rabbit.

'I came away early.' From the club, he means. Herb's voice is brisk with resentment. She smells whisky. Sauce for the gander.

'As did I.' Her laugh is brittle.

He gives her a startled look.

'Please, Herb. I'm sorry you've had to drag yourself away, but if we want to be home by dark, best we get on with it.'

It's been a while since Nell went out with Matthew on his rounds. He had to travel away to a family funeral, and then he took out the young graduate nurse who was gaining experience. Nell has woken early with a stir of excitement that won't let her doze on. Herb's side of the bed is empty and, unusually, she can hear him clattering in the kitchen. She sits up and pulls her woollen bed-jacket around her shoulders. She breathes, mindful of the rise and fall of her ribs, calling to mind the instructions she has recently read in a pamphlet from Peggy. It continues to rouse the uneasy question about meditation versus prayer, which is the conventional, the acceptable, method of communicating with the Divine. Meditation is not petition, is not an attempt to organise one's life with reference to a benevolent figure 'out there', but it allows a person to conceive of God as close, as even the Bible suggests, closer than breath.

'I reckon we *are* the Divine, each one of us,' she can

hear Peggy saying, 'like the cells in a great body. All the kingdoms of life, the animals and plants, our Earth, the planets and stars, make up this vast Being.'

Nell feels far from divine, aware of the tug, tug of her thoughts towards the morning with Matthew, the churn in her belly of thrill and anxiety. When once she has managed to stay cognisant of ten breaths in a row, she rubs her scalp with her fingertips and prepares to leave bed for the chilly room – just as Herb appears in his dressing gown, with tea for them both on a tray, and two pompom chrysanthemums in a sherry glass.

'Isn't it your birthday?' he asks when her eyes widen.

'If you say so.' It's a week away. She doesn't want to know if this is Herb's joke or his mistake. She sits back up against the headboard and takes the saucer and cup onto her lap.

Herb sits beside her, on the covers, with his bared shins and slippers on display.

'Crutching again this morning?' Nell asks. The small local shearing team were here the last two days and did the bulk of the ewes.

'Yes, they've left me with about fifty. We should be able to manage those on our own. I'd rather Tom carried on fixing the ridge fence. Cold snap later in the week.'

'You know I'm going out with the doctor this morning?'

Herb stares at her. 'I was counting on your help. Damned inconvenient at times, isn't it, your being at his beck and call?'

Jealousy then? The money, though. That's the

unspoken, unspeakable matter. It hurts Herb that he needs what she brings in, the scrap that it is, a tinny jingle against the great machinery of the farm.

'I'd better get cracking then.' Herb tips back his mug and reaches for his watch.

'Wait.' Nell touches his arm. 'Five minutes more?' She's not ready for him to rush away and leave her with the prospect of Matthew. There must be some bright nugget yet to be found between them. 'Have you read this morning's devotion?'

Herb sighs, but pushes into the pillow at his back. He picks up the small leather-bound volume. 'Abide in my Presence,' he reads. 'Be your hands ever so busy or your heart sore tested, nevertheless find ye amidst the daily round equanimity of thought, quietude of demeanour and clarity of intention, in constant sensibility of Me.'

They sit for a little while in silence.

'Do you find you can do it?' Nell asks.

'Do what?'

'Find that … that certainty of God's presence.'

Herb has one foot on the floor and is doing up his watch. 'At such times as this.' His glance at her is almost shy. 'Also, at the start or end of the day, I think of Him. In between, I trust I'm not left to my own devices, although my thoughts are principally on my work.' He stands and leans to kiss her forehead. 'And now I must leave you to your devices, and to our Lord's care. Happy birthday.'

'You know, don't you…' she begins.

He waits at the bedroom door.

'No, it doesn't matter.'

'I'll be back in an hour, if you'd leave my porridge on the warmer.'

Nell gets up and goes to the window. There's a light frost and it's only March, but sunlight is crackling through the pines onto the home paddock. At the wardrobe, she reaches for the navy linen; her hand seizes the new dress instead and pulls it to her face. The fabric retains a hint of the shop's alluring scent. Why not? Summer is as good as done and she hasn't worn it yet. Why shouldn't Matthew see her for once in another guise, not in the 'uniform' of navy and white that keeps her in her role. She'd like a bath, too. It's early and the twins are still in bed.

She runs along the passage in bare feet and turns the hot tap on full over the big iron tub. Spoons in lily-of-the-valley salts. Retrieves the best bath mat from the hall cupboard. The plushest towel, reserved for guests. Tosses the used ones into the hallway. Back in the bedroom, she lays ready on the bed the satin underwear ('What's that you're wearing?' Herb *did* notice, and asked the one time she has worn them. 'Let me feel. Where did they come from? Not very practical around here. Don't hang them out where the men can see.'), the dress and a new pair of sheer hose.

Walking out to the gate, she ties on the white apron that stands in for a nurse's smock and pulls her long, navy cardigan over that. Matthew arrives and gets out of his car. While he goes around to the passenger seat, Nell picks her way over the cattle stop. She smiles, seeing her green sandals balancing over the iron pipes. The flash of coloured skirt cheers her.

'Southerly change this afternoon,' Matthew says as she gets in beside him 'Best we're brisk. Straight up to the Dansey's Hotel.'

He reads his notes and eats toast with honey from a chipped plate.

'I hope you've had more sleep than I,' he mutters, scribbling notes on his pocket pad. 'The hotel rang me at five. I'd seen this woman last night, with a chest that seems to have deteriorated since.'

'I'm feeling fresh.' Nell eases the car into second to tackle the gravel slope. 'I have no other commitments today and Herb will meet the girls off the school bus.' The wheels spit stones and she makes the tricky double-de-clutch into first gear.

'Nice work.' Matthew says it without looking up.

Nell notes his close, careful shave, the jaunty red and purple tie she has admired before.

Nearing the hotel, Matthew drops the papers at last, onto the ominous pile of files at his feet.

Nell turns into the hotel's yard and makes for a park under the laburnum tree. She turns off the ignition.

'Thank you.' His look at last is warm. His glance takes in the splash of colour over her knees and above the pinny, and travels up to her eyes.

Nell feels a warm jolt as understanding flows between them, then he takes the file and opens his door.

'The chest' has indeed deteriorated. Matthew gives the patient a jab of penicillin and orders her to be lifted, unaware as she is, into the back of the hotel's van and hastened to the hospital in Oamaru.

The next stop is a farm worker's cottage where they let themselves in. Top and tailing in a bed, flushed and unhappy, are twins near the age of her own. Of greater concern, though, is the mother, who has pulled a flimsy mattress into the living room, so as not to disturb her husband's sleep, but is unable to rise from it. 'It's my head,' she croaks when Matthew bends close. 'It's lead. Burning lead. I can't lift it.'

In the kitchen, he tells Nell, 'We can't assume, just because the children have 'flu, that she doesn't have something else going on. She saw me recently with a persistent headache. I'll draw up a vial of morphia and we might need to send her to the hospital, too. Will you see if her husband can be found?'

Before they can stop for lunch, a child has vomited on Nell (she removed, rinsed, rolled up her apron and dabbed with a soapy cloth at the skirt of her dress), she has clutched a screaming and snotty child's face to her breast while Matthew inspected his ears, and has caught on the dress's waistband the not-quite-invisible spray from an over-tense boil being lanced.

'Pull over at the river, will you?' Matthew says as Nell drives them over dusty corrugations towards the Little Kyeburn.

She takes the track before the bridge and they bump down onto the grassy flat. Sun-gleam through a thin layer of cloud warms the air as she climbs from the car, and Nell feels suddenly as light as an angel. She takes off her cardigan and spreads it to sit on.

Matthew sits nearby and opens the packet of egg sandwiches his housekeeper has provided. He takes one out, then suddenly shakes it at Nell. 'You know I won't be contradicted in front of a patient.'

The words hit her with the cold thud of snowballs.

'I gave my physician's advice on fever reduction and you followed it with an anecdote conveying the complete opposite.'

The sick smell is wafting up from Nell's skirt. She shifts the cardigan over the flamboyant expanse, feels hectic colour in her cheeks. 'I spoke of my own experience. I have five children.' Matthew has none.

'As if my decades of training and patient care counted for nothing.' He stuffs his mouth with egg and bread, and throws the crust away.

Nell tucks her feet under her. What was she thinking of, wearing the sandals? She has a sandwich, too, made of Mary's dense wholemeal bread with the salty cheese she's made, but her mouth is too dry to eat.

Matthew is chewing and staring at the river.

He throws another crust. 'All you women in this bloody place, all intractably opinionated, with your old wives' remedies. Stuck in the damned past. Until the chips are down and you need actual medical care, actual scientific advice.'

Nell sees the angry jump of a muscle at his collar, the sneer that whitens his nostril. She's seen hints of this before, but chose not to take it in. Shame washes over her, double shame, but under it is anger.

In a trice, misplaced affection and wistfulness are retrieved. It comes to Nell as a revelation that she is able to turn on a sixpence. That she is old enough to snap her fingers and walk away. Nothing binds her. She will finish out the day, then tell him she won't be available next week.

Besides that, something is afoot with Herb and she wants to be on hand.

'Mummy! Here she is!'

The twins are on their bellies, Flick's head and shoulders inside the hill.

'Careful then. Don't try to touch her.'

Flick edges back and gives Floss the torch. Chloe, hardly more than a pup herself and mated on her first heat despite their best efforts to keep the farm dogs away, has taken possession of the excavated rabbit warren on the bank behind the woolshed. Herb cut away the front a few weeks ago to show the girls the extent of its tunnels and nests.

'Her eyes are glittering.' Floss's voice is muted by earth. 'Chloe? There's squeaking. Oh, pups! Don't growl, girl.'

'She'll be very hungry,' Nell says. 'We'll have to bring up food and water.'

The girls jostle ahead of Nell into the kitchen. Adam is dressed for his return to town and checking his face in Herb's kitchen shaving mirror. 'What're you up to, grubs?'

'Chloe has whelped in the disused warren.' It pleases Floss, having the correct terms to hand. Adam has occasionally admired that in her. Flick is more likely to twist about on the spot and whisper something enigmatic like, 'They might grow up thinking they're rabbits,' so that the facts have to be chipped out of her like coal.

'Well, good for her,' Adam says. 'Before you go beetling off though, Flick, do up this button for me will you, and Floss, give my shoes a once-over? Philip's coming for me any minute.'

Nell hefts yesterday's roast mutton from the corner safe.

'Do I have to, Mother?' The girls claim aversion to the dim wash-house cupboard where the shoe polish lives.

Adam cuts in: 'Hey, just do as you're asked, I'm in a hurry.'

Nell carves meat from the bone. She feels for them, but won't intervene. He'll be gone soon enough.

Flick does up the button, then makes his mutton sandwich, while Adam pores over a hand-written page. Floss scrapes a knife over the heels of his shoes, still on his feet but lifted as required, to take off the dirt, then brushes onto them Texan Brown. Nell senses her satisfaction in smearing on the colour, then seeing the shine rise as she buffs with the polishing brush. 'You over-identify with the children,' Herb has told her. 'You feel too much.'

'Oh Lord,' Adam shakes the page of writing, 'I promised cream. Ma ... too busy? Flick-be-quick, decant a pint off into a preserving jar and make sure the lid's down tight.'

Then he's out the door – 'Bye, fillies' – leaving the twins quivering, the usual. Nell kisses his cheek on the doorstep, waves to Philip, and watches Adam throw his bag into the boot.

Behind her, the girls twitter. 'He didn't even want to see the puppies.'

'Did he even say thank you?' They used not to expect it, but cousin Bea told him off recently for his bossiness toward the twins and Floss has started watching for it. She steps past Nell and yells, 'At least say thank you!' as the car rattles over the cattle stop with Adam inside.

He's gone for a whole half-term.

Nell wraps the bone in newspaper. When Adam goes back to the city, or off to the mountains (and lately he's talked of the remote Olivine ice plateau) busyness is the antidote. She half-fills a bucket with water.

As they walk over the lawn, Flick prattles, which the twins take turns doing when they sense that Nell is forlorn. They grow expansive and cast around for gems to offer. 'I think that if there's a girl pup, it will be obvious by its face, won't it? And that's the one I hope we'll keep.'

Past the woolshed, they go directly through the fence, Nell putting her gumboot on a lower wire and tugging up the one above so they can scramble through, then between them the twins do the same for Nell.

'Will Adam ask June to marry him?' Flick says.

Nell laughs as she reaches back for the bucket. 'I

don't know if that's the way they feel about one another. Anyway, they're far too young and Adam needs to finish his studies.'

'Isn't June a bit too…' Floss hunts for the word, '…too enthusiastic for Adam?'

'I like that in her. High spirits.'

'I heard him telling her off for having the fidgets while he meant her to listen to the Bartók.' Floss is walking slightly ahead in gigantic steps.

'Yes, well, June might not wish to comply with Adam's high expectations.'

'We don't always wish to comply with them,' Floss replies.

Flick glances at her mother's face before adding, 'No, we don't always.'

Nell puts a finger to her lips as they approach the warren. 'Let me go first.'

Crouched at the entrance, Chloe growls even at Nell, but she takes the bone and presses her nose to it, as if telling herself not to be cross. There's a rumble in her throat as Nell strokes her with one hand and shines the torch into the warren. 'One, two … four … six … eight nine ten eleven twelve … heavens, thirteen. Fourteen. At least.'

Flick is on tiptoes, hands clasped under her chin like Emily in *The Littlest Princess*. 'Fourteen! Chloe, you clever, clever old mother!'

Floss's face is glum. 'Dad said only two or three can live. One for me and Flick, one for the Barsteads, and maybe one more, depending.'

Flick is watching her twin, and her own face grows solemn.

'Don't say anything, Flick, when we get home. Let me do the talking, all right?' Floss tells her.

Nell reaches in and pulls three puppies writhing into her skirts. Two are silvery grey, like Chloe, the other crisp white with black head and tail. The girls take a silver one each and stare at the blind eyes, paddling paws. They hold them to their faces, to their throats. Floss tries to tuck hers into her singlet. Chloe is scraping meat from the bone and Nell says she needs more, with so many to feed. The girls can take two rabbits from the freezer to thaw, and bring them up. She need not spoil the moment with the truth about the fate of all but one – *one*, Herb has said with finality.

'Put them back before she's finished with the bone.' Nell stands and brushes off the knees of her woollen stockings. 'Then before you go riding, get out your school clothes for tomorrow so I can check them over, and you can give your shoes a clean.'

'We've only just cleaned Adam's.' Floss holds her pup against Flick's and kisses them both.

'Well then, you have your hand in. It won't take a jiffy.'

The spring school holiday has been grey and cold. It's a shame Chloe waited until two days before the end to whelp. Still, there's sun today and Nell promises they can have a billy and damper, and take the pony down to the river for a cook-up.

She'll go and strip Adam's bed and heat the copper to wash the sheets and the pile of farm clothes he's thrown into the wash house.

Lettie has gone to the study to look through the 'Children' file for her birth certificate. She has applied reluctantly for a secretarial course, since a friend has convinced her she needs skills beyond those of the farm. When Nell goes in to see how she's getting on, Lettie is standing on the sofa looking hard at *The Lorelei*.

'Actually, she looks better from further away. Up here, you can see all the brush strokes. Which only goes to show how clever the old girl is.'

'Mind. It's one thing for your father to call her that…'

'But really, Aunty Ilona's quite the talent, isn't she. The rest of us are drudgingly practical in comparison. I've noticed, too, she does whatever she feels like.'

'Comparisons are odious.' Nell shakes her head at her own parroted words. 'Anyway, I gather she works pretty hard. She's supporting them both with her flower paintings.' She wishes she felt less uncomfortable standing here with her daughter looking at a nude woman. Over the years, a mother forfeited the right to hold, feed, bathe and care for her daughter's body. And little by little, she also stopped seeing or touching it. Time has torn Lettie away. They're not a physical family, and while Nell might kiss a cheek or clasp a hand in greeting or parting, she suffers now. Lettie is entirely discrete: hands on hips, her slender, womanly body swathed in jumper, jodhpurs and thick socks. If she ever bares herself like the woman on the sofa, it will be to a man, to his gaze, his touch, his proprietorship.

Nell doesn't recall ever having seen her own mother's body, except once. As a child, she pushed the bathroom door silently ajar and saw her with slip pulled down, examining her breast in the mirror. She retains in this memory the alarming fullness of it and the jarring sense of wrong, her own wrong, in catching her mother out of role and unawares.

It's a relief to have Adam home again, for a long weekend. Herb has been in and out of his panics over the farm and now for a few days Adam will distract and jolly him along.

It's been a long term, he wrote a week ago, although his letter was suffused, too, with excitement about his studies in biochemistry and possible avenues of enquiry opening to him in his fourth year.

Nell wasn't home when he arrived and already he's taken a horse away up the back. She wants to catch the scent of his presence. She opens his bedroom door and stops. Books are piled as usual on the desk, his canvas bag lies unzipped and spilling shirts onto the bed. The floor, though, has been colonised, by a pile of ropes in various weights, a small mountain of metal loops and pegs, a wood-shafted ice axe, snow goggles, torch, balsa wood spoon and plate and, hung over the chair at his desk, a plump new khaki jacket.

Nell goes over and squeezes the puffy down, feels the resistance of tiny feather shafts. There is a sudden sensation beneath her fingers of blood welling from the seam. For a second, the shoulder is soaked and the cold iron smell is in her nose. She pulls her gaze away, up the hill, looking for Adam, then stares back at her hand clutching the jacket. Which is bland, unmarred.

Mountaineering is his new passion: his aspirations lead him to the edge of all he undertakes. It is simply her own fear, she tells herself, that has conjured the fearful image.

A shiver runs over Nell's neck as Herb comes in for lunch. The care he is taking. He bends to set his muddied boots side by side, pulls strands of hay from his jersey and drops them twisted onto the kindling box. He walks gingerly across to the sink to wash his hands. 'I have news.' He stops there, twining the towel in his hands.

Nell crouches to take the shepherd's pie from the coal range. The oven cloth is scorched and thinning; fast, she drops the pie dish onto the board beside the bread, straightens and takes off her pinny.

Seated now, Herb waits for her, smoothing the rattan table mat.

She serves, cuts bread, passes butter and for a while they eat in silence.

'I've found a buyer.'

Nell puts down her fork. 'I thought we'd agreed. To wait.'

'I can't. Coleman has to be paid. The bank. And the others.'

'We're not the only ones.'

'It's a sinking boat. I want to be off it.'

She shakes her head, can't seem to stop. 'Who is it?'

'Harry Parker.'

Enlarging his empire. 'So what was the discussion?'

'No discussion. It's done. We've sold.'

The chair flies out behind her. Nell finds herself in the middle of the kitchen. 'We've? No. *I* did not!' The room is whiting out. She puts a hand to the coffee grinder handle and drops her head. 'Whose money bought this farm?' she asks. 'Whose name is on the title?'

Herb takes another mouthful and chews it thoroughly. Army tactic: in the face of opposition, take your time. 'Two questions. Two answers. Largely yours. And mine.'

Nell steps into gumboots and drags a coat from the pile – barely aware until she finds herself at the water race two hundred yards above the house. It loops about the hillsides like a pencil line on a contour map, falling half a yard every few miles. It cuts the farm into two: above and below the race. She's too het-up to follow the tamed and twinkling water. The new fence-line marks the easiest route for her climb, straight towards the sky, the sou'wester at her back. Sheep run away to her left and, over the fence, heifers back off. Her chest and legs hurt but she won't slacken her pace. Not until the pup, Daff, appears at her knee, laughing regardless and dashing ahead. Then Nell turns and looks.

The farmhouse below squats square and obstinate in the remnant frost, puffing its chimney, which hardly spreads its warmth beyond the big kitchen. Herb will be wiping his plate with a crust of bread. Then he'll wait (and wait, will he?) for her to come and make a pot of tea, to put out fruit cake, cheese and an apple, sliced and cored.

Nell's gaze roams to the right, along the tops of the Ida Range, dusted with snow after the night of tearing wind. And scans left across the shades of blue that are the rolling, flattened Maniototo plains, to the Kakanuis – more than dusted, lightly coated in their march towards Mt Kyeburn at her back.

She turns and climbs again. To the chalk pit, she decides and she hugs into the fence now, so as not to lose her balance on the steep slope, one finger hooked around the wire, the force of breath dragging in and out. Everything she can see as she faces north, and a third of what lies behind, is theirs. Hers, rightfully, but of course she paid her inheritance over to Herb so he could buy the farm for *them*. She never dreamed he'd … The word makes her flinch. That he'd betray her like this.

And yet, why does she disbelieve? It's not the first time.

Herb's deal, sealed in the dead of winter – hands shaken after an evening of whisky with 'the chaps' – is with a landowner whose cash offer obliterated any remnant sobriety of thought in Herb. A mates' pact making no concessions to family.

They have five days to be out. Five days for Nell to pack up her 'domain' (the house and wash house, garage and garden shed), while the life of the farm goes on, with workers and visitors to be accommodated, and animals to be fed, put in or out, exercised or milked. And in the case of the old pony with staggers from eating infected hay (hay bought from a neighbour; Herb insists it would never be *his*), slung in a hammock and checked by day and by night (by Nell), injected, hand watered and finally shot.

There is no time to *sort* or *pack*. The verbs that bully her along are *seize* and *thrust, grasp, swipe* and *toss*. Occasionally *kick* or *elbow, burn and* even *bury*.

Every room is saturated with the life of the family. With actual markings: hand scuffs on doors; the ladder of heights on the bathroom wall. With emanations: the particular smells of each child's wardrobe, and memories conjured – in the sunny living room corner David curled, red-shawled and reading; on the verandah beam, Lettie balancing, with Adam declaiming from the canvas chair beside her. The twinny odour of their bedroom: pet mouse, cherry blossom talcum powder, ripe socks and apples. Every corner might detain or undo her, but there is no time to be undone.

Adam can come, for a single day. He puts all of his books into apple boxes, his extra climbing gear and clothing into a wool bale. He leaves untouched his childhood collections, microscope, puzzles and riff-raff. Throwing things away has never been Nell's forte. She *seizes* and *tosses* them into four more apple boxes.

Herb comes down from the hill late on the second morning with three strips torn from the palm of his hand when he fell with a roll of barbed wire. He refuses to wait for the doctor. While Nell cleans, straightens skin flaps, dresses and bandages it in the sunlit porch, the stewing apple boils over and crusts the entire stovetop, and the week's bread burns, all five loaves as dry as straw bales.

Coming for one evening from her job as a house-maid, ruthless Lettie packs from her room only what will fit into her school suitcase. She lugs her old exercise books, paintings and cardboard doll houses out to the bonfire pit. Nell rescues from it her own old teddy bear and Lettie's Enid Blyton collection.

David phones from his boarding school detailing the few objects from his room that must be preserved at all costs. They fill a pillowslip. The remainder of his clothing, toys, books and knick-knacks, *thrust* together, fill two large flour sacks.

For the twins, Nell heaves an old shipping chest from the garage, over the lawn and along the hallway to their room. She instructs them that by the penultimate day they must have put everything into it, leaving out only what they'll need for the night and the following day.

Herb is out of the house from dawn until dark and beyond, taking food with him, or snatching meals on the run. He is full of energy, elated by the prospect of debts cancelled and a fresh beginning – in what field, goodness knows, but he has been 'having talks', which has meant letters written in the late hours and others received from the city guild. There's no hurry to decide because for the next few months they'll live at Centrewood with Nell's mother, who has an ailment that is whittling at her body the way her mind has been whittled in recent years.

Most days a pain arises in Nell's belly. It grips her for an hour or two at a time, and bends her in half on a kitchen chair. Before sitting, she takes a flour bag and pulls out a kitchen drawer in order to sort the contents at her feet. Chilblains burn and itch, mouth ulcers and a sore throat banish equanimity. She has practically stopped sleeping or eating, living as she is on tea and alarm.

When Lettie has left the room, Nell opens her eyes, slips from bed and closes the curtains again. Back under the covers, she shapes her feet around the newly filled hot water bottle and sinks back onto the pillow, ignoring the teapot, egg, toast and little dish of marmalade on the bedside table. She stares at the pink roses sprigged with lavender and feels nothing. For the thrush trilling away in the birch tree nearby, likewise. Her eyes close.

Winter sun slices through the crack between curtains. Her breath plumes above her face. Somewhere in the house, far away, feet slap on floorboards, or thump over carpet, voices rise and fall. Nell doesn't know how many days have passed since she took to the bed. Or weeks. Possibly a week for every day of packing. The doctor comes and goes. She has been close to death, she is sure of that. She turns over and rearranges her feet on the hot water bottle, pulls the bed covers over her ear. To lie here is all she wants. Nothing, nothing, nothing more.

'It was horrible, Mum.' Lettie is the only one who uses that hard, dumb name instead of Mother. 'I was wild with you. Letting yourself go.'

Nell looks at her swift and dynamic daughter. She will not excuse herself; she was given no choice in the matter. 'You'll find that, in the end, you learn to forgive your elders.'

'Huh. Pfff.' Lettie gathers the silver cutlery from the table where they've been shining it and dumps it into the sink full of hot suds. 'And just so you know, I don't want any of this when the time comes. Stainless steel for me: knives, forks, teapots, toast racks. Life's too short for this nonsense.' The blackened rags and newspaper, the Silvo and teacups, the hours that have passed.

They've talked, though. And Lettie has told her more about Ian. He's going to come and visit them next week. They want to marry and take up a small farm together at Lawrence. Lettie's only nineteen but Nell can't recall her ever being dissuaded from a course she has set her sights upon.

Nell goes to take beef stock from the safe, which is the only thing her mother will swallow at midday, and butters a wafer of white bread in case. While the soup heats, she takes a bowl of hot water and a facecloth up to the bedroom.

At the window, Mother is sitting bolt upright, clutching at the rug over her knees. It's two minutes to midday.

'Let me have it. I've been waiting, you know.' She drags the cloth over her hands, back and front, then plunges hands and cloth into the hot water and holds them there while Nell grips the bowl.

'How many of us today?' Mother asks.

'The usual number: Herb and me, Lettie and the girls. You.'

'Thirteen then.'

'If you insist.'

'It's thirteen with all of us home. Four down one side, five along the other and two at each end. It's no fun sitting beside Father when he's in a mood. Crack on your knuckles with the bone handle. Crack on your head. Crack on the plate…' Her hands rise, and splash down with each 'crack'.

Nell gives her the hand towel. 'I'll be back in a minute with the soup.'

Downstairs she looks at her daughter. With open recipe books on the table, she is writing the week's menu into an exercise book. She insists she wants the practice – at everything she hasn't yet mastered in the domestic realm.

'I'm sorry, Lettie. It can't have been easy for you.'

'No. She hated everything I did. And she did this.' Lettie exposes a red weal across her collar bone. 'I never actually got her into the bath.'

'No. We seem to be past that now. I just give her a flannel on her way to the chair and instruct her to use it.'

'She can walk though. I caught her pottering about in the twins' room one day.'

'Poor old thing.' Nell goes to the stove and stirs the soup.

'Was she always a housewife?'

'I suppose so.' Even now, Nell is hazy about her mother's history, except that she married young. 'I'm afraid the women of the family haven't set a good example in emancipation.' She looks wryly at the dishcloth in her hand, wooden spoon in the other.

'But they ran households. As I shall soon.' Lettie looks up with a grin.

There are worse things to aspire to, Nell thinks. Home-making has developed many skills in her, and Lettie will be sure to make even more of it because she thrives on busyness and juggling, is continually stretching herself. Whereas for Nell's sister Stella it has been a kind of disaster. The intimate and relentless demands of family life overwhelm her and two or three times each year she collapses with nervous exhaustion.

Nell ladles soup into a bowl. 'Mother has always been a bit formidable. I think she imagined a finer life for herself, with more comfort and privilege than actually came her way. So she still acts that fantasy out when she can get away with it.'

'Don't we all.' Lettie hasn't even looked up from her list-making, and Nell laughs.

When Adam asks Nell if she'll come away with him for a couple of nights to the new Aspiring Hut, fear as well as joy supplies her answer. Of course, they won't climb a mountain, but she'll see him in his element.

Adam insists they leave before dawn on the appointed day. 'I'll prepare and carry the food, Mother. You simply need to pack your own clothes and bedding.'

Simply. Preparation is never quite that, in her experience. She's still lying awake after midnight, revising the list of items she yet wants to retrieve before they leave: the leftover shepherd's pie, a small piece of soap, her miniature sewing kit and awl. And do: write notes, for Herb about the dogs' tucker, for Jean about planting out the root-bound seedling lettuces, for the twins, to find and decorate a Christmas tree and keep the begonias watered in the sun porch. Mother has gone for a week to stay with Stella.

Adam is solicitous. At home, Nell is merely mother. Here near the end of the road, when they've bounced around gravelly hillsides, forded half a dozen streams and concluded that it's time to leave the poor old Singer parked nose downhill between matagouri bushes, she is his companion and a woman to boot. He loads his own pack to the gunwales and insists on pushing her sandshoes and water bottle into its outside pockets. He kneels to wind the mustard wool puttees around her boot tops, and lifts her pack onto her back, squares up the shoulder pads and tightens the straps.

'All right?' he asks, and Nell nods, ready to get walking, which will dispel the knot in her belly. Unease remains over the down jacket, and when at the last minute Adam sheds and shoves it under his pack flap, out of sight, she is relieved.

Since the day is gloriously blue, she's agreed to a detour: lunch at the Rob Roy Glacier. They leave Adam's laden pack at the start of the narrow valley, tucking the main contents of Nell's beneath it, and into hers go the shepherd's pie, two spoons, two apples and two tin plates and mugs. Adam shoulders the pack and gestures for Nell to take the lead. With the river roaring in the gully to her left and tree fuchsia flowers and ferns brushing her right side, she walks a while in silence.

'You've gathered an impressive pile of rope,' she tells him over her shoulder. 'And those metal things.'

'Carabiners and rock screws. We learned to use them on club trips. Larry, Dean and I have a couple of expeditions planned. I confess, Mother, to having brought you out on a reccy.'

'That's all right, as long as you don't mean for me to go anywhere perilous.'

'I don't court peril myself, Ma, any time. We learn always to balance capability against risk, caution against ambition. And we see it demonstrated by the top mountaineers in the club. They're splendid fellows, especially old Lex Harris with a mind as fine and dextrous as he is himself on a rock slab or ice face.'

A loud *crack!* in the valley ahead stops them in their tracks and Nell holds her breath through the long ensuing rumble.

'We'll be able to see the ice falls once we're clear of the bush,' Adam tells her.

He walks ahead and she enjoys observing her son: the clench and release of sinews below his shorts, the gait, both familiar and other. When did he become this man inhabiting the world largely without reference to her? There is such pain in being a parent. And yet now there is none. Adam is here with her in vibrant good health and generosity of spirit. Snatches of his whistling come to her and he turns every little while to check on her with a smile. She smiles back. The root-studded track calls for care, but she's happy with the simple task of minding her step, her head bathed in sun, a light breeze on her forearms and shins (she has borrowed a pair of Lettie's knee-length shorts and is astonished at the sense of liberation brought about by the disclosure of her lower limbs).

The glacier appears – a wondrous shock – the looming, vast accumulation of blue ice compressed and fissured and, even as Nell sits at their chosen lunch rock, up goes a puff of snow, followed by crack and roar as the puff becomes a cloud that plummets down a gully then billows over the cliff face below. Cries and laughter come from the party on a tartan rug a few yards away.

The bloodied jacket flies to Nell's mind and makes its own ice grip at her throat. Will it be in an ice fall? She can hardly bear to watch Adam spring away from her as she takes out the lunch: the swing of his arms, the fling of hair, the raw vitality of him leaping from rock to rock. He finds a vantage point and takes out his camera.

They arrive mid-afternoon at the new hut, huge and sturdy on its foundations of river schist. The opening the previous autumn was a grand affair, Adam tells her, attended by the who's who of the country's burgeoning alpinism, and followed by a day of lugging timber above the bushline for repairs to a wind-flattened bivouac.

'Sit, Mother, and I'll make us a cuppa.'

Nell goes to kneel on the bench seat in the high window. The valley spreads away in the foreground; bush-clad ridges rise steeply from it and, above them, Aspiring rears its angled horn. A telescope has been placed nearby and she stands to train it on the peak: sheer and white with sunless patches of blue ice.

'Next year, Mother, all going well.' Adam is at her elbow.

Her head makes a quick involuntary shake. 'Perhaps tell me about it after the event.' She takes the enamel mug of weak black tea – he's even found a slice of lemon to float in it.

'You mustn't put your head in the sand about this. You must accept that I'll spend as much time as I can in the coming years up here, gaining skill on ice and snow. Rock too. Some of the chaps are talking about the Himalaya.'

Nell blows, and sips. Why does he use the imperative voice? Must, mustn't. She will do whatever helps her keep her balance. A mind that constantly casts ahead is capable of brewing up calamities. She *mustn't* allow imagination to add its frenzied trimmings to portent.

'Tell me about it then,' she says, and he points out the bush ridge, the high rocky ridge, then the blue ridge of permanent ice that will be their route.

'You can come any time you want, you know. It's always a treat to have someone back in the hut, with hot food and water ready when we come down.'

Nell shivers. Someone who will be the first to know if the climb hasn't gone well.

She observes Adam's ease and affable greetings as one group then another arrives, the first from down the valley, the second from the slopes of Aspiring, whence they retreated in fright after one of their party fell (roped, as luck had it) into a glacier. She notices how Adam's tall, confident figure commands respect and attention from men and women alike.

Later, when they sit out in the day's last sun with mugs, the cocoa bobbing with lumps of milk powder, he is sharp. 'That chap who went into the crevasse, I'm not in the least surprised. He's good fun on club outings, but precipitate. He'll throw a pan of chops on the campfire while it's still flaming, or drive himself up a rock face before he's spied out the route. And the woman with him has a clever mind but, like him, she scatters her energies.'

Nell looks over at the party, subdued after their day on the snow. Harsh judgements notwithstanding, at least Adam knows 'precipitate' from circumspect.

After a night of twisting and turning in the unfamiliar

sleeping bag on a ticking mattress, with the rustles and snorts of sleepers around her, Nell is glad to hear Adam moving early and she tiptoes after him into the common room. While he turns his back over the kerosene cooker, she pulls on her outer clothes.

'What say we have just a cup of tea now, and stop when we meet the sun, for bread and cheese?'

She agrees, taking her mug again to the window, where a yellow hue outlines the peak beneath indigo sky. By the time she's drained it, dawn is daubing blues and greys on the mountainsides.

Outside, Nell breathes deeply the scents of damp tussock, sedge grass and matagouri that rise to meet her, with muffling turf underfoot and half-darkness a rug around her. She's happy to take the lead, following the indented grass trail and the white cotton strips tied to shrubs every fifty yards or so.

They keep their boots on to cross the river, which is ice-cold in the shadow of the mountain, where they also enter the bush. The track climbs at once, straight up the ridge, offering handholds of fern and sapling beeches. Adam means to leave her at the bushline for an hour or two while he ascends the rock ridge and spies out the mountain's flanks. Nell sends her thoughts into her boots and the pungent earth scents they release from the track, to the sweet array of foliage pressing up and sounding forth all the notes of green, moss and ferns, vines and creepers, striplings and mature trees, all alike clinging to the steep slope. Today she will, she must, find every scrap of the happiness available to her.

It has been both familiar and unsettling to live again at Centrewood. All through Nell's life, it has been a dipping-in-and-out place, with childhood winters spent chasing through the big, draughty rooms, or bundled up for headland walks, memories all tinged with impatience for spring and their return to the high county. It was the stopping place between school in Timaru and other family in Dunedin, it being more practical to stay there with her grandparents for a long weekend than to travel all the way up-country to home. Since then, it's been the halfway point between the farm and the city. They've all treated it like a motel at times, and Mother has encouraged that, always happy to see them for short stints.

Now Nell navigates the shifting ground between two roles: mistress of the house and servant. Mother has wishes, forcefully expressed, but her grasp on reality is loosening, and Nell finds herself tugged between truth-telling and palliating lies.

'I'd like to go out in the motor,' Mother says imperiously during the morning bathroom tussle over the facecloth (the steep-sided bath itself too hazardous, the shower so new-fangled Mother has forgotten her joy at its recent installation and, if coaxed inside, tries to fight off the falling water with yowls like a cornered cat's). Clad only in a long white singlet which shows off the bones of her back, she leans and wipes the fogged mirror. She leers at her own face. 'Atta-boy,' she says, then she turns and clutches Nell's forearm with a bony hand. 'So, will you arrange it?'

'I can...' Nell eases the facecloth from her mother's other hand and drops it into the sink of hot soapy water. 'Where is it you want to go?' She presses the empty hand to the rim of the sink. 'Hold on, Mother.'

'Don't Mother me, young lady. I'd like to take her to afternoon tea ... oh, you know, the one with the dog. Only she must leave it strictly at home. Spotty, with sharp toenails.'

'Stella, you mean?' There's no point in telling Mother that Stella and the children are on the West Coast now. That the dog is long dead, although its bumptious greeting ten years ago – the simple drag of its paw down their mother's stockinged shin and the subsequent seep and puddling of blood beneath her dining chair – gave abrupt and gaudy evidence that their mother was old, her skin friable, no longer 'the tough hide' (said Stella) it had been. They paid attention and saw that not only her skin was succumbing.

'She seems to think Dad's been phoning her in the night,' Stella told Nell recently, on their own weekly toll call. 'He told her to watch what was going on in the pantry. He didn't like the size of the grocery bill. Said that "those people downstairs are running a racket".'

Nell laughs. 'And so we are! I paid a monstrous price for the mushrooms she made me promise to buy for Hamish's visit. Then, Lord help us, we ate a few ourselves. And I paid David from Mother's own purse to dead-head her flowers and mulch her beds. Just so you know the kind of swindlers we are.'

'Well, there are some advantages for you, aren't there?'

It takes Nell a moment to catch on. She stands up and breathes deep, to contain the swill of her anger. Stella has no idea and Nell doesn't fill her in on the finer (coarser) details of what her mother's care entails, nor of Mother's more feral habits as body and mind slacken their hold.

'But speaking of money,' her sister says, 'do you think she could be talked into parting with eighty pounds so Rose can try out the new ballet school here?'

This is the kind of tricky dealing Nell loathes. She'd like her own girls to be able to 'try out' a few polishing skills too, but piano lessons for each grandchild have been the extent of Mother's educational input. Now Stella is asking her to override, to cajole, and utilise her mother's wavering mind on Rose's behalf – or not so much Rose's as Stella's, since Nell knows Rose to be horse-mad, and not bent towards the stage like her mother.

She waits until the half hour of chat is up, then she says simply, heart-thud notwithstanding: 'About the ballet fees, Stella – you'll have to ask her yourself.'

When Mother dies in early spring, Nell tastes a simpler, more spacious daily routine, punctuated by startling gusts of sorrow. The farewell has been a long one. The hunt for their own home begins.

Dear Mother,

You and Dad will be pleased to learn that I've been accepted into the doctoral course. I should be pleased, myself, but I woke in the wee hours this morning cold with the shock of realising what it will devour of the next few years, during which I also wish to expend quite some energy getting myself to the Everest region of Nepal. Nevertheless (back to the PhD) I think that by the end of that time, we'll be well on the way to developing a pig-based insulin that will ease and lengthen by many years the lives of diabetics.

Dad's cousin Jack called in the other day. What a forceful, restless soul he is. I wonder what fuels that vigour besides the urge to improve his land and play pranks. His entry to our living room, where Monty was polishing his blessed medal collection, was preceded by a shock of red hair, shaken about at the edge of the doorway – one of his theatrical props – followed by his grinning face. He has no sense of shame. Monty was completely flummoxed – he sat bolt upright, mouth open, blackened cloth in mid-air – but that's Monty for you. Anyway, he, Jack, was wondering if cattle were prone to diabetes since he's noticed the common human symptoms in a few of his (notably thirst and plenteous pissing).

Would you rifle through the canvas bag in the third drawer of my desk, for the map showing the Rangitata's upper reaches, and bring it when you come? Looking forward to taking you to tea (or, yes, I know, being taken – but I've scouted a dinky new tearoom we can visit).

Until soon,
A.

'Mrs Hamilton, please don't go up there. It's unsafe.'

Nell has stepped over the chair tipped as a barrier across the first steps of the winding stairwell. She has climbed over the three rotten treads (inferior wood used here and there; easily remedied). 'I do so at my own risk,' she tells the property agent. 'You needn't follow.'

He hadn't wanted her to see this house. He has been fixed on the idea that she wants modern, light and stylish. Which she would like, if there weren't so much barren ugliness mixed in with the newer homes he's shown her. Expanses of concrete paving. Banks of conifers. Tiny city kitchens.

Herb told her about the For Sale sign he'd noticed in passing, here at Ravensbourne, off the beaten track, and she insisted on being brought to see the house once the agent had dragged her through three or four hopeless properties: variously too soul-less, too public, too confining.

At the top she steps into the octagonal tower room with its eight window panels looking south into pines, west onto young beeches and elms and north to the swathe of lawn. The whole huge garden is hedged in holly. Nell is magnetised to the eastern windows, with their view of the harbour, shaken by wind, a deep, striated blue between the green hills. She kneels and spreads her elbows along the sill, with sun on her neck and shoulders.

Downstairs there is a thunderously large, dark and ugly kitchen (she'll paint all the woodwork white), a sprawling living room, chilly green drawing room and six bedrooms, with two cavernous bathrooms. It's wildly impractical, but here… This turret is hers. Her bedroom, her dayroom. Here she will be at ease.

Her mind is made up and Herb will have little choice in the matter.

'Yes,' she tells the agent. 'Will you draw up the papers and bring them to us today?'

Colour is needed in the rambling house, and more light. Nell has wall lamps put up in three corners of the living room to augment the spread from the ugly chandelier at the room's centre. She paints the three small bedrooms in soft yellow, the larger, cream ones can wait, although each has one wall painted in vines and exotic flowers. No one wants to use the formal drawing room in the southeast corner of the house, and a rumour has come from one of the neighbours that its builder, once the work was done, hanged himself from the copper beech outside. The tree itself is beautifully formed and benign, but that portion of the garden is likewise unpopular.

Nell invites the women who live on either side of their property to afternoon tea. Myrtle and Ann have barely met before, but in the sun porch swap tales concerning the local school, recent flooding and complaints about service at the corner dairy.

They ask about Nell's children, and then whether Herb is at work today. They are overly impressed by his status as mayor of West Harbour. They fall silent and stare too hard at the fine china set Nell has brought out. Nell wanted to treat them, but sees that instead she has overdone it. She finds herself stilted and awkward.

Not much since schooldays has she fallen into fellowship with women as a group – into the ease of a netball team, the camaraderie of bridge players or coffee clusters. These groups have sprung up as the war's austerities have fallen away, but Nell feels she has lost the knack. This invitation was a mistake.

'I'm sorry,' she says after a swelling silence. 'Please will you take a daisy each with you? I've grown more cuttings than I can possibly use.' She'll give them two of the blue ceramic pots intended for the front doorstep (overdoing it again). She stands to fetch them and her hip catches the tea tray; teapot, saucers and emptied cups slide with the tray cloth and smash onto the brick paving.

Myrtle and Ann swoop and console, chirp and tut in sympathy. Instead of going home, they ask for another cup of tea in the everyday teapot and cups. They begin to confide and grow amusing. They have both noticed her handsome sons (Adam coming and going from university, David from survey school). The broken tea service has broken their reserve and behind it is collusion; they propose another tea party soon, at Myrtle's place, inviting a couple more neighbours, too. 'And let's all bring garden cuttings,' says Ann.

1952

Begonia-growing is a luxury, like lapsang souchong tea and hot baths foaming with lily-of-the-valley, but such are essential to wellbeing. Nell has laid a shelf the whole length of the sun porch, using pillars of bricks for support. In the long row of soil-filled planters she has nestled the hairy tubers with their pink snouts. She speaks aloud her expectations as to colour, form and timing. 'You'll adorn our Christmas table, my dear. Along with salmon and gold, you'll make our centrepiece a shock of flame. So put your little toes down deep and drink up the colour red.' The habit is one of the few she's glad to have received from her mother. It comes with a warm feeling in her arms and throat, this talking to plants, and making vivid in her mind what wants to come into being, which it occurs to her might be the benign face of clairvoyance.

David is down from Christchurch for the weekend, and Lettie has managed to leave the farm for a few days with year-old Tory. With Adam living at Ravensbourne while he saves for a climbing trip, Nell gets behind his scheme to have the whole family ferried across to Broad Bay for Saturday lunch. The Oaklands have been urging them for … well, it might be years now. 'As many as you can rake together, truly! You might be our very favourite family and we'll have Dottie at home, so we can have a good old sing-song too.'

Saturday is a rare cracker of a May day, meaning one that starts fine and still and stays that way until dusk. How extraordinary it is to have all five of them gathered under one roof, six counting Tory. Last night they pushed the two big sofas into a V before the fire and for an hour or more (until Lettie began to wilt and baby to wail) Nell could take in her fill of them. All evening, they listened to one another, were kind, respectful and encouraging.

This morning though, for all their mild banter in the big kitchen, old habits are sneaking back, the misgivings, the small suspicions, the assertions or abnegations of self. Nell lets them know she's aware, and works to keep the atmosphere easy.

'Adam, I do think you might refill the honey jar yourself. Flick hasn't had a chance to sit and eat yet. You know where the tin is.' This accompanied by a warm nod for Flick to put down the jar, a warm squeeze of the arm for Adam.

Or, 'David, are you going out already? Please, I want to hear more about your workday, and what it entails. Come, I'll top up your tea.'

'Here, let me hold her,' to Lettie, who is not yet out of her nightwear, and whom Nell heard getting up at least twice in the night. 'Go and have a nice hot bath. We've plenty of time.'

Fruitcake, shortbread, coats and rugs, a bundle of late roses and a roll of *Soil Association* magazines to pass on to the host, Tory in her pushchair: all are manoeuvred down the road to the wharf, and onto the ferry when it comes alongside, chugging and puffing smoke.

'Look at them,' Nell tells Herb. They have wound up sitting together at the stern, looking over the heads of their family and other passengers. 'Where have the years gone?' Herb gives her a wry look. 'Spun into gold.' He nods at Lettie and Tory, and Nell is delighted. She takes his arm and smiles.

They have been happy together, and unhappy, in pretty much equal measure. As most of the couples Nell knows have been. One or two have seemed to exceed the common measure of one or other, and one or two have parted ways, as she and Herb have not: she wonders if this is because she made a choice somewhere, or failed to make a choice. Or if there was no choice, if their life together was decreed by forces beyond any personal control. They have allowed space between them, though, in this matter or that, for the sake of their own interests or the other's. If Nell sometimes feels herself to be wiser than Herb, more cognisant of the people and influences around them, more aware of the stitches required to keep the fabric of daily life intact, then she has been filling in gaps for him, as he has done for her when it comes to a grasp of politics, of how money works in the wider economy, of how to go about setting the world to rights beyond home and neighbourhood.

The engine chugs steadily; they are all being borne together over the water. Herb is here beside her and for this moment they are of one mind. Nell sees with bright clarity that he could not be, could not have been, anywhere else. He is for her as he is for himself. She is fitted in place, as he is. And they have done their work upon one another. Chiselled, abraded, chipped and smoothed. Angered and soothed, antagonised and calmed. Known, awoken, integrated and interlocked. It could hardly be otherwise.

1954

When Floss wakes to find she has her first period, Nell agrees she can stay home. Flick's anxiety about catching the train and walking the mile uphill to school on her own is such that Nell agrees that she can stay, too. She chides herself only briefly. She is lenient with the twins. Much easier in herself these days, though, and that is surely a good thing. She's glad that they had 'the talk' again recently. The girls have known what to expect, and besides, they witnessed the hormonal flares and fluctuations of their older sister.

While Floss sits hugging a hot water bottle and giving instructions, Flick makes a batch of cinnamon scrolls, then helps dice carrots and potatoes.

When he comes home for lunch, Herb is surprised to find his daughters sitting down with them to hearty bowls of minestrone soup.

'So, you can both afford to take a day off?' he asks.

The girls glance at Nell, who tries to give him a warning look, but until his hunger is appeased, irritation won't be shaken off.

'What are they teaching you anyway? Floss, what's the capital of Italy?'

The girls look equally stricken.

'Vienna?' Floss ventures. Her embarrassment at being wrong rises in a red tide, deepening the birthmark on her cheek. She bows her face to the soup.

'Flick then. Twenty-four times three.'

Flick shakes her head as if there were an insect in her ear.

'The French for pass me the salt.'

She passes it and murmurs without looking at him, 'I don't take French.'

'Latin then.'

Shake, shake.

'Please, Herb.'

'Please nothing. I pay fees for these two to have some useful knowledge tipped into their dear little heads. Floss, one hundred divided by three.'

'Thirty-three and a third.'

'That's more like it. Flick…'

Her shoulders twitch and she presses her spoon to the table.

'Find India.' He reaches behind him for the miniature globe he keeps on the sideboard for their occasional enlightenment.

Flick runs her hand in confusion over the Pacific Ocean.

'How do you spell rhythm?'

A tear stains the green cotton table mat beside her soup bowl.

Herb spoons up his soup.

'You have to keep them up to it,' he snaps at Nell.

Later, when he's gone off to the greenhouse, Flick stands in the doorway and runs her finger around the latch plate. 'Nothing comes when he asks me,' she says. 'Nothing at all. I'm just stupid.'

'It's fright,' Nell offers. 'Shall we take our tea upstairs?'

They exchange a twin look, eyebrows up. Nell has been assiduous in her claim on the turret and although she is sure that furtive visits are made by each of her children, as long as she is home, none dare ascend.

'I'll carry the tray, Flick, if you'll bring the teapot.'

The girls look to her for guidance as to where they should sit.

'Cross-legged on cushions, like three yogis. Or two, since my legs won't cross as readily these days.'

With her bed behind them, Nell puts the tray on the low window ledge in front. From the floor, they can still see the harbour, quiet and grey today under a heavy nor'west sky. The cold change is due any time.

Floss and Flick enter into a conspiratorial mood, especially when Nell tells them that David is bringing a young woman home next weekend.

'He must be keen on her. He's never even mentioned a girl before now.' Floss butters a circuit of her broken scroll.

'What's her name?' Flick waits to take the knife and copy.

'Barbara. You two could prepare the flower room for her. What would you do to make it ready?'

Flick looks at the ceiling. 'Take out that awful picture of the man.'

'Awful?'

'You know. He's leaning gloomily on the gate, but something else is wrong. The hills are too straight and the light is too ... shiny.'

Nell looks at her with interest. Academically, Flick has no confidence. She shies away from anything requiring concrete thought or tight definition, but the sketches and doodles with which she hems newspapers, pamphlets and schoolbooks, and the pencil always behind her ear, show where promise lies. Herb won't countenance art school for his daughter. His sister Ilona, after training in fine arts, and stints painting at St Ives, in Paris and Tahiti, 'consorting with lord knows what Bohemian types' now lives on Waiheke Island, married to a divorcé, and paints her days away in bold, celebratory oils. Nell has a Tahitian one on the wall up here: a woman in red muumuu strolling under palms beside a blue estuary. She is statuesque, brown, bare-shouldered and, besides the occasional Māori wife travelling with the shearers, unlike anyone Nell has actually met.

'We could swap the gloomy man for something a little more … proportional and cheerful, if you like. What else?'

'Dust, sweep and mop, shake the rug, fresh sheets, fresh flowers.' Floss is ever the pragmatic twin.

'Find books?' Flick has noted Nell's habit of selecting one or two with the guest in mind.

'You could do all but the sheets and flowers today – as you say, Floss, fresh is the word.'

Floss pushes away the hot water bottle and tops up their teacups. 'What else do you know about David's girlfriend?'

'Well…' Nell sips and gazes out at the sky, and sees David at the local Easter dance a year or two ago:

blushing and diffident, but watched by the girls as long as Adam wasn't anywhere near to steal the show. 'Barbara is his boss's daughter, so we'd better not alarm her. She writes a column for some paper or other, and I hear she's rather good-looking, with a brother at the med school here.'

'She won't think much of us then.' Floss is putting protections in place.

'You know David; she won't be unkind.'

'Are they here yet?' Flick throws the wet scrap bucket under the sink and takes the eggs trapped along her arm to the pantry.

'You've only been gone ten minutes.' Nell is arranging hard stems of rowan berries into a brass tube vase.

Floss goes to the door. 'Come on, Flick, let's go down to the gate. Nonchalantly.'

The letterbox abutting the holly hedge is a sturdy double. They'll clamber up and sit with their heels kicking the 8 and the redundant 10 as they listen for a Humber straining up the hill.

Nell checks the bedroom. The twins have done a creditable job. The sheets are pulled taut, pillows plumped, eiderdown rolled just-so, and the picture that offended Flick has been replaced by a fantasy from the twins' bedroom of violet and fuchsia irises painted in vivid slabs of oil, by Ilona. Flick's arrangement of red button crysanthemums with dark purple penstemon wands is idiosyncratic and striking.

Nell looks into David's room. The twins have been a

little more perfunctory with his bed. She lays on the end the few letters that have come for him, and a copy of *The Sea Around Us*, which Adam has insisted the entire family must read. David can go first.

Downstairs, the table is set, the steak and kidney pie in the oven, cauliflower ready to be steamed, parsley minced. Herb will be in his room, writing reports until David arrives.

The girls return. 'Only two cars went by. Flick was getting cold.'

Nell aches for them in this moment: their swings at fifteen between responsibility and childishness, between puppyish exuberance, quivering watchfulness and the occasional attempt to make statements of their own.

'Tell you what,' says Nell. 'A letter came from Adam today, which I haven't opened yet. Shall we read it together?' She retrieves it from the mantel shelf and sits at the kitchen table.

The letters are, of course, arriving weeks after they were sent. This one was posted at the stop in Panama, but by now the expedition team will be in the Himalaya, filing around mountainsides, acclimatising. Adam was asked to join the trip set up by the now-famous Hillary, their goal an unclimbed, horrifying ice behemoth. This requires courage, faith and deep morning breaths on Nell's part, when she wakes in a flush of panic. For now, though, they laugh at his précis of the other passengers. *Tiny Miss Higgenbotham in knickerbockers has known the name and habits of every bird seen (and unseen, but suspected) since we left Auckland and is on her way to enlighten the infants of Calcutta.* They know the way he can egg certain people on until they bloom into their full eccentricity.

'Will you get it, Nell?' Herb's voice comes from the desk in his bedroom.

Nell takes off her apron and strokes back her hair. She walks the long hallway and opens the door to early-June sunshine and the postman.

'They wouldn't fit in the mailbox.' He puts a string-tied bundle, dozens of letters, into her hands and she stands there, swaying on the step, as he walks away down the winding drive. She lifts the pile to her front, then she holds it out straight. A strangled sound rises in her.

Back in the kitchen she grinds coffee, heats milk and hears the silence of the house. The girls have returned to school, David to Christchurch, Lettie, Ian and the baby back to the farm. Herb's council work has taken him into its embrace.

The kitchen nook catches the morning sun and Nell sits at the little table side-on to the window. It's so quiet, she hears the *zt* of the scissors cutting the string. Cream and blue envelopes slide apart. She spreads them with her hands and picks out familiar handwriting. Peggy's. Pat's. Cousin Eda's. She holds them to her face to staunch the tears.

The scene plays itself again and again. Again and again, she allows it, as if by paying close enough attention, some detail will alter; events will fall another way and she'll hear Adam's socked feet sliding over the floor behind her as he comes to bunt his beard to her crown. 'Morning, Mother. How'd you sleep?'

And she'll look up at him, a laugh will shriek from her throat. 'What on earth are all these then?' and she'll fling the letters out through the open window. 'What a ghastly nightmare!'

A week ago: Adam telephoned to ask if she needed anything. He was leaving the lab early. Even in the hallway, she could hear the drum of rain on the roof upstairs and the splash of overflow from the rickety corner of the verandah. Somehow, she didn't caution him. It must be, she'd later think, because she had no memory of his motorbike going out that morning, imagined he'd caught the train to town. If she knew, she'd have *urged* him … But then – how can it be? – she had such a lovely afternoon. *Delectable;* she recalls summoning the word. She was sitting out in the porch at the little sewing machine table where she writes letters, the last few begonias drooping their heads nearby. A pot of tea sat in front of her, and her pale blue porcelain mug, mohair rug around her knees. She had one of Adam's records playing almost as loud as he played it (Sibelius, she'll never be able to listen to the violin concerto again) over the drum of rain, ink pot lid raised, a new cream pad cracked open beside a letter from Peggy full of questions Nell had time that afternoon to ponder and reply to. She lost herself in the texture of recent days, in the insights gained through coaxing herself to observe her children (as she does her flowers) without interference now that they're all grown up or near enough, having learned to unhook her clinging thoughts.

It grew cooler and she pulled the mohair rug around her middle. She refilled and cradled the little round mug and stared out at the bank of chrysanthemums beginning to sprawl under the weight of rain. The violin was surely describing the free nature of flowers, of her children, of her own self if she could truly let go and become impartial; they told her it was already accomplished ... and then the music ended and she went on sitting. Probably she was smiling. *Smiling.*

Banging! at the door. An axe into the silence.

'Mrs Hamilton! Are you here? Please! Get a coat and come!'

A wet boy she didn't know was heaving for breath in the hallway. He grabbed an umbrella out of their hall stand and flicked it open for her as he exited. He cried in his cracked boy-man voice: 'Accident ... go down Adderley.'

She has no memory of getting there (but somehow she arrived in Herb's coat; where was Herb? Where were the twins? She no longer knows). Now she can see herself running after the boy, trees shaking and throwing drops *tears* all over them and some voice telling her to stop, slow down, not to go any further. She must have run all the way down the long puggy driveway, along the rough footpath, or the road – did she run straight down the centre? – after the boy – was he holding the umbrella for her, or was she? – *slow down, Nell, turn for home* – and from the bottom of the pedestrian zig-zag she saw the little crowd gathered at the foot of Adderley Terrace, a couple kneeling, others standing. There was no motorbike to be seen and Nell's heart leaped. This had nothing to do with her. They'd called the wrong mother.

Then a man, Bert someone, rushed at her: 'My fault … cycled straight out, he had to swerve…' He grasped her hand and almost bunted her with his bowed head. 'I'll never forgive myself.'

She flung his hand from her. She had seen the corduroy trouser leg, the sock and the shoe.

Everything fell away – the rain, the onlookers, her own life – as she crawled over the footpath, running her hand over Adam's ankle, his shin, trouser leg, oilskin coat, hip, side, shoulder, beard… His woollen scarf had been wound around his head and eyes but it could not staunch the dark seep over the wet asphalt.

Nell is not sure she can leave the car. Not because of the rain thrashing at the windscreen, nor because she is numb and cold to the core. She looks at Herb with his hands clutching the steering wheel although he has parked the car beside the cathedral. He turns to her and his eyes are black with dread.

'Nell,' he says.

They look at one another across the abyss.

'Here's your umbrella, Mother.' Floss to the rescue.

The minister urges them to go around and up the main steps, rather than slipping in through the side door. He has outlined his belief that grief requires the full ritual, and they are in no condition to contradict him.

David runs down to meet them as they climb, rain-coat held over his head. He has come with Lettie and Ian. He takes Nell's other arm. She is practically being lifted up the steps, which is not necessary for her, though perhaps for them.

The organ is playing Handel's *Largo*, which Adam would hammer out lugubriously, ironically, on the piano when he felt the family needed a mirror, or an echo chamber, for their collective mood: urging them to 'take stock and buck up!' There will be no stock-taking today, no choices made. They are well under, being hauled by a sluggish and powerful current.

Fifteen minutes before the start, the cathedral is already packed. (Later, they will enumerate the groups and clubs: the climbers and trampers, the university faculty and students, cathedral and university choirs, the acclimatisation people, the debaters, the aunts, uncles and cousins, neighbours and the friends he gathered up everywhere: all those warmed, charmed, challenged, awed, chagrined or delighted by Adam.)

Herb's sister Pat has offered her own black hat, with black half-veil, but Nell is glad to find herself without it: the eyes turning to catch hers as they walk up the aisle need to be answered. She can nod. She can hold her mouth in a small smile of thanks that they've come.

The hymns, the homily, the summary of a life delivered by David, all slide around her, brown water spiked with lacerating branches. 'Oh God, our help in ages past, our hope for years to come…' Such lines have delivered courage before; now, something painful and strange. She is not seeking shelter from the stormy blast, nor her eternal home. The only object of her desire lies – incredible! – in the casket. How can that vigour and laughter, that swift and comprehensive intelligence, how can it all be stilled and laid down?

Somehow, the end comes and everyone stands. Herb and David go to the head of the coffin, with Lettie's Ian and Adam's friend and colleague James behind them. The organ's long opening chord to a slow rendition of 'Thine be the Glory', induces the men to move their feet. They sway and tilt under the weight of her son. Nell gathers her daughters. They cling and jostle after the coffin. 'Endless is the victory thou o'er death has won.' Grief streams from the people turning in the pews, from the friends, the lovers for all she knows, from acquaintances and the curious: all feed the brown river. The four men, and all of them, are bent and tumbled in the torrent.

A month later, Herb brings a large paper parcel into the kitchen. Unbeknown to Nell, he collected it from the hospital weeks ago. If she has wondered at all what happened to Adam's things, she assumed them disposed of, burned in the hospital incinerator with used dressings and bodily detritus.

'Wait,' she tells him when he goes for the scissors. 'I need tea.'

She makes a pot and checks the fruit cakes in the oven – cooking and baking, their practised routines and substantiality, have given her ballast these last weeks, although she can hardly eat – and then they sit at adjacent corners of the square table.

Nell can't speak. She pats her breast for the hanky tucked into her brassiere. She watches Herb snip the string then pierce the brown paper and cut because there's another layer of paper and white hospital tape, too.

They pull back the paper and flatten it around the tidy, terrible pile. On top, with his pipe and tobacco, is the Argentinean wallet, butterscotch with tiny silver gaucho knife and so new it affronts. Nell's hand closes on the folded singlet underneath. She presses it to her nose. Herb lifts the flannel shirt onto the table, both hands over it. She has never seen Herb cry, until now; his face is lifted momentarily in a soundless wail, then he turns away and sobs, also without sound.

Nell stares at his back. Nothing in her goes out to him. Not even her hand to his quaking shoulder. Grief is a cage.

Under the shirt are the corduroy trousers. Nell delves in the pockets and snatches to her face the handkerchief, unfolded but barely used. The smell of tobacco. The smell of him laughing in the porch, reaching up to slap the rafter.

The oilskin coat is pressed flat over his shoes, water-stained but dried, and under them is another parcel.

The down jacket is wrapped around itself and tied with a piece of narrow gauze bandage. It puffs open and topmost is the collar, the shoulder, the seams impregnated with the cocoa colour of dried blood.

❦

The winter is long and ghastly. Rain bashes at the house, seeps into walls, obscures the sky and prevents any semblance of pleasure on Nell's walks, which are daily, long and solitary. She takes the back roads, scrambling up and down, through lanes and walkways, anything to avoid the main road with its trundling cars, trucks, onlookers and *that corner*. The sorry letters keep trickling into the letterbox, one from a friend who refers to Adam's trust in the 'Path of Life'. And she thinks again of the theosophists. Is solace to be found there, in *the path*? The one she finds herself on currently she wants only to repudiate. Nell hasn't returned to church since the funeral. Peggy has been a brick, but she is preparing for her own journey to northern India. Intrepid, she intends living as the monks do, for a few months at least. But the ideals – of being a lighted vessel, of finding the lighted way – are of no help when all is dark within and without.

Visitors come, family, friends, Adam's university colleagues, and Nell plays the hostess, impeccably: she feigns interest in their doings, assures them that she is getting on all right, pours tea and presses baking on them when they leave.

After each walk, Nell sheds her coat in the porch, shoes beside the coal range, and climbs the stairs to her tower. Only here is something approaching solace to be found – or if not solace, silence that is tolerable – in the mohair rug she wraps around herself, the big cushion she sinks onto, in the flower she keeps renewed in a cone of greenery (this week a burgundy hydrangea, the last of the season) on the round table. Arms along the low window sill, she stares out at the trees, at the harbour if cloud allows, at birds scurrying across the winter skies.

The scene will change. The weight will lift. She knows these things. Everyone tells her so. Herb tells her so. They all talk of recovery. Though, after the initial spill of memories and admiration, few speak directly of Adam. And Nell tells no one that she wishes only to go and join him.

Herb is off at the council chambers and after a brief sort through her wardrobe (it's been years since Nell bought anything new; she will force herself to town and find a blouse or two and a cardigan) Nell takes the hoe down the driveway to scratch up weeds from amongst the narcissi and tulips. Thank God for flowers, for the persistence of green, for these darling wood anemones raising their pale blue heads amongst cloven leaves.

Suddenly a young woman is crouched beside her. Jennifer. Nell looks at her and they stand up together.

Jennifer tries to speak, but her face contracts and her eyes well and overflow.

Hugging is not Nell's way, but at this moment she would rather not look into the tragic face, so she pulls her close.

'I loved him,' Jennifer sobs into Nell's shoulder.

Nell looks into the sky above the holly hedge. 'Yes. I'm sure you did,' she manages to say.

And in a year or two, Jennifer won't, or not quite so much; that space will be taken up by another love.

Whereas, for the rest of Nell's life the pain will be fresh and piercing whenever her thoughts alight on his name, his face (all the faces of his twenty-eight years), his vitality.

Oh, the ghastly self-absorption of grief.

'Come on inside.' She takes Jennifer's elbow. 'We'll boil the kettle.'

The twins are terribly good. Too good, Nell knows, but what, really, is to be done about it? They tiptoe and anticipate; they murmur and ache to please. The house is often silent. When he gets home, Herb talks about the intrigues, squabbles and occasional triumphs to emerge from his days on the council (he has given up trying to urge her along to stand beside him for mayoral functions – 'Not yet,' she still feels it within her right to claim). But Nell, once she has coaxed from the twins a little about their school day, retreats back into the quietness she has let grow up, like the holly hedge, around her. Adam is in every room: standing and swaying lightly beside the gramophone; grinding coffee beans in the kitchen, then pulling out the square glass receptacle and brandishing it for the aroma; sitting halfway up the stairs to her turret and reading in the plank of sun that falls through the skylight onto book or papers; perched on the bath's rim, soaking his feet back to warmth after a long motorcycle ride. His bedroom has been straightened, dusted, and often she puts a vase of native greenery on his desk, but the room has become a kind of shrine she can enter only when there is no one in the house, because sometimes all she can do in there is wail.

Tonight, Flick and Floss have prepared the shepherd's pie – put the mutton through the grinder, made up the white sauce, mashed the potatoes – with steamed celery and glazed carrots. They've set the table just so, with a little dish of relish and two yellow daisies in a tiny vase.

Herb begins with a tale about Mr Robinson's dog, which turns up now and then outside the chambers, looking for his master. Floss offers a story from the school science lab and urges Flick to do her imitation of the dressmaking teacher's tics. How hard they try to beguile her, to make her smile, to never make reference…

Adam balanced on the back rim of the red-painted chair as he explains the habits of native trout; Adam applying salt and pepper to his meal, ambidextrously; Adam commanding or cajoling a twin (depending on the day) to fetch his book or a cup of tea.

When silence falls again over the table, Nell says, 'We can't stay here.'

Herb stops. He lays down his knife and fork and looks at her. After all these years, when at home, he puts himself at her disposal.

'With your mayoral term ending, we could be closer to town, to the girls' school. We don't need all these rooms,' she says.

The matter and the true reason for it, are not discussed, now or later, but Herb goes to see a real estate agent and the sale of the old and a hunt for the new are set in motion.

1956

Dear Mr and Mrs Hamilton and family,

I learned only very lately of Adam's passing, and feel that a friend I loved and worthy brother has passed away. He stayed for a few days with me at Bombay, on the way home from his Himalayan adventure. In these few days and later I learned to appreciate dearly the fine outer and inner character that was his.

To you all, who must love and miss him, I send my heartfelt sympathy and the humble consolation that an Indian friend shares a small part in your loss.

Adam would not have liked us to revel in the sorrow of our personal loss. He knew somewhat to live in a world that transcends the barriers of incarnate life. Today, at the Vaishak Full Moon, we in India celebrate the 2500th anniversary of the passing into eternal life (Nirvana) of the greatest of India's sons: Gautama the Buddha. Even in his passing he has left behind a wonderful heritage of love and understanding for all mankind. In a very much more junior key, Adam is now part of that one Life. In our love for him let us forget our sorrows and share in the calm enlightenment that comes from accepting the ever-just and merciful law of eternal righteousness, which transcends race and time.

Sincerely yours,
Sohrab Hakim

p.s. please send me a happy photograph of Adam

'Please, there are a couple of seats left.' The usher touches Nell's elbow and points out a chair in the middle of the front row. She looks around for Peggy, and sees her on the far side of the room, seated between two men and talking. It serves Nell right for being indecisive when Peggy asked her to come. She'll go and find her afterwards. She feels tall and uneasy walking up the centre aisle, then having her head right in the middle, but at least the screen is well above all of them.

'It might be said that Roerich's art is not of this world.' The speaker at this public meeting hosted by the theosophists is a member recently returned from India. 'I couldn't help wondering what part elevation played in the ethereal quality of his watercolours. Certainly, I felt the effects as I made my slow ascent of the Kullu Valley where Roerich spent his autumn years.'

As the projector whirrs and speckled light fills the screen, Nell pulls off her gloves and smooths her hair. Adam gave the family an entertaining account of his visit to the valley, to the boarded-up Urusvati Himalayan Research Institute with its priceless collections of stuffed birds, herbs, medicinal plant seeds, minerals, art, archaeological relics, maps and Tibetan manuscripts, which were little by little being transferred to Russia. Nevertheless, the caretaker had opened a room for Adam, in which hung the nine paintings they are about to see.

The first few are disappointing – religious icons in standard colours, with borders and gilding, and there's one of the banner the artist created to urge for preservation of the world's art treasures in times of war. Then a couple of the mountains make her sit up in appreciation for the depth and distance they convey, and yet, they are foxed, the colours no longer true, and have been nibbled by insects. The speaker outlines the influence on the artist of his namesake St Nicholas.

'This last painting had been sealed up and packaged for transport to Russia, but somehow was left behind.'

The slide-holder shuffles and clicks.

Nell goes still inside. Blue on blue, the vision opens to them and she is plunged in headlong. Adam might be the tiny figure perched on the foremost hillock, or she herself might be, gazing out into the blue void which is framed by peak after peak floating as if in space and still, beyond, up they rise. 'Crowned with glory' comes to mind because she will need to capture this later in words and what more apt can be said about the great white (blue) serrations, ice-bound mountains to which the eye and the heart fly like filings to a magnet? Here. This is what lured him. Not merely mile upon mile of upthrust rock and snow, but *this,* this essence conveyed across time and canvas, captured on a tiny slide, and delivered in a burst of light to this hall filled with middle-aged people who will never in a lifetime (Peggy excepted) visit the Himalaya, but who in this moment are transported…

The speaker leaves the slide there as he winds up his talk and the secretary announces tea in the back room. Nell sits on. She is wrapped in elation, which she'll later name for herself as Adam's elation, and is loath to disturb the wrapping. Anguish will reassert itself soon enough.

'Of course I know of you, Lady Balfour.'

'Eve, please, Mr Brasch.'

'Charles then.'

The arrival of visitors, one planned, one spontaneous, requires Nell to cut a quick caper. 'Do sit.' She gestures at the two fireside chairs. 'Charles, did you know that Lady Eve has written detective novels as well as her books and articles about "the living soil"? Lady Eve, Charles grew up cheek by jowl with Herb's family, but more importantly, he's also a fine writer. He corrals our nation's best literary offerings into a quarterly – is it? – magazine.'

'Oh?'

Nell goes for tea and cake, the green tea set, white cane tray with gingham cloth, glad to know they'll find their way and that she can do what she does best: listen, observe, and prompt if necessary.

When she returns, Eve is saying, 'I'm glad I played at writing in the twenties with my friend Beryl – you know we published our novels as Hearndon Balfour? – because it meant that when the time came, I brought some skill and a sense of drama to bear on my fascination with dirt.'

Charles laughs and Nell sinks gratefully onto the sofa.

'How did you come to be here?' Charles looks at Nell, too, who tilts her head at Eve.

'Nell's Herb has been my most energetic New Zealand

correspondent, as a member of the Soil Association. When he heard I was coming south, he proposed a visit. So here I am for two nights, and mighty grateful of the respite from travelling and giving talks.'

She smiles so warmly that Nell feels a blush rise. Eve has bonded with her – to use Eve's own term – and has made it apparent that she would rather poke about in the garden and local lanes with Nell than linger indoors with Herb, who is inclined to stretch mealtimes and tea-breaks into lengthy discussions, or discourses.

There was a time when Nell would have felt her self disintegrating in the presence of two such talents (although Charles, a dozen years her junior, has never added self-importance to his influence and generosity), but hard circumstances have shown that her part, as far as she can discern it, is to walk alongside whomever life brings to her door. To walk, and also to stand. To stand firm, to stand when others shy away, or lord it over her; to bend, to sway, but not to fall, or if she falls, to rise again without self-recrimination, enabling others to do the same.

Her guests eat heartily and enjoy a second pot of tea, with much laughter, then Charles takes his leave (and from his bag a slim book for Nell, titled *Three Poems*). Eve suggests that she and Nell go out and plant the broad beans. 'And if the house sale hasn't gone through by spring, you and Herb can enjoy the harvest. I want to tell you about my travels in Turkey, where I fell in love with the marvellously versatile broad bean, or bakla.'

Adam would have enjoyed Eve, Nell thinks, as would Peg; Eve's inclusive, far-ranging mind and generous spirit conjure their own. How blessed Nell has been in the company that has found her in this lifetime. She fishes gardening gloves for them both from the basket in the porch, offers galoshes and jackets. Warmth spreads under her ribs as they tread the gravelled path to the vege patch.

1959

Peg is home from India – and Tibet, of all places for a woman to travel on her own. Seizing the opportunity to drive together to Christchurch in Nell's new Volkswagen Beetle, they decide to make a three-day feast of the journey and go inland up the Pigroot and across Dansey's Pass, then over the Lindis Pass, cleaving to the foothills, stopping at rivers and viewpoints, dreaming and revelling. Although they have mapped out hotels along the route, they've brought bedding with them (Nell has Adam's down sleeping bag), stretcher-beds and a fly, 'Just in case,' Peg said, eyes alight.

All the first day they talk of friends, family and places, the mood of the time and their own adaptations to it. They stop above the Kyeburn Valley to take in the old run, to sense the scope of the twenty years Nell lived on the skirts of the folded hill ranges under this enormous sky. As they penetrate inland, the talk follows suit. They delve and feel out the sympathies and antipathies that have grown in them, and the sense they have of meaning and purpose behind those.

As the sun lowers and lights to gold the high, bare Lindis hills around them, Nell asks Peg if they might not simply drive off into the tussocks for the night.

Newspaper, a broken-up box (Peg hollering and jumping onto it from the car's bumper is a sight to make Nell laugh for years afterwards) and handfuls of tussock generate enough flame in the thermette to boil water for the billy. Peg has made a hearty brown-rice salad (Nell enjoys the sweet tinned corn, the chives and boiled egg, but discreetly palms the rice husks from her lips; no wonder the grain hasn't caught on in the public imagination). The evening is so still and dry that they open the stretchers under the sky and lie back to watch the light fade and stars wink into being.

'I'm sorry I haven't been here for these hard years.'

Nell turns her head on her pillow to look at Peg. 'I knew you were with me. I've cherished your letters, which always put grit in me, or light, or … or fire when I seemed to be dying of cold. And really, there's nothing else to be done, is there, except to go through it?'

'I know you haven't gone through blankly or blindly, though. You've let the inner work proceed, at great cost, and to great reward. Whether you see that or not.'

Nell feels that she doesn't see. The cost, yes, the reward if there is to be one, not yet – except that sometimes, out of the blue, wonder and gladness ignite in her, burning like the pure straight flame on a Bunsen burner, impelled up from the belly, stoked in the heart, and driven on into the ethers. She herself is both the glass vessel in which this occurs, and the one who observes it.

In the deep dusk, Nell can just make out that Peg is watching her, and nodding.

They lie awake, listening to the starry silence and then to the low grinding hum of a car climbing the road, winding in and out of earshot, until at last the beam of its headlights flares along the fence and through the tussocks. It slows, as if reading the scene – thermette on the roadside, car nosed into the hillside and a casually waving hand (Peg holds hers in the beam) – and dawdles on toward the pass.

Then Nell urges Peg to say more about the series of months she spent in silence in a remote monastery under the severe tutelage of some kind of 'master'; of the ensuing months doing service in the adjacent asylum for indigent women; of her weeks in a tiny concrete-walled room in wintry Darjeeling, racked by dysentery, before she could gather wits and strength enough for the journey home. Peg is still gaunt, but her spirit is undimmed.

Nell shudders, sure she would have succumbed early, in any of those arid circumstances, to despair. Cold, boredom, sickness and ugliness: these she resists still, and it shames her to know it.

'What I've realised though, Nell, is that I didn't have to go to such extremes. I reckon if I'd stayed home, life would have dealt me the same sort of hand but in a different guise. I would have suffered deprivation until I said yes to things exactly as I found them. I would have been given some grim old woman or other to look after, until I said okay to the grim old woman lurking within. Even here, I probably would have got sick and stayed sick until I stopped fighting.'

'"…for I have learned, in whatsoever state I am, therewith to be content."' Nell is surprised to find the words ready in her mouth.

'Yes! And don't you think that must include where-soever and with whomsoever?'

Peg is speaking direct to Nell's heart. The stars blur together. 'With *and* without,' she murmurs. Without Adam. With Herb. In the instruction lies the capacity and with Peg's encouragement she will lay hands upon them both.

Meanwhile, the little Bunsen flame is burning bright. It greets the Pointers and the Southern Cross above; it winks at the Belt of Orion and flares towards the fat golden jewel of Venus ready to descend behind the western hills.

1960

The new house and garden, the latter embracing a green gully half an hour's walk from the city centre, are retrieved from neglect. The villa is painted inside and out, sunrooms built at each end of the house to catch warmth at either end of the day, fresh carpet laid and old lino replaced with cork squares. Nell claims the small bedroom facing like a ship's prow into the southerly winds that strike the house after each warm nor'west spell in the country's 'seven to ten day weather cycle'. She paints the walls in soft sage-green, sews up curtains and bedcover in a leaf motif of wine-red on cream. Guilt (that the twins are using the old bedding that does nothing for the mauve curtains in their room) she pushes from her. She knows at last what she needs and will not be badgered into good works or sociability when her soul cries out for beauty or silence. Once she is settled and established in herself, she will find, like over-wintered begonia tubers, the urge to strike new shoots and take on new tasks.

'Mother?' Lettie is visiting with her littlest, Babs, and she appears at the bedroom doorway as Nell straightens the last of three small watercolours. 'I've been calling through the house, Mama. You really are quite deaf, aren't you?'

Nell shrugs and smiles.

Lettie runs her hand over the bedspread. 'Babs is asleep at last so I'm going out for fresh air.'

Nell nods. 'Take your time.' She listens hard as Lettie goes. And hears the creak of her foot on the loose board, the blackbird outside the window, and she's sure that last night she heard wind scraping the tamarisk against the weatherboards (she'll get the secateurs right now and cut it back). It's true that she's noticed a reluctance to converse with more than one person at a time, that she loses the thread quite easily, but how much, really, is she missing? If she wants to hear music better, she simply turns up the volume.

Perhaps deafness will come as a relief. When she failed to hear Lettie's urgent voice unsettling the house, Lettie had to come and speak with her face to face. So what if Nell no longer hears every bit of prattle or news? She bends to straighten the bedside rug and picks up a fallen hanky. If she waits for others to answer the phone, she will less often be caught up in small-talk with someone who wants Herb. It doesn't seem so long since the phone call was like the telegram, used for stating only the necessary. Now people use it to natter. Herb natters, as far as she can tell. He and old Wattie talked for an hour the other afternoon about the fluoride business, then on to golf, then the pruning of currant bushes. She could hear all that well enough as she sat darning in the sunroom next door. But if she wants to talk with someone, she'll invite them over, or go and visit. Which besides makes them easier to hear.

Nell opens her bedroom window, then tiptoes along the hallway, hesitating outside the drawing room where Babs's pram has been parked. Silence. She creeps inside and across the plush rug. Her granddaughter is perfect. Naturally. She has turned towards the window, sun-dapple like a wand accentuating her beauty, playing on the pulse of her temple under dark and downy hair, on dark lashes, pink lips that pout then make a gentle sucking, on the hand beside her face that splays then curls back to rest. What will show in her of Lettie or of Ian? Of Nell or Herb?

What will they see in her of her uncle Adam?

'Herb, do you think the tent will fit in the Volkswagen?'

'Are you off somewhere?'

'I thought I'd take the girls up to see the old places. Flick doesn't go back to college for another week yet.'

It's not an expedition Herb would countenance. For all his rigour (cold showers followed by press-ups and sit-ups, and once she found him – a sight imprinted forever – hanging by his toes from the shower rail as he dried himself off), he doesn't enjoy the petty discomforts and inefficiencies of camping when he has a perfectly good house to sleep in and plenty to get on with. When they moved to town, he retired from the mayoralty and took up a campaign against fluoridation of the nation's water supply. He has delved deep into the abstruse principles of the British Israelite Society, fuelled by a drive, Nell suspects, to improve on their known ancestors – hers dour, word-shy Yorkshire farmers; his from the treeless Scottish isles. He asserts that all of British stock are members of the 'lost tribes of Israel' and that their claims, if she's understood rightly, supersede those of the current Jewish diaspora. She's always glad to see him leave his bedroom-study for the garden and a good dose of earth and substantive reality.

As for her own beliefs, she hews to no known path, and for the first time in her life is not sure it matters to what schemes her thoughts attach. The universe is so vastly greater than any set of ideas can express and therefore so is God. And anyway, since Adam died, she understands that grief alone, that unexceptional ordeal, has bound her at last to the whole human race. The dark face of love, the tempering counterbalance to all joy and pleasure, the wound that never heals, has brought her to a more pungent, a broader and more vital state of perception than any provided by religious principles.

Later that afternoon, Herb calls her out to the driveway. He has managed to pack the canvas tent into the boot space and beside it the three fold-up stretchers, thermette and billies. 'There's room still for your bedding, a bit of fodder, a slim pair of twins ... and you can load up the spare seat.'

The smell of canvas and sacking intoxicates, as it did in childhood when it spelled time out from chores, Mother in the best of moods, sun and rivers. It lifts her. 'Thank you, dear. I'll talk to the girls tonight and see if we might get away on Wednesday.'

Nell looks around. 'Do you think we might need these?' She nudges with her foot the heavy wooden tent poles still lying in the grass. They're longer than the car.

Herb rolls his eyes. 'Clever-clogs. All right. If we're going to make do with the German tortoise, it's probably time to get a roof rack. I assent.'

He wants her to go, whether for his own sake or hers she won't dwell on, and so, whether or not the twins come with her, Nell will go. The road beckons, and the wide skies of her past.

Another decade, another committee. Nell had sworn never to go on one again, but it was irresistible to join the group setting up a croquet club on the corner of their street. As children, they played the game with parents and guests on summer evenings: the thwack of mallet on ball, the faint comedy of adults rolling balls through hoops, with hovering associations to Carroll's Alice wielding a flamingo. Anyway, Nell enjoys the company, the sedate but strategic game, and the fact that they are a cohort beginning something together, encouraging new-comers, setting their own rules, if not for the game, then for their club interactions.

Alone at the clubhouse one day, getting out the cups and saucers, splitting and buttering date scones in advance of the afternoon's game, she hears voices outside and finds a couple on the lawn looking around.

'Can anyone come and play?' The woman clasps handbag to hip, pressing the other hand to blouse and pearls under a tailored jacket.

'We welcome new members.' This is the approved line; they are trying to dissuade casual players from turning up on club days. They wish to create a skilful team capable of inter-club competition.

'We've played a fair bit on our home lawn,' her husband says.

Nell looks at him and her breath catches.

Those polite and sleepy eyes, the scar at the corner of

the mouth, hands still smoothly youthful and clasped over a cane.

She can't be certain that he recognises her, though his head draws back and his shoulders square as her own recognition breaks.

'We have an open session on Tuesday evenings, when newcomers are welcome to make a start…'

'Bridge night,' says the wife, as if that's the end of the matter.

Simon is looking away over the lawn, towards the sea. 'All right then, dear?' turning back to his wife. 'We'll leave it for now, thank you.'

Nell feels only relief as they walk away.

It's possible that, back then, he had no compunction, no sense of trespass, but she'll never know because, as she recalls events, the next morning they uttered not one word to one another as they drove the sheep down between the bluffs and home, as hard and as fast as they could without active cruelty. She craved and hated in equal measure the boy-man she barely knew, whose hands had been intimate in ways that now she shudders to recall and that went beyond what Herb ever attempted. Simon stayed out in the shearers' quarters after that, cooking for himself, and by the time Nell returned from a stint in the city with the volunteers (packaging cakes, socks, books, pens and paper for 'the boys'), he had gone.

That portion of her life, a large portion it must be admitted, when the body, the imagination, the love-longing flared and burned and had to be accommodated, has passed into a kind of dream. How peculiar to have been so seized, so irrational ... and yet she can only think so if she forgets that she is part animal, all of them are, and if the sensual pleasures of earlier years have lost their siren appeal, now there are deep, hot baths, begonias, morning coffee, silk nighties and fine shoes to appease the sensualist in her. Along with the thwack of her mallet striking dead-centre of the ball.

1963

David and Barbara are apologetic about leaving so soon after her arrival, but this was the plan, that Nell would turn up in time for them to attend the surveyors' dinner and dance. It has meant driving north all day, and after a quick cup of tea, seeing to the children's baths and meal while Barbara gets dressed up, while David changes suits and polishes both of their shoes. The four children look in wonder at their mother, scented and glowing in emerald-green, and glittering at ears and wrists. Little Michael is given a last hug and has to be pried away with shrieks and then a long, high scream.

'He'll be fine,' Nell assures the parents. 'Really. Don't look back.'

She hopes she's right. It must be six months since her last visit when Mikey was five months old. To him, she's more or less a stranger. Still, what is familiar lies bone deep: it is in the way she responds to the children, she who mothered their father, and of course that father has attracted a woman who also feels familiar. Nell has observed that the ambience of a family doesn't alter vastly from one generation to the next, and after his bowl of mashed veges and bottle of warmed milk, Mikey is happy enough to nestle into his grandmother's lap, to play with her fingers (swivelling the wrinkles across her knuckles, chewing on the three rings) until he succumbs to sleep and can be laid in his cot-bed.

The older two return after dinner to their papers

and pencils on the coffee table, and Nell is grateful for the chance to sit now with three-year-old Kit, who has lugged to the sofa a formidable pile of pictorial books on the natural sciences. He and Nell pore over enlarged images of frogs and dragonflies, of rare gemstones being prised from their niches of origin; pictures of horses and riders of Mongolia. As Kit rifles, in the last book, through photos of the Himalayan mountains, she sways back to see the rapt look on his face – within moments he has found the photo of his uncle, her son, leading a pitch across the high snow face of Baruntse. The child's forefinger presses on the climber at the rear, then hop-hop-hops up the ice-blue footsteps to Adam who is leaning out, hip to the slope.

Nell all at once recalls Adam's efforts as a child, climbing the clay bank behind the house – gouging foot-holes and banging in tent pegs for hand-holds – and as she tells Kit of it, he comes willingly enough to brush his teeth and climb into bed, assured that he may sleep with the book tucked under his pillow.

Grace has made her own, the size of a match-book, with a crudely stapled centre, and has sharpened a pencil in order to write on it in tiny letters – except that she has only recently started school and all is hazard and guesswork. 'How do you spell *plenty*?'

Nell writes on the scrap paper beside her. 'Plenty of what?'

'Plenty of ponies. Is that a good name?'

'It sounds like one I'd want to read.'

Grace crouches over the table. The P takes up a

quarter of the cover. The y has to be made very slender. There's no room for i, e or s, so they go on the inside cover. Nell smiles, remembering. What a job it is, to find proportion in life, to make room alongside all that's inevitable for what's wanted or needed for one's own sake. And then, of course, more than half the knack is to learn what can be left out. Plenty of Pon has its own charm.

Grace's older brother Guy, tongue between teeth, drags a charcoal pencil over the page as his eyes flick at the open *Lion Annual* beside him. A creditable Batman has taken form, but Nell notes that Guy has tilted the figure, which is upright in the book, so that it looks poised for flight. The blue cape has been altered, with hairy orange spots added, until it resembles the wings of a great moth.

Nell strokes their two heads and tells them they have a few more minutes before bed. Time for her to put the dishes through the sink, turn on the heater in her tiny chilled bedroom and pop a hot water bottle between the sheets. Knowing that Mikey wakes at five thirty regardless of who has been out carousing the night before, Nell will go to bed when the children do, and wake in time to scoop him up at first cry in the morning.

Flick, on the other side of the kitchen table, wipes her eyes with the heel of her hand and stares into her teacup. Halfway through her fine arts degree, she has come home at midterm certain that she can't go on. Although her abstract works in oils (trees, hills, pools of dark water) seem to Nell startlingly accomplished, she has had trouble meeting deadlines for the academic papers.

'Are you finding life in the flat distracting? There must be a lot going on.' Nell pushes towards her the plate of buttered toast with honey.

'Oh, no. They're all lovely, mostly.' Flick reaches for a piece, but drops it on her plate and licks her fingers. 'It's my own fault. Anything is preferable...'

'Preferable to facing the blank page? I know ... your brother overcame that very fear. He said he simply made himself write something, anything at all, because as long as there were words on the page they could be shaped.' It's strange how vividly Nell has been recalling such conversations with Adam. She herself has increasingly found writing a chore, and leaves as much correspondence as she can to Herb.

Flick is giving her a hurt, almost fearful look. She's right to. Adam would never have had the patience to coax his highly strung, imaginative sister through this inward battle. Comparing her efforts to Floss's is similarly futile. Floss is away teaching in a country school and – influenced by Adam's keen interest in natural sciences

– intent on making that her specialty.

'Also, there are the little ones across the way.' Flick looks out the window. 'Barbara is up to her elbows.'

David and Barbara, expecting their fifth child, live close enough to the art school and Flick's flat that she is the logical answer to the question of who will help out in the weekends, or babysit evenings.

'Does she ask you often?'

'Well, she always says only if I have the time.'

'And you find it hard to say no.'

Flick blinks at tears. 'I know how busy she is.'

'And we know how busy you need to be to complete your own work.'

'Yvette rang her the other day.'

'Who?'

'My flatmate Yvette. Barbara had telephoned to see if I could come because she and David had tickets for the pictures. I said yes, and Yvette got cross and said I had to stay and do my assignment. I didn't know what to do. I was paralysed. Yvette rang Barbara – crossly – and said I couldn't come. Then I felt so awful I couldn't think. Couldn't write a thing anyway.'

Nell looks at her youngest daughter, now pink in the cheeks and nibbling at a torn-off crust. She is water in motion, wind in the leaves, a licking flame. All of these likenesses have occurred to Nell at times and she feels anxious herself at the thought of her daughter struggling to conjure and pin down in writing a solid idea about art with its themes, she imagines, as abstract as her own persona.

Herb comes in for his morning tea and asks Flick what she's going to do with herself today; since she's here, he could use a hand to clear out the greenhouse.

Flick flicks about, looks at her mother, is on the verge of agreeing.

'Flick...' Nell corrects herself: '*Isobel* is having a do-nothing day, Herb. She's home for a rest. If she wants to come out later, she will.' Nell rises to refill the kettle and get out the cheese and relish.

She wonders if all parents feel so impotent with their adult offspring. Of course, she reminds herself that she has done her work and that her children must now employ the equipment she and Herb put at their disposal. She supposes she is not alone, however, in suspecting that her job was done imperfectly (and certainly that her husband's was), that she fell into habits, using the very formulae she took exception to in her parents, because in the heat of a given moment, they flew to hand ('Go to your room until you can put on a pleasant face.' 'Because I said so, and that's final!'), as unconsidered as breath.

In addition, each child has its own personality cross to bear: Floss a stubborn certitude that closes as many doors as it opens; Flick the other side of that coin, indecision and dithering, which likewise mean that avenues lie unexplored, or only to the point of adversity and then are abandoned.

As Flick pours their tea (they have moved to the porch, reached by the late morning sun) Nell brings out a writing pad and pen. 'Let's make a plan of action that will see you through to the end of term. Taking into account what you stand to gain if you stay the course, what you might lose if you leave. And also taking account of your willingness to please David and Barbara.'

Family must not stand in the way of any woman's achievement. Nell gave up nursing for her mother. She gave up the farm for Herb. It hardly bears thinking about what else her left hand has signed away without her right hand's knowledge.

After croquet (she has won the club cup for the second year running) Nell walks home along the lane. The late afternoon sun slants through the trees and casts gold over the leggy stalks of the burgundy hydrangeas at the gate, over the yellowed bean leaves on Herb's bamboo wigwam, opportunistically set up in the middle of the lawn when Nell pulled out an ancient rose. She'd been going to replace it with a weeping cherry, and she will. Still in her whites, she skirts the house and takes the concrete steps down to the glasshouse. She can't help smiling whenever she steps into the merry mayhem. Her begonias have 'gone bananas', as Lettie said last summer. They leap and sprawl, dangle and wag in every shade of yellow, red, pink and orange on the chest-high shelf and, amidst the medley, the rose-form whites startle the eye and quiet the heart. Her heart. Nell finds comfort here in the thrust and surge of life. Their irrepressibility tells her that he is not gone, he is only sleeping, like a tuber in the soil.

1966

Nell sees up ahead the stand of native beeches, then the big iron shed. She pulls off the road and climbs out of the VW (stiff! after five hours' driving, the last two without stopping) to open the gate. She parks in the shed, beside the farm truck, then she goes out and looks around. With the highway at her back, the Makarora River valley is spread before her, the homestead on the far side, nestled under the vast wooded mountainside and set about with green paddocks. To the east another river valley opens with, at its head, a rearing slab of snow-plastered rock. Straight ahead, a horse and rider, no, two horses, one riderless, are coming through the river. For a moment the water is around the horses' bellies, then out they come and soon they're cantering up the faint track that weaves through tussock and matagouri.

Nell settles into the big saddle and takes the reins. Jumbo lives up to his name and it takes a minute or two to settle to his roll and sway as she and Ian thud down through the scrub, he on his lighter chestnut. Both horses are laden with the food, clobber and Christmas gifts she brought in the VW, and thank goodness she thought to put her own things in a canvas bag instead of a suitcase. Ian has it over the pommel in front of him. Being shod, Jumbo's hooves clash and grind on the river stones, while Lady's bare feet make lighter, hollow clops as she picks her way. Such details of understanding are never lost,

Nell reflects, like the intricacies of harness and saddlery, the nuance of huffing and ear flicks. It's wonderful to feel she understands horses still after all this time. It must be almost twenty years since she's ridden and her legs will burn tomorrow, but it's heavenly: the smells of matagouri and dried river mud, the sweet air blowing down the valleys and now, abreast, the horses lean back on their haunches and slide down the gravel bank into the main stream. For a moment water swirls under her stirrup irons and Nell reaches her hand into the ice-fed river. She splashes her face and grins at Ian.

Ahead, on the home straight, three of Lettie's girls are perched like restive hawks on the gate. 'Yahoo, hooray!' their cries come. Babs, the youngest, with her legs hooked over the top rung, rolls upside-down and waves before her blouse falls over her face and arms. Her hands touch the ground, feet follow, then all three are down and pushing open the gate. How they've grown!

'Wait,' Biddy cries. 'Take us too. Hello Me-ma! Bring him up close.'

Jumbo knows the routine. The girls remount the gate and he sidles against it. Wiry Babs grabs a handful of mane and slithers in front of Nell. Biddy and Jac slide on behind the saddle. Nell laughs out loud as Jumbo takes up a gentle amble and they all bump and sway together. Heavenly, too, to be encased in granddaughters, and here comes Tory the eldest through the garden gate.

So starkly she sees in the girls the qualities of her daughter divvied into four and embellished – generosity, bossiness and pluck, dreamy sensuousness, grit and hilarity, studious thoughtfulness – and bodied forth in these lithe and lovely girls, all with their hair cut short. Bare-legged, bare-footed, they have dispensed entirely with the flounces, white cottons, hair-brushing and boot-lacing that slowed or stymied a child fifty years ago (*and* created small moments of intimacy, care and closeness with adults that these forthright creatures seem able to take or leave).

Lettie appears as Nell dismounts (the girls have slipped like mercury from the horse and are carrying inside her canvas bag, the laden saddlebags) and Nell holds her and breathes her in. These fleeting, precious exchanges nourish her through the months of absence.

'Mum, you're a trooper. Sorry you couldn't come over in the truck today.'

'It was heaven.' Heaven is the only word for now. Soon enough, she knows she'll find herself frayed by the girls' energy, irritated by the dynamics (Ian's needling of his daughters and Lettie's self-imposed labours bordering on martyrdom – these are familiar and it's painful to see them played out in this subsequent generation), exhausted by the pace they all move at. Great swathes of her own life were like this, when caring for bodies food clothing warmth health farm were all-consuming and she wonders who that woman was, the Nell who managed it all.

'Now, Mum, you're not to do a thing this evening, except turn up for dinner. The girls have chores to do now, so go and make the most of it. There's heaps of hot water if you'd like a bath.'

Driving down to the city, Nell turns the VW left onto George Street and finds herself in the thick of things, slowed to a crawl. Students are marching in the opposite direction, with coats, scarves, mittens and banners. Their breath plumes amongst placards and chants pronouncing: Troops out Now! War is Hell. There's a *pock* on the roof above Nell's head; egg yolk and white slide down the side window. She will assume that the sleek black car in front of her is the intended target since broken shells litter its roof, and something like tomato relish sullies its back window. A young woman dashes up and runs alongside its passenger window, smacking at the glass and, when the car speeds up, she spits after it.

Herb has tried explaining to Nell the necessity for Western intervention in Vietnam, but he might as well be rapping sticks together. Nell doesn't have to attend a war to know that it's hell, that it solves nothing, and serves only to entrench the antagonists in damages and antipathies, for generations. Aeons.

At the shoe mender's she looks out of his George Street window at a group of stragglers who might be debating whether conviction will carry them on to the Octagon, or if they'll dash away to their next lecture. Nell asks the cobbler (as Herb still calls him) what he makes of the march.

'Had a young soldier bring his boots in for me to fix. I was sorely tempted to glue burrs in the toes. Loosen the nails and make his training a nightmare. But, of course, it's not the young fellas' fault. They're just following their blood. It's the politicians' feet need nailing to the floor.' He ducks down to look under the counter.

Nell considers. 'Are the young people out protesting not also following their blood?'

The man stands and presses her favourite shoes to the counter, resoled. 'So they are. But...' he consults the ceiling, 'they've made theirs run contrariwise. They've given the matter some thought. The mob goes off to war and the thinkers stay away.'

Nell looks at the cardboard tag and opens her purse. She's pretty sure she knows what Herb would say on the thesis of warriors versus thinkers. Of course, she loathes war, and the students loathe war, but really, she, the students and the cobbler have only their aversions and opinions to offer up. The machinery of endless, repetitive war is oiled and kept running by men who are welded to their ideologies and intentions. She puts a pound note on the counter.

The cobbler fishes for change in his drawer. 'Shoes should be good as new for a few years. Nicely made and nice to work with.' He counts the money into Nell's hand. 'I was glad of this trade in the last war. They told me to stay and make boots rather than put on a pair myself.' He gives her a nod, then turns back to his work bench.

Tucking the shoes into her capacious bag, Nell wonders if there is something in the make-up of the human race itself that depends on the outlet and the demolitions of war, since it seems unable to imagine or desire another way through conflict … and yet, at its root, is war even about dissension or greed? Herb believes in evil, that it exists as his God exists, independent of man. Maybe he's right. It would make a kind of horrid sense: that evil has roamed the earth since time began, goading and abetting men to fight, and only ever being appeased – momentarily – by the prodigious shedding of blood.

Outside the shop, Nell repositions her hat. What a morbid train of thought she's taken. The road is steaming in the sun and the demonstrators are singing, the last of them a block away now. Two tea-shop assistants are carrying a round table onto the footpath. Why not, she thinks. She won't sit outside in the melting frost, though. She pops inside after the girls and the bell tinkles behind her.

'That's about deep enough, I reckon.'

Standing beside the square hole, Nell and Floss look down on Herb's cap, level with the grassy edge.

Floss laughs. 'It should take a few years to fill.' She and Nell have been wheeling away the excavated dirt to make a small mountain beside the infant hawthorn hedge.

Herb lifts the handle of his spade to Nell, who holds tight and leans back as he kicks his toes into the earth and climbs out beside them.

'Ready for lunch then?'

Egg and bacon pie, served on paper napkins outside Floss's little caravan. From the picnic rug, they gaze directly at Mt Kyeburn and Nell recalls the day they climbed it with the children.

'You two hadn't turned up yet,' she tells Floss. 'I suspect it was the start of Adam's love affair with the mountains. Do you remember, Herb, how he kept hooting and leaping over tussocks as we came back down?'

When Adam is conjured, everyone goes still – Nell feels the silence, a tightness at her centre – and she aches for someone to embellish, to say something that will keep him present. Could they not reach out together and net him with words? Or even with some expression of the pain they have each hoarded this last decade in their own secret recesses? Between them, they could bring him into their midst, the whooping, hollering Adam of that day, or any one of his many selves. Floss manages to say, 'I wonder…' but then they all look away, and Herb says, 'I do recall after one such outing we came home to find a family of geese had moved in to the children's paddling pool. And talking of geese…'

After lunch, Floss and Herb work on making a wooden platform around the hole, for the dunny which a local builder will deliver in the coming week. This is Floss's acre, bought on the edge of Naseby, ten minutes' drive from the old concrete farmhouse. Today they have borrowed a car with a tow bar and brought Floss's dinky little caravan up, selected a sheltered, sunny spot for it and chocked its wheels into place.

Nell takes herself for a walk up to the ridge where the view opens out, where every fold and gully of Buster and Kyeburn is made vivid in the blue nor'west light. The hills, tawny, breathing, are a body she can no longer lay claim to, no longer hold. Twenty-two years since they left the run; thirteen since Adam died. The dearest things are torn away. She herself is thistledown, two feet her only contact with earth, the sky above vast and fathomless; where will she next alight?

Macrocarpa striplings have been planted alongside the track. Nell grasps a tender tip and pulls, breathes into her hand, to return herself to her senses. Still her arms ache to hold … or to be held? It occurs to Nell she might be aching for the clasp of earth, that a part of her might be yearning for her own death.

1970

Nell has the house to herself, for three whole days while Herb is up in Christchurch for some church business (she grows hazy about the specifics of his trips away, of his meetings, his letters to editors and appeals to politicians) and to see the grandchildren there. She regrets that those five young ones see more of him than they do of her, but he has always known how to entertain children, to keep them in the palm of his hand with tales and magic tricks, as long as it's not for more than an hour or two at a time. They drop at his feet, agog, listening and drinking him in. She admits to herself that she has little facility with children in a gaggle, children who are awkward with their elders, or who try too hard to please them, which covers that family, beloved though they are. Or perhaps she is the awkward one. Perhaps it simply means that she is tired. In short, she has stayed at home to luxuriate in the empty rooms, the unplanned days and the silence.

After the first cup of tea with toast, and still in her dressing gown, Nell takes the newly arrived plans outside and opens them beside the sturdy implement shed. Using a small inheritance from Aunt Liz, she is having it further strengthened and a studio room built on top. Reminiscent of her tower room, it will be painted white and filled with light, with generous windows to east, west and south. Small ones to the north because a) there is the house and the front door, and b) because although

Nell will enjoy the room when she can, it will primarily be for Flick's use, and too much direct sunlight is trying. Flick gave way before finishing her fine arts degree, with the *promise, promise, promise* that she will paint every weekend, as long as her current training as a Karitane nurse allows, as long as she is not called to work away.

Nell's feet go cold with the sudden memory of standing on the concrete pad of the Maniototo house, the scraping dismay of having to build it from the ground up in that unforgiving country, with a baby. How she wanted to be looked after, just a little bit, as she looked after Adam. Oh, Herb always asked too much of her (she asked a lot of herself), and back then, she found it in herself to deliver. Until she couldn't. When they left the farm, she no longer could.

The plans in her hands are simple and satisfactory. The door looks a little slight, as do the steps up the outside. But she hasn't the energy (or the funds) to plan for anything grander. She pencils in a bank of shelves, some with doors; they might as well be built at the same time.

Then she goes inside and runs a bath, opening the new bottle of Blue Grass bath oil Lettie bought for her recent birthday. She runs it deep and lays ready a crisp fresh towel, throws a facecloth into the water. Bliss.

In the soft light of the overhead heat-lamp, she attends to herself. Sinks right under, shampoos her hair, then rinses it from the green plastic jug. Scrubs softened skin from her toes (she'll sit in the sunroom afterwards and cut the nails with the new horrid but necessary podiatry clippers), pumices elbows, knees and heels. Notes dwindling hair 'in the corners' and wonders if the kind of bruise she feels underneath is another haemorrhoid forming. She has ointment for that.

She lies back and closes her eyes as she soaps her hand. It's a while since she last checked her breasts as her newish lady doctor urges her to do. The left one feels all clear. She soaps the left hand. Sees the breast in quadrants. Presses all four with all four fingers. Then her hand travels up towards the armpit and stops. A piece of grit. Rounder. Perhaps a cherry pip, only larger. She presses back down into the upper, outer quadrant and sure enough, there's another one, larger again, and somehow craggy. The image that comes to mind is of a whiskery little tuber. Her own begonia.

She is not surprised. Somehow, she's known it was there, but has managed to distract herself, to procrastinate, half in dread half in hope, because her love for life is tempered, because she senses that since Adam went ahead she has, over the years, already half pulled up her roots.

Nell's cotton-gloved hand grips the arm rest as she is thrust back in her seat with the crescendoing roar. She thrills to these moments when Earth's pull is denied; loves flying, as she discovered late in life, and even went up in a glider when David learned the art a few years ago, before having children and deeming the risk too great. Beside her, Herb has his forehead pressed to the window so he can watch the cows sheds sheep river trees appear and dwindle below them. He flies often up the country to meet with gangs of opinionated men: the British Israelites, the anti-fluoridators, or the army officers. Loath to retire fully, on this trip to Auckland he'll visit the boss of his latest part-time syndicated venture, in credit control. Debt collection in other words, an occupation and a class of man despised since the time of Jesus. Nevertheless, he is dapper and optimistic, while Nell is delighted to be up in the clouds and able to give a kind smile to the damp-faced woman across the aisle before she closes her eyes.

Stepping out of the airport in Auckland is a revelation: the air close, warm and sweet. Nell has to throw off her coat at once, and wishes she'd worn sheerer stockings. Why has she never considered, in seventy years, living in the soft, embracing climate of the north? Herb has brushed aside the offer of a trolley and strides towards the taxi stand with their suitcases one in each hand. At seventy-four, he considers himself to be in his prime and is willing to show it. 'Where do your people come from?' he asks the fuzzy-haired taxi driver, and on hearing the name of the Melanesian island, turns up a wartime tale of Kiwi heroism.

Around the time of Nell's surgery, Herb was kind and businesslike with her, matey with the medical staff and teasing with the nurses. Since then, he has all but forgotten that Nell lives with these new losses: of a breast (how terrible – and yet, who cares? hundreds, thousands of women silently lose breasts and – she recently read with incredulity in an African aid magazine – far more intimate parts of their anatomy) and of her future beyond a year or two. Because she has let him forget. She pops a bit of foam into her brassiere. The disease and its outcomes are hers alone to weather, and she will do so with all the silent stoicism she can muster. If she needs to talk, it will be in letters to Peggy, whether or not they are actually sent.

'You do look well, both of you,' Herb's sister Ilona has met them in the lobby of their hotel. She kisses Nell on the cheek and takes her brother's arm, steering him towards the door. 'I'm taking you for tea.' Ilona lives and paints on Waiheke Island to support herself and her older invalided husband. None of the family has ever been invited to visit her there, and she and Herb both hope it might happen this time.

In the dim coffee house with rickety chairs and tables, Nell makes for the window where at least there is light and some tropical thing with pink flowers curling behind the glass.

Ilona talks expressively and obliquely. ('I need to get more pigment while I'm in town, and a pineapple or two.' 'I don't suppose you've read any of John Berger's essays?') She is evidently itching to light up, so once their pot of tea and date scones have arrived, Herb stands and eases up the sash window and Ilona puts a slim cigarette between her lips. 'Only twice a day,' she tells them, 'but mid-morning is one of 'em.'

They give her news of children and grandchildren, but Nell understands that their doings are of scant interest to a woman with none of her own, who has travelled and enjoyed the stimulating world of art and artists. Croquet and flower gardening are small, humble conversational offerings. And Herb's rumination on the comparative merits of the mayors of their two cities brings overt boredom to his sister's face. When he has slaked his thirst, Ilona leans and puts a hand on his arm. 'Herb, be a darling and run a message for me?' She gives him one of the new ten-dollar bills ('What's this in pounds? Five, or twenty?') and directions for the dry cleaner's.

When he's gone, she scrapes her chair closer to Nell's and her voice lowers. 'Now you can tell me the real news. How are you doing?'

And Nell finds herself telling about the surgery and imminent radiation treatment. 'And that will be enough,' she says. 'I won't take the experimental potions on offer. I can accept...' She lifts her chin.

Ilona is watching her face. She nods. Doesn't flinch or deny, for which Nell is grateful.

'You must ask to see Doctor Dawson, though, or Mister, I suppose he is, if you change your mind. My friend Susan had him. Absolutely trustworthy, and a damned sight less patronising than most of the medical crowd.' She's suddenly a little distracted, looking for something in her satchel, but Nell feels understood, not least because Ilona knows Herb so well.

'I won't ask you over to the island. Harley's got the aches pretty bad this spring and besides, I can't stand it when he and Herb get onto their war talk, their political hoo-ha and bon-homerie. Come up on your own in autumn, after the summer heat, and I'll put you in the wee sunroom. Although truthfully … I don't know how much longer we'll be there, with his heart. He talks about moving nearer to a hospital.'

Herb has scorned and despaired of his sister's choices in life. She went against the accepted moralities of the church, and twenty-odd years ago Herb was party to the dissolution of her engagement to a German when he (Herb) found out that the man was married. Or had been married. Or was simply German. Didn't matter which. There was too much against him, and Herb had only to slip him a suggestion about Ilona's party-girl reputation at art school to see a cooling off of the arrangement. Ilona later said that it was the interference itself that turned her suitor away, and of course she never forgave it.

Nell smiles at Ilona's red linen shirt, turquoise beads and modish bob. At the hitched skirt and neat brown knees crossed beside the table. How drab she feels herself to be. How slow and fuddy-duddy. When did colour and verve, or even simply nerve, slip from her grasp? She has the wit, though, to drink them up in Ilona, to appreciate their minutes of gossip before Herb returns, then to ask, 'Tell me, Ilona, where can I go to find something pretty for the girls?'

'Are you on the new phone?' David asks.

Nell squeezes the orange hand-piece, taps it lightly

against her hearing aid. Its companion-perch is screwed to the wall beside the kitchen table. David's children wanted her to have one matching theirs, so it arrived with the two eldest for Christmas and three months later it has finally been wired in by the phone man.

'It works just like the old one,' she tells him. 'Sounds the same.'

'But it's in the warm room, at least, and doesn't weigh a ton.' His voice she can readily make out, but it was hopeless trying to fathom what the children said earlier. Was it two or three she talked to? She has worked out a little stock of patter so that (she hopes) they feel heard.

'Anyway, we're all well, the two at new schools making no complaints, Barbara and I having golf lessons. We've decided to subdivide and sell later in the year...'

Life going on, in other words, and Nell sees the snippets of news in comic-book frames; the books of their lives, turning page by page. And to think that once she was deeply embedded in her own book – you might say she was the ink, the colour, the asterisks and exclamation marks, but now she is the disinterested reader of others' books (not *un*interested, she wants to say), and soon will be the one lying down, eyes closed, never to read, or be read to, again.

'...and brought home a pup. Mad little thing.'

Nell startles, returns. 'Do send us a photo. And of the children. We missed the younger ones this summer.' And this summer has been her last, she is sure of it.

David has said something. 'I see,' she answers – appropriately?

'Floss seems to be doing a fine job in Wellington,' she tells him. 'Very stimulating for her.' But who will insist she stay up there, once Nell has gone? She has warned Herb not to try and lure her back to look after him, but she must relinquish *this too*. 'And Flick is managing to paint between jobs. I like having her here in the studio. Although she's met someone.' An accountant, of all unlikely types. Nell half-hoped Flick would find herself another artist (she's envisaged a potter, a worker in stone), someone who could teach her by example to wrangle and tame her nervous energy.

Nell bends to one side and presses her palm to the table. Her back. It's an hour before she's supposed to take more pills. 'Thank you for calling,' she tells David.

After pills, and half an hour on the carpeted drawing room floor with one pillow wedged into her waist, her arms wrapped around another, Nell is ready to move again.

Down in the sunny orchard, she sinks onto the grass and opens Lettie's fat letter. She no longer needs to tear them open as soon as they arrive. She has learned to save and savour. In news from the Makarora Valley, Ian is learning to fly. Two of the girls are off at boarding school, the younger two provoking the home governess to sobs and pleas. Good for them, thinks Nell. Her own anarchic streak has finally broached, if not on her own behalf. No girl should be bored by her teacher. None should be told what her limits are. And no person (inevitably female) should be coerced into looking after others while her own talents go to waste.

Of course, she should have instructed her younger self thus. What she has told her daughters and what she has demonstrated are not one and the same.

Nell hears the snap and rustle of twigs and grass and Herb appears. He has the basket from the car and the picnic rug, which he throws down beside her. He has filled the thermos and little milk bottle, brought down her favourite teacup and his own. Alas, there are no teabags to be found in the basket, so he goes back up and while he is away Nell takes out the packet of photos that arrived with the letter. They're from a film Lettie says she found years after it was used, half of it able to be developed.

The top photo, half drawn out, reveals the coif of Adam's windblown hair. Nell pinches her nose at the shock.

She waits until Herb returns, this time with the teapot in its red knitted cosy.

'It looks like the day we all went up the Kyeburn from Centrewood. It was your birthday.' Nell hands him the packet. 'Adam's new camera and our first colour prints, remember? We all took a turn with it.'

Herb takes the photos out right away and Nell watches. His eyes open wide. He thumbs the lenses of his glasses.

Together they look through them: Adam is, all of them are, golden on the riverbed. The tray with the remnants of Herb's birthday cake is set on a driftwood stump. In one, David is holding a terrier, she can't recall its name, in another Adam is standing on his hands.

They've built a wigwam from driftwood and the three older siblings look to be doing a Cossack dance beside it while the twins hold their mouths in laughter.

'It was the day Lettie found the moa print in the river, as we all thought. Remember?'

'What else could it have been?'

Nell holds up the photo she saw first: Adam tilted forward, one foot on a log and arms out like wings. His face catches the low sun and Mt Kyeburn behind him is drenched in gold.

Herb's hand covers hers, holding the picture. 'They shall not grow old, as we that are left...'

Nell shivers ... but no, she will not be irritated. She will be here on this warm rug with Herb. With all of them. Bees have come to investigate the blue wool and others can be heard in the borage behind them. Afternoon sun crowns the sycamores and the macrocarpa with flames. When Herb goes to take his hand away, Nell turns her own and holds on.

Acknowledgements

Many, many people have enabled the writing and publication of *Nell* – my gratitude grows along with the realisation: my grandmother herself, née Eleanor Preston, whose influence is evident on every page. My good father Andrew Todd who was my cord of connection to her. My 'young' twin aunts Fiona and Ione who have been generously involved at every stage of my life. Aunt and godmother Elespie was a living spark from Nell in her generosity and strength. Grandfather Bruce kept us kids in thrall and demonstrated the power of a good story. Uncle Colin Todd was the stuff of legends and the family's hidden sorrow.

Thanks go to Creative New Zealand for a writing grant in the first Covid year. To Mike and Rose Riddell and the writers of Oturehua for the retreat of 2020, where Paula Wagemaker saw this 'necklace' of cameos I was starting to string together. To Craighead archivist David Batchelor who generously furnished me with photos and snippets of the school's history. To Emma Neale who read my first draft and wrote a report to be cherished. To my mother Elizabeth Todd who gifted me her discerning eye and who also liked what she read. To my next expert readers, Claire Beynon, Pam Morrison, Paddy Richardson, Raymond Huber, Alex Huber (who also proofread), Sophie Bond (who is also line editor and my PR pro), all of whom heartened me and *Nell* with their thoughtful comments. To Mary Hammond who read the midwifery scenes, and Lex McMillan the farm scenes (nevertheless, I take full responsibility for any deviations from reality in these). To the Cloud Ink team who approved of the manuscript, made astute suggestions and the offer to publish, and have been a delight to work with. To Fiona Farrell for reading the final manuscript and bon mots. To Caroline Pope, who worked with many opinions and came up with a fine cover. To Paul Stewart for meticulous care with typesetting and more. To each member of our writing group, more precious as the years go by: insightful, clever, generous every one. To my siblings and cousins who shared Nell, our 'Bunny', and have provided variously encouragement and sparks of inspiration. To dear family and friends already named, and those unnamed but likewise treasured, without whom life would be implausible.

About the author

Penelope Todd of Dunedin is an award-winning author of fiction
– the YA *Watermark* trilogy; *Peri, Box* and others, *Island, Amigas*
(co-written in English and Spanish) and much-loved memoir
Digging For Spain: a Writer's Journey. She has gained residencies
at the Iowa International Writing Programme, Chateau de
Lavigny in Switzerland, in Spain and Argentina and at the
Dunedin College of Education. She is the publisher at Rosa Mira
Books, and works as a freelance editor and literary assessor. She
is nourished by friends, family and garden, and by going into the
hills and harbour, summer and winter.

www.penelopetodd.co.nz

About the publisher

Cloud Ink Press Ltd is an independent publishing collective based in Auckland, New Zealand. We use a collaborative process to publish high-quality works across a range of genres.

www.cloudink.co.nz